THE DARK OF THE ISLAND

ALSO BY PHILIP GERARD

Down the Wild Cape Fear: A River Journey through the Heart of North Carolina (University of North Carolina Press, 2013)

The Patron Saint of Dreams (Hub City Press, 2012)

Creative Nonfiction: Researching and Crafting Stories of Real Life (Waveland Press, 2004; Story Press, 1996)

Secret Soldiers: How a Troupe of American Artists, Designers and Sonic Wizards Won World War II's Battles of Deception Against the Germans (Plume, 2003; Dutton, 2002)

Writing a Book That Makes a Difference (Story Press, 2002)

Writing Creative Nonfiction (edited with Carolyn Forché, Story Press, 2001)

Desert Kill (William Morrow, 2000)

Hatteras Light (John F. Blair, Publisher, 1997; Scribner's, 1986)

Cape Fear Rising (John F. Blair, Publisher, 1994)

Brilliant Passage: A Schooning Memoir (Mystic Seaport Museum, 1989)

THE DARK OF THE ISLAND

PHILIP GERARD

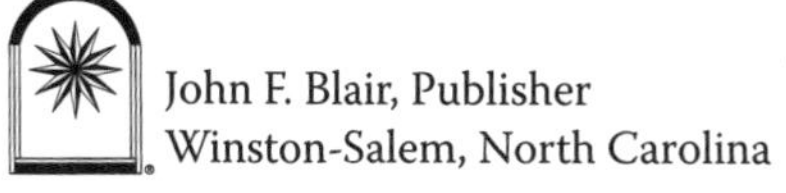
John F. Blair, Publisher
Winston-Salem, North Carolina

JOHN F. BLAIR,
PUBLISHER
1406 Plaza Drive
Winston-Salem, North Carolina 27103
blairpub.com

Library of Congress Cataloging-in-Publication Data

Names: Gerard, Philip, author.
Title: The dark of the island / by Philip Gerard.
Description: Winston-Salem, North Carolina : John F. Blair, Publisher, [2016]
Identifiers: LCCN 2015039236| ISBN 9780895876607 (softcover : acid-free paper) | ISBN 9780895876614 (ebook)
Subjects: LCSH: Family secrets—Fiction. | City and town life—North Carolina—Fiction. | World War, 1939-1945—Veterans—Fiction. | GSAFD: Mystery fiction.
Classification: LCC PS3557.E635 D37 2016 | DDC 813/.54—dc23 LC record available at http://lccn.loc.gov/2015039236

10 9 8 7 6 5 4 3 2 1

Design by Debra Long Hampton
Cover Design by Anna Sutton
Cover Image: "Rosebud Pier at Night," ©bradmcs/Flickr

For Jill

NORTH CAROLINA

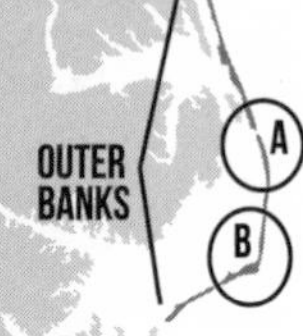

AREA A DETAIL

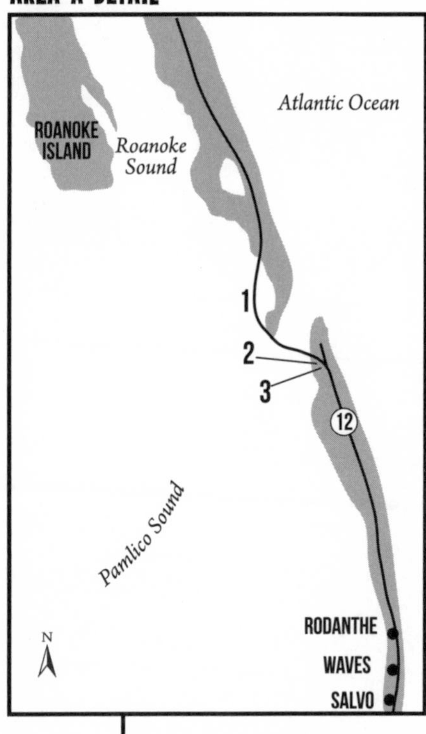

AREA A

1 Bonner Bridge
2 Caroline Dant's house
3 Dant's Marina & Garage

AREA B

4 Tim Dant's boat found here
5 Littlejohn's favorite store
6 original Hatteras Lighthouse
7 inflatable boat lands
8 Lifeboat Station #17
9 Merchant Marine Cemetery
10 Family graveyards
11 *Lady NorthAm*
12 *NorthAm Rascal*
13 Lord's Manor
14 *Island Times* office
15 NorthAm drilling platform

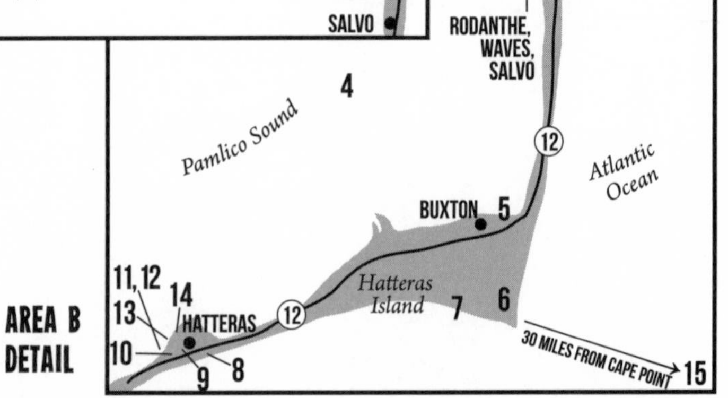

CONTENTS

Author's Note

The Hatteras Island portrayed in the following pages does not exist except in the imagination of the author, who has felt free to alter its geography and inhabit it with fictional characters, none of whom has a real-life counterpart. Their forbears live in the pages of *Hatteras Light* on the same imaginary island, which has shifted and settled over the generations, a vivid mirage between sky and sea.

PROLOGUE

CHICAGO, 1940

The crowd of workingmen surged into the Bund Hall in a draft of whirling snow. They filled the rows of wooden folding chairs and flowed down both side aisles and across the back, dammed against the walls, shifting and murmuring. Nicholas Wolf stood in the restless mob at the rear and stared, mesmerized, over rows of dark cloth caps and gray slouch hats.

There were no preliminaries, no warm-up speeches, no local dignitary to introduce the Great Man. He appeared all at once from stairs behind the stage, rising like an apparition to the silver fist of the microphone.

A lean, commanding figure: Charles Lindbergh, the famous aviator. "The Lone Eagle," the newspapers called him. A figure of stubborn courage and dogged self-reliance who had no patience for the weak, the uncommitted, the timid.

Nicholas Wolf noted the high forehead, sharp nose, and fierce eyes—a man of action, not just words. Lindbergh stood proud and tall on the platform, hands jammed into the side pockets of his long brown leather flier's coat, knife-creased jodhpurs tucked into spit-shined cavalry boots. Just standing there, he seemed to possess velocity, his momentum propelling him forward into history.

Behind Lindbergh hung the giant red, white, and blue shield of America First—red for courage, white for purity, and blue for justice.

Lindbergh stood silent for a long moment, head turning slowly, nodding, as if doing a final check list before launching into flight. The crowd settled and hushed, straining to hear.

And then Lindbergh began to speak.

Nicholas Wolf listened with his whole body, hands clasped on his cloth cap. Without even being aware of it, he leaned toward the voice, drawn by its magnetism. Word by word, rhythm and sense, the speech entered his hands, and his fisted fingers crushed the cap into a soft ball.

Lindbergh spoke in decorous phrases about patriotism. A good word, he said, a strong word. A word rooted in *father*, as in *Fatherland*. A patriot was responsible for his country the way a father was responsible for his family. The patriotic thing to do, he said, the best way to keep America safe, was to keep her out of a war against Germany.

He swung his arm, hammering home his theme with his fist.

He argued for neutrality. But when he spoke of the Jews, his coded message was clear to Nicholas Wolf.

"The greatest danger to this country lies in their large ownership and influence in our motion pictures, our press, our radio, and our government," he told the crowd, and it roared approval.

Nicholas Wolf had nothing against the Jews. Some of the best machinists in his shop at the Pullman Works were Jews. But he read the papers. It didn't take a genius to see that America was leaning dangerously toward war with Germany. And that was all on account of the Jews advising the president—Lindbergh was right about that much.

Pullman was building a record number of railway cars, and that could be for only one reason: to carry troops.

More ominously for Nicholas Wolf, the plant was now manufacturing tanks, whole flatcar trains full of battle tanks rolling east toward port cities including New York and Philadelphia and Norfolk. Tanks were not weapons of defense but of invasion. The plant was building them to roll across the plains of northern Europe.

Lindbergh spoke in a high tremolo of a voice quavering with passion, and the hot stage lights painted a sheen of perspiration on his forehead.

"The three most important groups who have been pressing this country toward war are the British, the Jewish, and the Roosevelt administration," he said, counting them out on his fingers.

It was the Jews who were pushing the government to take up arms against Germany. Yet here in Chicago, as in Philadelphia and St. Louis and New York, tens of thousands of hardworking, loyal German-Americans manned the stockyards and factories. What of their heritage? *Stay out of the war,* he was telling his countrymen. *Don't listen to the Jews.*

"We cannot blame them for looking out for what they believe to be their own best interests, but we also must look out for ours," he said, his voice reverberating. "We cannot allow the natural passions and prejudices of other peoples to lead our country to destruction."

Roosevelt and his Jewish advisors were drumming up war fever out of wild exaggerations and lies, casting Hitler as some kind of monster intent on taking over the world. "The Germans claim the right of an able and virile nation to expand," Lindbergh explained, palms out—who could argue?—"to conquer territory and influence by force of arms as other nations have done at one time or another throughout history." Adolf Hitler was merely satisfying German honor, righting an old injustice.

Nicholas Wolf listened, rapt, nodding along without even realizing he was doing so.

"There is no Genghis Khan nor Xerxes marching against our Western nations," Lindbergh insisted, his color rising with emotion. "This is not a question of banding together to defend the white race against foreign invasion. This is simply one more of those age-old struggles within our own family of nations—a quarrel arising from the errors of the last war—from the failure of the victors of that war to follow a consistent policy either of fairness or of force."

In the flood of words that followed, Nicholas Wolf heard poetry, Lindbergh praising German strength, German will, the ideal of a greater Germany that would triumph over the complacent British and the decadent French. Lindbergh had traveled all over Europe with his eyes and ears open. Hermann Göring himself had presented the Great Man with the Commander Cross of the Order of the German Eagle.

Now he was delivering the news of the future.

"In England, there was organization without spirit," he said. "In France, there was spirit without organization. In Germany, there were both." Nowhere else in Europe, he said, had he found such personal freedom.

Lindbergh spoke to Nicholas Wolf's heart, to the hearts of all Germans. He was a man who understood pride and purpose, honor and destiny. Lindbergh was an Aryan who had made a difference in the world, who had shown what an iron will and a steady nerve could accomplish. Everyone had told him it couldn't be done, a solo flight across the Atlantic with no margin for navigational error, no time for sleep, trusting to fate and the weather. But he had defied them all and made his destiny. Nicholas Wolf could see it in his luminous eyes, unblinking, focused as searchlights.

"The majority of hardworking American citizens are with us," Lindbergh said. "They are the true strength of our country. And they are beginning to realize, as you and I, that there are times when we must sacrifice our normal interests in life in order to ensure the safety and the welfare of our nation."

It was duty, plain and simple. That's what Nicholas Wolf heard. *Sacrifice.* "It depends upon the action we take, and the courage we show at this time. The time to act is here!"

The cheering and applause rattled the wooden walls and rafters till the whole place thrummed.

Half an hour later, outside in the ticking silence of a soft snowfall, on his way home, cap pulled low and straight over his brush-cut blond hair, filthy snow slushing under his boots in the murky November twilight, Nicholas Wolf was marching.

His purpose was clear now. He had never felt so sure of himself as at this moment, Lindbergh's noble challenge still resounding in his ears.

He would not return to his post at the Pullman Works on Monday. They would have to find a new foreman for the machine shop. He had been wrestling with this decision for more than a year, ever since

Hitler's troops had reclaimed Danzig, taken Poland by storm, and proclaimed the Thousand-Year Reich.

In truth, it seemed clear to him now that he had been consumed by it for all of his life in America. His heart ached to return to the Fatherland, to be part of the revival of a great nation, his nation. He had left only because, in those lean, chaotic days following the Great War, it had become a wasteland, a pile of wreckage ruled by vandals and criminal gangs.

How was an honest man to find work in that wasteland? To make a future? What choice but to leave such a ruined place? But now Lindbergh's words filled him with resolve: *The time to act is here!*

It was time to go home and do his part. But he could not take Marlena and the boy, Johann. Not in a time of war. Later, in victory. In vindication.

At home, in their apartment over the candy store, he poured a shot of schnapps to celebrate his decision, which calmed his heart. He lit his pipe and puffed extravagantly, breathing in the sweet cherry aroma. Resolve settled upon him like the grace of God, a quiet coal-fire certainty smoldering within.

Marlena sat with him but did not drink, found no cause for celebration. Nine-year-old Johann—whom she insisted on calling by his American name, John—lay asleep behind a closed door.

Nicholas Wolf believed he had not made much of his life. Factory foreman, true, at the age of thirty-seven. Yet Lindbergh had crossed the ocean and made history by the time he was only twenty-five. Nicholas Wolf knew machines and could make men work hard. But there was no glory in his life, no grandeur, no hope of a shining future. He was no Lone Eagle. If he kept on this way, he would live out his years in the German-American enclave and retire on a modest pension and die—all too soon—unremarked and unremembered.

"I do not like the strange light in your eye when you talk about that creature," Marlena said evenly, twisting a linen dishtowel in her small hands. Hitler was always *that creature*. This was an old argument, and she understood that tonight she had lost it, but she would be heard. "We are Americans now. We do not bite the hand that feeds us."

"We are just refugees here." The force of his own voice surprised him. So did the emotions stirring inside him, a clarifying anger, a contempt for his circumstances, as if he were already gone and looking back with amazement that he had settled for such a small life.

"Oh, Nicky, not after so many years."

"Too many years."

"You passed the test. You took the oath. We are citizens."

As he threw back one more schnapps, she could see him lighting up with purpose. His head tilted back and his profile showed definite against the window light, his features composed and strong as she rarely saw him: the jaw set, the ridges of his cheekbones sharp under narrowed eyes.

"There is a higher claim on my loyalty."

In that moment, she loved him and despised him at once. The kindness was gone from his eyes, but there was always the terrible pull of love, the way she felt incomplete without him. They were finished with words. And with the words gone, they disappeared from each other and passed a terrible, wakeful night in silence.

He left in the morning, walking away with one old leather portmanteau clutched in his left hand, snowflakes dusting his squared shoulders like ash. He had looked in on his sleeping son and kissed him, and that was all the explanation the boy would ever have from his father. He left behind his beloved guitar, built by another German, Christian Frederick Martin, but he carried his Hohner harmonica snapped into a shirt pocket. He would have music with him on his journey.

Marlena watched him from the second-floor window of their apartment, still feeling the stiff pressure of his embrace, still smelling the cherry sweetness of his pipe smoke. His broad, gray back grew smaller and smaller, at last vanishing in the haze of snow.

She did not weep. She would have years for that.

Nicholas Wolf rode the Panama Limited down to New Orleans, sleeping for the first time in one of the Pullman cars he had spent so many years building, then slipped aboard the *Tara Maru*, a tramp steamer bound for South America. From Buenos Aires, he shipped across the Atlantic as a machinist's mate aboard the steamer *Austerlitz* to Vigo and found his way overland through the middle of Europe to Munich. Whenever he could, he posted a letter home. In this way, his itinerary became known later. Nicholas Wolf went to a lot of trouble to find the war.

Abruptly he stopped writing. Marlena never heard another word from him.

Then, in 1942, she received a telegram from the American government saying that Nicholas had died in the service of his country—*this* country, the U.S.A. The telegram said only that he had been reported killed in the Merchant Marine, which wasn't really the military, so there would be no pension. There were no further details.

But what did she want with a pension? What she wanted was to know.

For many months afterward, she sent letters to Washington to find out how he had died, where his body was buried, but she received no answer. Somehow the truth was lost in the mammoth bureaucracy of the War Department. There were just too many dead men to account for them all accurately.

Two years after Germany surrendered, a neighbor, a former American officer stationed with the occupation forces in Berlin, made contact for her with German officials. They found him: Corporal Nicholas Walter Wolf, 120th Infantry Regiment—a German regiment. He was officially listed as killed in action.

But then came even stranger news. According to the German records, he had died aboard a U-boat when it was sunk by an American bomber off the coast of North Carolina, at a place called Hatteras Island. No bodies were ever recovered. There was no further record.

How had a corporal of infantry died on a submarine? And how could he be claimed by both countries?

The thing was impossible.

CHAPTER ONE

CHICAGO, AUGUST 1991

1

The adventure began for Nick Wolf with a simple choice: tundra or island. Two deserts, one cold and distant, the other lapped by the salt sea. And what he was choosing was not what he thought he was choosing—simple geography, another job at some remote drilling site—but knowledge. Every new posting was an adventure into himself.

As usual, it was Fannon who gave him the choice. Nick was just about to head upstairs to a retirement reception when Fannon leaned in the doorway to his cubicle, loose and lanky, grinning crookedly, his collar open and his yellow silk tie askew. "You ready for another adventure, mate?" He was almost forty, but his freckles and uncombed reddish hair gave him a boyish look. He had a sun-drenched roguish manner about him that women found irresistible. "Bloody icebox or sandy beaches—take your pick."

Nick Wolf had known Fannon for as long as he had worked in the oil business and didn't know him at all. Fannon was all on the surface, a great pal to drink beers with while watching the World Cup, but a man whose private life, if he had one outside the company, was a mystery.

Fannon seemed Australian but never mentioned home in any specific way. He exuded an indefinite air of having grown up in boarding schools and yacht clubs, wore no wedding ring, and talked once in a while of pretty girls he went out with, but it was all in a bantering small-talk way that revealed nothing of what he truly loved or believed in or wanted out of life.

Some people were like that, Nick had learned, and he didn't press the matter. There were plenty of Fannons out in the world who didn't have much of an interior life—what his grandmother, his Oma, called *der kern*, a soul. The kernel of a genuine personality.

But he liked working under Fannon. He could trust his judgment on the job. And private was private.

"That's the deal," Fannon went on, and lit a cig. "I know, mate," he said, grinning and waving the cigarette, "*verboten*. Can't seem to get housebroken, yeah? Afraid all those nights at the smoke shack in fifth form wrecked me." He flicked the spent match onto the carpet and said cheerily, "Blue Team is bound for Anchorage and points north, and Red Team is off to the sunny coast of Bumfuck." Each team consisted of a cadre of geologists, engineers, boat drivers, roughnecks, tool pushers, assorted utility workers, a rig master, and supervisors such as Fannon—everybody the company needed to get a project up and running.

And one public research specialist, Nick's official title. He thought of himself simply as the company storyteller.

"Your call, amigo."

"What about you?"

"Me? Had my fill of Eskimos, mate. Reckon it's the sandy bitches for me."

"You mean beaches."

Fannon grinned.

"Let me take a look first, see what we're getting into. When?"

Fannon flipped a wheat-colored project folder onto Nick's desk and smiled, showing straight white teeth. "Now." He turned up his left wrist and checked his Rolex Submariner. "Wheels up in about four hours."

This was news. "What, no recon?" There was always a reconnaissance before sending in a full team, months of prep work to set up a staging area and quarters. Nick always liked to lie low for a few weeks before the company showed up—meet the locals, get his bearings before the waters were roiled. He'd never even heard about this project until now.

Fannon shrugged. "Parachuted in for a bit about six months ago, all on the QT, then got pulled out. Job was dead in the water, so they told me. Politics and financial hijinks and whatnot. Then, presto! OPEC squeezes production, the price of crude shoots through the roof. Somebody in Washington pulls a rabbit out of the hat, and the permits suddenly go live. God bless the bloody Arabs."

So after two years of waiting for the permits to be approved on the lease, bingo. It was an all-at-once kind of business—Nick had learned that a long time ago. Nothing happened, then suddenly everything happened at once. Still, it was a strange beginning. He felt as if he were entering a story already in progress.

"What are you not telling me?"

Fannon let out a long breath of smoke, then leaned close across Nick's desk. "Okay, mate, between you and me and the walls. You know how it goes: This could be nothing, nothing at all. A waste of time and money."

"But you don't think so."

Fannon smiled slyly. "We got some new reports. I think this could be it, Nicky. I think it could be big."

"How big?"

His voice came out as a hoarse whisper. "Game-changer big."

Nick sat back, nodded slowly. "And if it is . . ."

"And if it is, I want somebody on the ground I can bloody well trust, yeah? We'll have to move fast. We can't let corporate fuck it up. You know Funderburke—he'll question every bloody requisition. It's a short season before the hurricanes, and we've got to make our strike before we start losing time to the weather."

Funderburke, the senior auditor, was famous for being a skeptical stick-in-the-mud, the guy who ruined every party, always wanted one more report, one more question answered, before he would sign off. And the company hierarchy was total nineteenth century—one guy at the top, and below him Funderburke. A dictator and his number one. Funderburke was the narrow end of the funnel, the gatekeeper. Nothing got approved unless Funderburke signed off. Nick was one of the few people the old man trusted to give him straight answers, one of the only people he would take at his word. And the only such field man.

"So you want me to run interference with Funderburke."

"Only if you can tear yourself away from the fucking Eskimos, mate."

Nick checked his watch. "Speaking of Funderburke, you coming upstairs to see him off?" Funderburke was finally set to retire, and today was his official send-off, though he'd be around awhile longer as the company sorted out who would take over his desk.

"Nah, I hate sheet cake. Anyhow I got to stop at La Grange on the way out of town. Last minute thing, as usual. Some special gear they want me to carry down. I'll be pressed as it is." The company kept a secure warehouse at La Grange for housing core-drilling samples from all over the world, as well as sensitive technical equipment.

"Hey," Fannon said, "if it turns up a dry hole, then you get to lie on the beach and drink Coronas while we add up all the money we're losing."

"I hate to go in with so little prep."

"Christ, don't you get it? We had to keep this under wraps. Tiptoes, mate. Go in soft and quiet, no big deal, just one exploratory well. And if that's all it turns out to be, so be it."

"But if it hits . . ."

"Yeah, if it hits." Fannon grinned big, eyes flashing like he knew more than he was telling.

"What about the locals—any hostility there?" Nick opened the folder but continued looking at Fannon, trying to read the truth in his eyes. Some of the supervisors had a habit of papering over the rough spots—they were all can-do guys. Nobody wanted to be the first to point out what could go wrong. That wasn't the path to promotion. But Nick didn't care about promotion. He had all the job he wanted. And if there was any bad news, he wanted it up front so he could do something about it. That was a big part of his job: to know things, then to advise the bosses, and ultimately Funderburke, how to use what he discovered.

If the local environmental group was upset, could the company offer a donation of wetlands for preservation? If residents objected to increased traffic by heavy trucks, could the company mount a training program to hire local drivers?

Usually he went in long before the rig so he could suss out who the players were. Sometimes it was a mayor or senator, but just as often it was someone without any official standing who nevertheless carried the real power—a local tribal chief, the head of an old and revered family, once even a priest. He needed to know the local press, the city council, the bureaucrats who handled traffic and zoning, and, always, the environmentalists. Then he would pass off his research to a front man—or more often a front woman—who would go on camera as the face of NorthAm. And one of the vice presidents—coached by Nick, who always remained in the background—would fly in to meet the players who mattered.

The other part of his job, the part he liked best, was simply to write about the operation, to tell the company's story artfully and with enough clarity to celebrate the benefit it was bringing. He filled pages of press releases. He wrote gripping narratives for the company newsletter. And the annual shareholders' report routinely carried the newest version of his most important narrative: the innovative success story of a lean, responsible, old-fashioned company.

Fannon had an unflattering name for what he did. He called Nick "the carnival barker outside the tent." But instead of luring in the rubes to see the geek show, he lured in the investors—bankers, brokers, day traders, rich guys looking to get richer, mutual fund managers in need of a reliable investment. There was an advantage in telling a good story about yourself to the right people. They didn't just want to invest in a company or a product—they wanted to invest in your story.

Nick didn't care what Fannon called him. He believed in the story and was good at telling it.

Fannon blew out a long drag. "Not so bad—a few old hippies and fishermen. The rest just don't want us to fuck up the tourist trade."

They were drilling offshore then. He looked hard at Fannon. "Are we going to fuck up the tourist trade?"

"Nah. It's just the one hole, exploratory."

"For now."

"Can't even see the platform from the beach."

Nick might as well be on hand in case the exploratory hole turned into a bonanza and the team needed him up to speed in a hurry. But gearing up for extraction would still take time—to assemble the equipment for long-term lease, to file the thousands of pages of regulatory paperwork, to hire a large, experienced crew.

Nick scanned the first page inside the project folder. "Jesus, man. You're kidding."

"What? Something wrong, Nicky?"

Nick slapped the paper against his hand. "This place, that's all. Of all the places on the planet. How weird is that?"

"Hatteras Island?" Fannon cocked his head. He hated not knowing things. He spent his life being in the loop. "Wait, that's the place you told me about, yeah?"

"Yeah, Hatteras." The name sounded strange in Nick's mouth, though he had heard it all his life. He thought it might be an Indian word. He stared at the name on the folder. His Oma used to whisper it like a curse that shouldn't be spoken out loud. He sucked in a breath. Just a sand bar of an island, really, narrow and bent and low, no high ground, off the coast of North Carolina. Part of a protective string of such islands called the Outer Banks. Sand and sea oats and tourists and fishermen. He had studied the map for years, knowing he would never go here.

Fannon said, "I take it you're in."

2

Nick had lost his Pacific tan over the last two months, holed up in his cubicle at the home office of NorthAm, on Michigan Avenue fifteen glass stories above the clamor of the city. *Debriefing,* his supervisors called it.

He spent his hours writing reports and analyses and talking points about the new oil and gas discoveries in the Andaman Sea, ginning up a public-relations campaign to emphasize "environmental stewardship" and "green technology"—all routine stuff, the long, slow glide after the intensity of twelve-hour days overseas. He enjoyed the solitary nature of it.

Even at the office, he typed on his notebook computer, the newest available—a durable six-pound machine that wrote his stories invisibly onto floppy disks that were not floppy at all but hard, flat plastic squares of data. He could print them out using his portable machine, and from anywhere in the world mail the disks to corporate headquarters.

He liked the feel of the keyboard, the soft *click-click* of the plastic keys. He had started his reporting career on a manual typewriter, and it took practice to break himself of the habit of pounding the keys to make words appear by punching an inked ribbon onto paper. Now the stories floated on a glowing screen, ethereal, never set in type until he was completely satisfied he could do no better.

Then his reports went to corporate, and usually without much alteration were cycled back out into the world of small-town newspapers, briefs for lobbyists, shareholders' reports, and the like.

Cyrus Hanson Jr., son of old Cyrus Hanson, who had founded NorthAm as a wildcat driller in Texas back in the 1940s, had hired Nick. Hanson was great at running the company but spoke only in numbers. He tended to be taciturn and private, hardly talked even to his own family. He was smart enough to know he needed somebody eloquent who could tell the company story in plain words.

He had read Nick's newspaper articles on aldermen's meetings and zoning hearings and all the crucial, dull machinery of city government and marveled that he made his subjects actually seem interesting. One day, he summoned Nick to a meeting at NorthAm headquarters and expected to wow him with the opulent surroundings—hand-rubbed mahogany paneling, ten-foot-high windows that canted outward like those on the bridge of a giant ship, the desk he sat behind, a single slab of black granite that weighed over a ton. But Nick was not wowed, only bemused. He stood slanted against the dark wood doorframe, hands in his pockets, smiling crookedly, waiting for Hanson's pitch.

Hanson held up a recent copy of the *Tribune* and said, "If you can make this crap seem exciting, then you can turn the NorthAm story into *Moby Dick*."

Nick didn't bother to remind him that in Melville's opus, the ship went down with all hands but one. He liked Hanson—and he was ready for a change. Cyrus Hanson made his point and doubled Nick's salary, and all at once Nick was, as Cyrus called him, "the company storyteller."

NorthAm specialized in difficult projects—remote locations, sites made perilous by political unrest or extreme weather or geography, unusually deep wells.

On the Andaman project, it had sunk four wells. The only hitch had come on one deep well. The bit penetrated a field of cool methane slush, which expanded with the heat of the whirling drill. The hole blew up in a small way and began leaking oil into the pristine sea, the vacation paradise of James Bond Island, and the sugary beaches of southern Thailand. The platform was wrecked, but most of the crew—all but three local men—got off in the lifecars. The crew drilled a relief well and got it under control and capped the bad well, and that, too, was in Nick's report. He had gone over the data to make sure the well was under control and spent a long time getting the words right so the company could talk honestly and accurately about what had happened and how it was fixed for good.

Luckily it had happened far from American shores, and he knew from long experience that Americans weren't interested in anything overseas. But lose control of a well off North Carolina—that would be a different matter. That would mean headlines in the *New York Times* and the lead story on every TV network and federal marshals hauling the guys in charge to the congressional hearings chamber.

So he might as well be where he could keep an eye on things. He was getting restless anyway, ready to get out in the field again, to lose the tie and put on cargo shorts and boat mocs and breathe again.

Before heading out, he rode the elevator up to the executive floor to pay his respects to Ned Funderburke, who was retiring after almost half a century. He had been around when old Cyrus brought in his first gusher. He was the fiduciary conscience of NorthAm. No replacement had been named yet, but rumor was that there would be some changes to modernize the corporate structure, and Fannon was on the fast track to become a VP. He had taken on more and more operational control in the field as Hanson got older and stayed close to home.

Nick arrived just as Funderburke was finishing his remarks to a smattering of applause and polite laughter. Funderburke was a small man with a hard little belly who wore tailored dark blue suits with suspenders and a bow tie. As the old guy stepped away from the mic, Nick waved, and Funderburke's blue eyes lit up. Nick was one of the few people who liked him. Fannon and the others found him rigid and opinionated, grated at his rambling war stories of the old days in Texas. But Nick didn't mind. Sometimes the stories found their way into his reports, reminders of the rock-solid integrity of the whole enterprise. And the older man made him feel a reassuring continuity with the past.

"Nicky," he said, clapping a short arm around Nick's shoulders. "You missed my best joke."

"You can tell it to me when I get back. I'll buy you lunch."

Funderburke leaned close to his ear. "It was Fannon, wasn't it? He kept you downstairs."

Nick grinned. "He's all right, just an asshole sometimes. He was prepping me for a trip."

"Speaking of trips. That Andaman project." Funderburke held him with his unblinking eyes. "You saw the men taken care of with your own eyes."

Nick nodded. "I was on the search boat, and later I made the rounds at the hospital."

"Good. Were you also in the control room when the cap went on?"

"No, but I got there right after. Fannon showed me the data and the raw camera feed."

"Fannon." Funderburke shook his head. "So it's cleaned up? For sure?"

"Yeah," Nick said. He squeezed Funderburke's shoulder. "It's all in the report."

"I can read," Funderburke said, and smiled. "But I'm old school. I wanted to look you in the eye."

"You know my rule."

"Yes. Never write what you didn't see for yourself."

"So I've got a plane to catch. And so do you."

"Yeah, Cabo. God help me, I'll probably rot in the sun down there. But Gloria will like it."

"Gonna miss you around here."

"Maybe you, nobody else." He shook Nick's hand with both of his and held it in a surprisingly strong grip. "It's a good rule, Nicky."

3

Nick slipped home to his garage apartment and packed in no time: one big bull-hide duffel, a soft briefcase, the old Martin New Yorker guitar he had carried around the world in its canvas gig bag. Left behind in Chicago all those years ago, it had belonged to his grandfather, Opa, his namesake.

Cabbing his way to O'Hare, Nick stopped to see his grandmother at the assisted-living home in Evanston, a brick monolith that was surprisingly modern inside, with pass-card doors, indirect lighting, and blond oak floors, neat and trim as an architect's model and smelling heavily of flowers. It always unsettled him. She should be living in an old-fashioned, cozy row house with high windows filtered by lace curtains, saggy, soft furniture, and a screened porch—something from the old neighborhood.

Nick at thirty-five was a little taller than average, handsome in an ordinary way except when he smiled. He had the wide-open grin of a little boy on Christmas morning, his Oma always teased him. She said he had his grandfather's smile, and because he had never known his grandfather the compliment unsettled him. He had studied the one sepia photo his Oma had of his grandfather, showing a stolid, set face with a thick brush-cut mustache and no smile. "You should smile more often, Nicky," she would chide him. "Always with that same sad face, not like in the old days."

He knew what she really meant. Not since that awful morning during high school when everything changed. Since then, he had not truly connected with anyone. He was friendly, but he had no true friends. Girlfriends came and went, but none stuck. He kept some part of himself always separate, aloof. His Oma would wink coyly. "A pretty girl, she loves a man who smiles at her."

His blond hair was going darker with age. He was strong and agile enough except for a creaky right knee blown out by a collision at third base when he was in high school. Winters, it ached in the damp chill that blew off Lake Michigan. Another reason to go south.

She was expecting him. She always seemed to know when he'd arrive, always managed to be sitting right beside the phone whenever he called, at whatever hour. There had always been that intuitive connection between them.

The door was ajar, and he stepped in with a greeting. The beige carpet felt spongy underfoot. She was sitting in a rocking chair by the window, a black woolen shawl laid across her lap despite the heat, a tiny woman with a fluff of white hair and a face like a kindly nun. Yet she had once been an iron workhorse of a woman, who'd spent forty years at the Pullman Works wiring sleeper cars. Her hands were small and cramped now, bony and arthritic, but they had always touched him with exquisite gentleness.

"Oh, Nicky, I had the dream again—it was so real."

He kissed her cool forehead. "It's only a dream, Oma."

"Ach, it was on the beach again. Standing there, looking out to sea. And his face, Nicky—so real! He was watching me from across the waves, like in a movie."

He held her hand. "Did it frighten you, Oma?" He thought that each time she dreamed, it distorted the memory of her actual past before the war, so long ago now, until after a while she would not recognize truth from dream. Maybe she already could not.

She looked puzzled, shook her head slowly. "No, not this time." A look of wonder lit her face, softened the creases. "That was the strange part. This time he was . . . he was smiling." She looked up at Nick, and her pale blue eyes seemed enormous behind her old-fashioned gold-rimmed glasses. Her face was fixed in a kind of beatific daze. "I know what you think of an old woman's wishful dreams, but this was real."

Nick nodded, unconvinced.

She said, wonder now in her voice, "He was at peace."

"There. You see."

She shook her head more vigorously. "But I am not." She recovered herself and laughed. "I am being a terrible hostess." As was her custom on these visits, she poured Goldwasser into tea glasses and served them both on a tray, which was already on a side table. She had it sent over from Keonig's once a week in a ribboned box, her single luxury.

Nick jostled the glass and watched the flakes of gold stir and settle in the amber liqueur as in a snow globe. It was strong stuff, aromatic with herbs, and he closed his eyes, drank, and felt an immediate, pleasant flush.

She had brought with her what she could from her former residence—a well-worn club chair, a four-poster bed, and her prize: a Black Forest steeple clock made by Franz Hermle. It had been a wedding gift from her friends at the factory, a legacy of the old country. Her family had owned one like it, hand-built from dark cherry with a steepled top and twin conical towers on either side. The bottom half was encased in ornately frosted glass, behind which a brass pendulum measured out the hours. Carefully wound, it could run for eight days.

Nick sat back and listened to the tireless ticking of the clock, now settled on the mantel above an electric fireplace.

"And where are they sending you this time, Nicky? You never come anymore unless you are also going." She smiled at her little wordplay. She had come over from Danzig in 1935, a child of the Great War, a hungry girl of twenty, and spoke all these years later with the same thick accent in which she had stammered out her first words of halting English: "Mister, you want hire me? I work good."

"Another island."

"Ach, always an island with these people! Not back to the cannibals and the *schwartzes*?"

"Oma, please." He laughed. She had a fixed idea that islanders the world over were black savages. "No, Oma. This time, I'm staying in America. The East Coast." He hesitated a beat, and she cocked her head, waiting for the rest. He might as well be honest. "Hatteras Island."

"Nicky . . ." She put down her tea glass and leaned forward, touched his bare arm with a feathery hand. "Hatteras?" She whispered the name slowly, drawing out each syllable as evenly as a sigh.

"I know, Oma." He'd been everywhere, to thirty-six states and twenty-two foreign countries—deserts and rain forests and islands and lonely peninsulas on the edge of frozen seas. He would count them off whenever he had trouble sleeping. But in all his travels, he'd never set foot on this particular island, so strangely famous within the family. Truth to tell, he had avoided it. What good would it do to go there? As a boy, he had never heard the name spoken without feeling a vague anger and sadness well up within him, because it caused his Oma so much distress. Somehow the name itself contained a fatal mystery.

He used to write it out in block letters and rearrange them as anagrams, trying to unlock their bitter truth: *AT HEARTS. RATS HATE. STAR HEAT.*

But by manhood, other trials had overtaken him, and he had outgrown all that. Hatteras was now just a name on a map, a place he had never been and did not plan to go. Until now.

"Your grandfather. Opa. My Nicholas."

"There's nothing down there, Oma. That just happened to be the place where the U-boat got caught." It had sunk many miles off the beach, he was sure, out in the deep water where the U-boats hunted and were, in turn, hunted by sub-killing planes. He had seen maps and charts in the books he had pored over as a boy in the public library, trying to understand his Opa's strange history.

"You can maybe discover something."

"We're going down there to look for oil. I'll have my hands full." That was stretching it, he knew. Fannon had all but guaranteed the trip would be a vacation, not the usual grind—unless they got lucky. But he shied from making promises he couldn't keep.

"My poor Nicky." She touched a mottled hand to her brow, then resumed sipping her Goldwasser. Her hand trembled with memory.

Which one did she mean—her lost husband or him?

"It's just a coincidence, Oma."

She said, "There are no coincidences in life, Nicky. There are only patterns you don't recognize yet."

Then she lapsed into silence, her head nodding. He'd been afraid of this, what his news might trigger. Her memories were sometimes more real to her than her life in the here and now. It happened more and more often these days. The staff was careful to avoid using the word *dementia*, but he understood she was slipping, mind and body.

He gently eased the glass out of her hand and set it on the lace doily covering the side table.

4

Nick leaned back in his chair, swigged the last of his drink.

He had grown up in the western suburbs, not far from here, had learned a smattering of the German language during visits to his Oma. Then, coming back on the expressway from a weekend foliage tour in Door County, Wisconsin, his parents were killed by a drunk driver.

He was staying over with a friend from his soccer team, glad to be away from his parents for the weekend. He and his soccer pal had stayed up late watching movies in the den, and when he woke Sunday morning his friend's mother was standing in the doorway in her bathrobe, tears streaming down her face.

He sat bolt upright, knew it was bad, as bad as bad ever got. All he could say was, "Which one? Which one?"

And the boy's mother only cried harder and held out her arms, but he could not accept her embrace. He dodged past her and ran outside in his sweatpants and T-shirt, bare feet pounding on the cold sidewalk for seven long blocks to his empty house.

He was seventeen.

After the double funeral, he moved in with his grandmother, into the apartment above the candy store where she had lived for all those years after her foolish husband, loyal German that he was, marched off to fight for the Fatherland. "If I move, how will he ever find me?" she always explained, for death could not be final and real for her without a body to bury. And for all her husband's stubborn faults, she had loved him with her heart's heart. She had been so young when he left her. And some part of her must have believed her own stubborn love could bring him home.

Sometimes he himself had half-expected his grandfather would appear like a shadow at the front door, an aged stranger in a gray uniform, in whom he would recognize his own sad face.

Nick finished his senior year of high school among strangers. Whenever he got the chance, he sneaked off to Comiskey Park to watch the White Sox, reliving some of his best memories, long afternoon doubleheaders in the bleachers with his dad. His dad always rooted for the Sox—what he called "a workingman's team"—even though they hadn't won a World Series since 1919, the year of the Black Sox, the big fix.

Soon enough, Nick went off to study journalism at Northwestern on a scholarship he earned delivering newspapers. But he wasn't cut out to be a local reporter. He was far too restless for that. Since joining NorthAm, he had mostly lived out of his duffel in far-flung places that might as well have been the dark side of the moon. It was a life that never seemed quite real, as if he were playing a role in a movie, masquerading as a rugged man of the world, hiding in plain sight.

Some days, he felt as if he lived nowhere, that he belonged nowhere, that he was a free agent floating through the world, stirred this way and that like the flakes in his Goldwasser. On good days it was a romantic notion, and on bad days it just made him feel homesick for a place that wasn't even there anymore—maybe never had been.

Even his name, Nicholas Wolf, sometimes seemed strange to him, a name that belonged to somebody else, whose life he was only impersonating.

His Oma was his one touchstone to his boyhood, the only living person who could say it had ever really happened at all. But the old candy-store apartment was long gone, the whole block bulldozed for a freeway ramp. The landscape of his youth was erased, indistinct even in memory now.

And all the places since then seemed to blend together into a generic foreignness. The same stink of diesel and cigarettes and wet concrete. The same patched-together, improvisational feel to the shanty boomtowns on the edges of nowhere, peopled with contractors, fishermen, fixers, local hustlers of one kind or another, soldiers of fortune, a few lost souls who had washed up there when their money or luck ran out.

In those shifty places, where secrets sloshed like sewage in the open-air gutters, a tawdry kind of capitalism was always at work—everything for sale, shares to be sold, leases to be negotiated, fixes to be arranged, claims to be filed, fortunes to be made.

But never his own.

Now he watched his Oma sleep, her face relaxed in dreaming, the worry lines smoothed out, her breath coming in long, peaceful sighs. From time to time, her hand fluttered and her mouth opened as if to speak, but the only sounds were her quiet breath and the precise ticking of the steeple clock, its pendulum swinging behind frosted crystal.

CHICAGO, 1936
5

Nicholas Wolf was entering a Pullman car late in the afternoon, just before the end of his shift. He was to inspect a set of faulty hinges and try to figure out a better design. The car was oddly dark inside, and he heard muffled noises at the far end, in one of the sleeper compartments. He trod lightly toward the far end, a ball-peen hammer in his hand. He had brought it along to pop the pins out of the hinges. He stopped before the curtain of the last berth. He drew it aside.

A young woman was pinned onto the bed. Two men were holding her down. One had a big, bruised hand cupped over her mouth and the other clamped onto the partition. Her eye was swollen, and there was blood on her lip.

The two men looked up, taken off-guard. He recognized them from the electrical shop. He understood at once what was happening and saw that it had not gone very far. The young woman's clothes were mussed, but she was still dressed. He did not think or say a word. He swung the hammer against the hand on the partition and heard bones crack. The man leaped up in pain and rage, and Nicholas dropped him with a fist to the eye. The other man put up his hands, palms out. Nicholas swung the hammer anyway, and the man fell to the floor holding his hand.

"Go away from here," Nicholas said. "Take your friend."

"Take it easy, it's payday."

"Not for you. No more for you." He was breathing hard. He could have killed them, still wanted to, and they had seen that in his eyes. It was a revelation to him, that he could be a man whom other men feared. He had acted wholly on instinct, and now he had discovered at his core a man who could do whatever he had to do.

When the men had gone, he reached into his back pocket, pulled out his red kerchief, and carefully dabbed the blood off her lip. She sat up, and her face tightened into a sob.

"There, there, none of that," he said. "It is over."

She blinked back tears and wouldn't look him in the eye. "I am so ashamed."

He laughed shortly. "What a crazy thing to say." He jerked his head. "It is they who are the shameful ones." Then he said, "I am Nicholas. They call me Nicky in the machine shop."

Slowly she raised her eyes and looked into his. "I was . . . I was wiring the carriage lamps."

"I know," he said. "Tell me your name."

"Marlena," she said.

"There, there," he said, soothing her brow with his rough hand. "There, there."

6

A few weeks later, Nicholas Wolf was working behind a crew repairing a faulty coupling on a Pullman Tourist Car, checking the quality of the welds. At the other end of the long car, he spied a willowy figure—Marlena?—stepping tentatively across the tracks inside the great shed. Behind her, the high square of light from the open door leading to the transfer table haloed her, so he could not see her face for all the light. She was just a small, upright shape, slim curves and a nimbus of dark hair, a wooden toolbox that seemed much too heavy for her suspended from her left hand.

The transfer table was in motion. It was a stretch of track fitted onto a lateral engine so the track could move sideways up and down a row of a dozen other tracks, taking a car from any of them and delivering it to the track leading into the shed, where it could be worked on out of the weather.

Marlena hesitated before mounting the high step into the car, as if she were not sure she could step so high carrying such a heavy burden. Nicholas saw a dark shadow loom behind her—a new car was rolling into the shed, propelled by gravity. There was no engine noise, and the racket of welding and hammering would have drowned it out anyway. He dropped his toolbox and sprinted down the tracks toward her.

She looked up, puzzled, then almost afraid. She was all in shadow now, the railroad car bearing down on her.

With one arm, he swept her off her feet, then leaped onto the step of the Tourist Car. She grabbed a rail and held on with one hand, her other still tightly gripping her toolbox. Nicholas felt the gust of air as the new car whooshed past almost soundlessly.

She steadied herself on the platform of the car, still holding onto the railing with one hand, and set down her toolbox and took a long breath.

Nicholas smoothed her dark hair off her face as he would a child's, and smiled. "You must always watch," he said gently.

She was shaken and still afraid, and maintained her strong grip on the railing. "You saved me. Again."

He took her trembling hand and kissed it lightly. She glowed with survival, her eyes fiercely bright. "Yes. And for that, you must marry me."

He did not wait for her to say no. He went inside the car to check some fittings, walking its length without feeling the floor under his boots

And in a matter of weeks, they shared their first breathless night together, his voice husky in the dark, whispering over and over, "*Du bist die Liebe meines Lebens*"—"You are the love of my life."

From then on, he whispered it to her every night, and every night she whispered back with utter certainty, simply, "*Ich liebe dich*"—"I love you."

CHICAGO, AUGUST 1991

7

Nick lingered a moment in his grandmother's room, listening to her breathe softly, her chest barely rising and falling, watching her face relax into deep sleep, into peace. Her hand had stilled. This little place was her last home. She knew that as well as he. And she was the last of his blood kin. When she was gone, he would be alone in a world that had never claimed him, and no part of which he had ever claimed.

He could not see the face of the clock on the mantel, so he checked his watch—a good diver's watch, the only luxury he owned. It was time to go. He tucked the shawl snug around his Oma, kissed her cool forehead. Her lips mouthed the familiar words, though her eyes remained closed. He murmured into her ear, "*Ich liebe dich auch*"—"I love you, too"—then clicked the door closed quietly behind him.

He paused for a moment. Standing outside her door felt like standing outside every door in the world, all of them closed to him, none opening into his own home.

He checked his watch again. He had a plane to catch.

CHAPTER TWO

HATTERAS ISLAND, 1991

1

She expected he would come someday. Because they all hoped so hard he would not, his coming was, in her mind, inevitable. There was nothing mystical in her certainty, just cold calculation. The world was in motion. Nobody stayed put anymore. If enough strangers came to the island, sooner or later one of them was bound to be part of the story.

Until now, she had never known who it would be. His name didn't matter. He would be the Someone who would upset everything. The Someone who would look backward, opening up settled matters. All these years later, it was still the foundation of everything. The invisible current running underneath the placid surface of their lives, like the memory of a storm in a distant place, a great, dark wave far out at sea. When it reached shallow water, it might break violently, overwhelm everything.

Well, she considered, *it won't be easy. I know his name now, and I hope he is ready.*

And am I ready? Is any of us? Is such a thing even possible?

There was no telling what would happen, who he would turn out to be, besides his name. In some strange, awful sense, they were giving themselves into his hands just by allowing him onto the island. As if that were their choice.

And there was no telling what she herself would do—what any of them would do. *We will act as who we are,* she mused.

And who is that?

The loyal granddaughter who will protect my grandfather, no matter what.

She closed the reservation book and sent the maid upstairs to make up his room. Then she changed into a gray linen suit and prepared to chair the ten o'clock meeting of the board of directors of Royal Enterprises—every single one of them family, including her grandfather. All the news she could talk about was good news: highly profitable investments, two new shopping plazas opening on the north island, rentals booked solid in four hundred units two years out at an average rental of two thousand per week, with another fifty units coming on line any day now. Cash flow was strong and getting stronger every day. The value of Royal Real Estate alone was appreciating at almost thirteen percent per year.

But the numbers, all the dollar figures and profit margins, meant little to her. Maybe she simply took for granted all she had. Mostly it felt like a great weight on her shoulders, responsibility for a heavy name and the lives of so many people.

The running of the various companies was managed by some of those other people, trusted cousins. Her job was merely to preside over the corporation, to be the one who perched atop the pyramid and took the long view, steering things in the right direction. The one who carried on her grandfather's legacy.

The one saving grace was the Royal Foundation, which funded college scholarships for island kids, supported the senior center and the emergency clinic in the village, rebuilt the library after the last bad hurricane, and one way or another provided financial help for many of the poorest families on the island—almost always anonymously. She didn't mind signing those checks. The foundation had its own staff to keep the paperwork straight and all the accounts current.

And in truth, there was no need for her to manage the inn personally. But it grounded her, kept her close to him, felt like clean, honest work. Made her believe her life was simple and complete. Sometimes, for hours on end, it could allow her to forget who she really was, the burden that one day would fall entirely on her shoulders.

One day, maybe soon, but not yet.

2

From the time he was an infant, Isaac Abraham Lord had started each day at sunup, eyes wide open. He missed very little. Now, eighty-seven years on, he hauled himself out of his narrow bed at dawn and pulled his old gray flannel robe around his shoulders. He carefully tucked the corners of his blanket around the thin mattress and placed the single down pillow neatly against the headboard.

The day came up hot even before sunrise, but the chill had settled deep in his bones. He fingered the small cross around his neck, silver against his black skin. *O Lord,* he prayed silently, *make me an instrument of Thy peace.* He raised the cross to his lips and kissed it.

He started a kettle boiling for tea and stepped onto the back porch of his one-story board-and-batten cottage to sit and wait and watch the snowy egrets and clapper rails feeding in the back marsh. The clapper rails dove and stayed under a long time, emerging far away from where they entered the water, able to fly underwater. He always marveled at their ability to exist in two different worlds at once.

What would it be like to fly through a sky of water?

The egrets pranced around the marsh in elegant high steps, as if on a parade ground. Wherever he looked in the world, he saw an unutterable beauty, divinely inspired. It filled him to overflowing, lit a candle of joy inside his heart, and came out of his mouth in the words he spoke from the pulpit every Sunday morning, words that brought tears of rapture to his congregation.

Where there is hatred, let me sow love.

The sky seemed to waver, the thin gray clouds rocking like the sea.

He still had so much to do, but he understood he had little time left. He had long been shadowed by a sense of the days and hours ticking down, the mainspring inside him loosening and loosening until it would give up its hold altogether and, at last, come to rest. He was tired all the time now and would welcome such rest.

He felt only one regret: Long ago, he had been entrusted with a letter he had never delivered.

Where there is injury, pardon.

Strange, after the thousands of good deeds and unselfish acts over his lifetime, that a single thing he had done—or in this case left undone—should have festered like a sliver in a finger, a little sting he felt every time he touched something. Over it had grown a hard and callous part of himself, a part that gave him no pride.

The letter had been handed to him many years ago by a fisherman whose pregnant wife was staying with her parents at the other end of the long island. For all Isaac knew, it contained routine news, pleasantries, and household business. It was not unusual for islanders to communicate this way, even with their own families, especially if, like this man, they were temporarily separated by miles and the demands of weather and season that respected no personal interest. They must fish when the fishing was good, and stay out as long as it took to fill their holds, and their families understood and accepted this fundamental fact. The letter bore no address—in those days, Isaac was postmaster as well as preacher, and he knew every family and house on the island, and rarely required postage for local delivery.

But the letter had been misrouted by one of those strange accidents that interfered with the predictable unfolding of life. Distracted, in a hurry to make the run to the mainland ahead of a gathering nor'easter, he slipped it into the wrong sack, the off-island sack. As simple as that. The two sacks were standing open side by side, and he put it in the wrong one. And by such careless missteps were lives changed forever.

He had carried it to the mainland himself on the mailboat, all unaware. The letter passed from hand to hand in the main post office unopened and unread, and then came back to him a month later, like a message in a bottle. Someone had recognized the single name on the envelope as one common to the island.

And by then, everything had changed. He would never deliver the letter. Could not.

It was better that way, Isaac had believed for a long time. No good could ever come of it, only heartache and strife. He kept the letter in the top drawer of his pine-wood dresser and visited it nearly every day, each time renewed in his belief that he was doing the right thing by holding it, by not delivering it.

But why keep it at all then?

He had asked the question of his conscience often. *Why not simply destroy it?* And the answer, delivered in the still, small voice in his soul, always came back the same: *Because you have no right.* He did not truly understand the answer, but he lived with it.

At last, in great age, he had heard that still voice of his conscience, the whisper of divine guidance, telling him what he must do. The voice came to him in moments like this one, quiet moments of reflection, when his alert attention to the world itself became a pure prayer.

The same voice had called him to preach.

He had been walking the beach after a storm and found, washed up on the wrack line, a small leather-bound Bible. He picked it up, and it fell open in his hands to Malachi, the last book of the Old Testament: "I will send my messenger, who will prepare the way before me."

The book of Malachi, of all passages. In it, the prophet foretells a judgment on the people who have strayed from the covenant, who have enriched themselves at the expense of their neighbors.

For Isaac Abraham Lord, it was a call to righteousness tempered by good works and mercy.

The small voice stirred inside him, and he felt words forming in his throat, words to say to the ones who had troubles, who had lost loved ones in the war, who were suffering in their secret hearts, who were wanting in courage or faith or hope, who lacked generosity of spirit. And he heard the voice tell him, *You are my messenger.*

And so he became, listening always for the voice to guide him through his years. And now the voice had told him, *A new messenger will come. From off. Yet he will not be a stranger but one who has dwelt among you, and you will recognize him.*

Isaac could not parse the riddle, nor did he try. The letter was addressed to a person who had never existed, and yet Isaac knew—as the messenger would know—who must receive it. So he had left written instructions to his son, Diogenes: *Give it to the messenger from off.*

He must trust his son to understand his meaning and fulfill his covenant. He must trust him to recognize the messenger when he appeared.

Perhaps that would make it right in the eyes of the Lord. For his sin was compounded: Isaac had read the letter. Steamed it open over his teakettle and carefully unfolded the three loose-leaf pages, line after line covered with small, carefully penciled handwriting. Only then it was too late, for the letter was both a confession and a suicide note.

He had sealed it up again and never told anyone what was in it—never revealed to a soul that he even had it.

Where there is error, truth.

He had done all that was possible for an old man to do.

And now he sat, watching the birds in the back marsh as the water heated for tea. The light went hazy. A great roaring stillness came over him, as if the sky had suddenly melded with the ocean, and the air held the density of water alive in his ears.

Time stalled. Out on the marsh, nothing moved, the egrets and clapper rails frozen in place.

His breath caught in his throat. A hollow pain spread inside his chest. His mainspring was loosening its coil and letting go.

Isaac felt his body suddenly lighten.

He tried to stand but could not, as if his legs no longer had the bone and muscle to lift him, as if the substance of him were evaporating.

Where there is despair, hope.

The world started up again. The birds moved over the marsh, but the marsh was suddenly far away, behind a screen of silvery mist.

He exhaled the pain in his chest, and it was gone. He no longer needed breath.

Where there is darkness, light.

The light came up gauzy and brilliant.

Inside, the teakettle screamed.

And where there is sadness, joy.

Isaac Abraham Lord rose out of himself then and into the light.

3

The company turboprop shuddered through a violent thunderstorm just west of Roanoke Island and set down on the slick runway, slewing into taxi mode. Nick stepped down onto the wet concrete apron, which was hissing steam into the heat, and felt the humidity press on his shoulders like familiar hands. The place was nearly tropical, but the heat was clean, wind-burned, like some parts of Africa where he had been.

Fannon tossed him the keys to a slate-blue Land Rover bearing the NorthAm logo on the door panels, a stylized gold compass rose with a dark blue arrow pointing north.

Fannon wore a company golf shirt with the same logo, but Nick dressed in sun-faded khaki cargo shorts and a blue sports shirt unadorned with anybody's logo. He knew by now that strangers didn't talk easily to men in uniform. And nobody in a place like this confided to a man wearing a coat and tie.

Nick tucked his duffel, guitar, and briefcase in the back and settled into the driver's seat. A couple of local hands wheeled over a large metal case on a hand truck and hefted it onto the rear cargo deck with a thud.

"Careful with that," Fannon said sharply.

The men shoved the metal case firmly inside and closed the tailgate and shuffled away muttering.

"What are we hauling along this time?" Nick asked.

"No idea, mate. They said it was fragile, some kind of calibration equipment or whatnot. I'm not a fucking engineer, am I?"

"I remember once in Nigeria they had me carry in a box like that," Nick said. "Turned out to be a case of eighteen-year-old Glenlivet."

"Don't I wish," Fannon said. He leaned a bare arm on the passenger-side window sill and said carelessly, "Take it easy on the curves."

From the air, Nick had noted the single ruler-straight road that ran south toward Hatteras. He laughed. "What curves?"

He pulled into a steady stream of tourist traffic—minivans and campers with license plates from Ohio, Virginia, Delaware, New Jersey. They drove through Manteo, a village of strip motels and low-slung cottages, and over a causeway and a high modern bridge from which Nick caught his first glimpse of the ocean, gray and corrugated with rough waves.

"Breezing up out there, ain't it?" Fannon said.

Nick just nodded. The wind pushed and tugged at the boxy car, and he held the wheel with both hands till they came down on the other side into Whalebone Junction and turned south, following Route 12 onto Bodie Island, a marshy sand bar inhabited only by birds by the thousands: Canada geese, pintails and canvasbacks and mergansers and mallards, plovers and pipers, herons and egrets, gulls of all stripes.

"This'll be part of the fuss, Nicky boy. Sooner or later. We're driving smack under the Atlantic Flyway."

"A migration route, eh?" Usually Nick spent weeks prepping for a trip, absorbing the local geography and culture, alert for potential problems and opportunities. But he hadn't had any time to research this place—unless he counted his whole life. Fannon had come down briefly to lease docking space, and that was all the official prep.

"Oh, yeah, it's a regular freeway for the little feathered fuckers."

Nick laughed. Fannon pretended to be a nature hater, part of his fuck-all manner. But in the only unguarded moment Nick had ever caught him in, he had seen Fannon weep over swans smothered in an oil spill in the Med.

He'd make a note about the flyway, though. Any spill here would be devastating. They'd need to have a good plan, one they could talk about with conviction. The way they had handled the unlucky mess in the Andaman Sea. You could fool people for a while, but in the end it was always more effective to coax out their fears, figure out an answer you believed in, and then talk straight. People craved reassurance, but it had to be genuine.

And then you had to do what you could to make it right. People also craved justice.

Nick believed in his work for NorthAm, in the responsible manner in which the company did business. Drilling oil was dirty work, no argument, but how could you live without oil? The whole world ran on oil: ships, planes, automobiles, home furnaces. And what could you build without plastic? And how could you make roads without asphalt?

There was a right way to go about it. You could do things that would soften the footprint, minimize the disruption. Some of the majors didn't operate that way. They just charged in and took what they wanted, paid off a few local bigwigs, and made their killing. And they left behind a mess. That wasn't how NorthAm operated. Once he'd made the mistake of saying this out loud over drinks at an industry seminar, and the guys from the majors just laughed at him. One of them said, "You believe in Santa Claus, too, sport?"

His job description didn't even exist at the majors—they were all about spin, high-powered PR, and VPs who would gang-tackle the local interests and throw enough money around to make the troublemakers go away. The guy at the conference had snickered at Nick's unofficial title of "company storyteller." To him, that meant *journalist,* and journalists were either the enemy or somebody to be shined. To him, "public relations" meant slick TV ads featuring attractive women cooing the virtues of "clean energy." Beauty shots of wildlife preserves, breaching whales, rafts of ducks bursting into flight, saccharine narratives about preserving the quality of life Americans expected. And, of course, money—lots of it—doled out liberally to politicians and decision makers. For the majors, it was a cynical business.

Nick was no cynic. He was aware of the costs, the things those TV commercials never showed: dead fisheries, ruined beaches, tarballs overwashing into marshes, dirty refineries, the disruptive traffic of heavy trucks, the danger of pipelines rupturing onto fragile permafrost. The thing was to anticipate those, minimize them, warn the right people, make the best plans.

It was a fine line, trying to preserve his personal integrity—the sense that his life and his job somehow came together in a unified whole—while serving the company's bottom line. But he had Funderburke on his side, and ultimately Cyrus Hanson. They were old-school, principled men who took pride in their record. The work was too hard if you didn't believe in it, at least to a point.

Nick copied this onto the front page of every project journal: "First, figure out what you already know. Second, use what you know to figure out what you don't know." As far as he could tell, that was his job. The geologists and engineers handled the technical end. What he had to figure out was the community—the people in their homeplace—then put what he discovered into words that painted the big picture: *Can we work here? How do we get this community to buy into our project? How do we talk about it in public? And just as important, what can we do for the community in return—how can we make this place better off than we found it?*

Maybe it was corny, but it was also good business. It gave him a grip.

4

Marlena Wolf dreamed of waves rocking her. No one else was with her, yet she did not feel alone. In the dream, she was carried far out to sea in a little boat, almost to the horizon, under a deep blue, cloudless sky—then woke ashore in her own bed, disappointed that the rocking had ceased.

Yet she felt closer to him than she had in many years, and this cut her with a sharp pang of loneliness, as if he had just left and it was still not too late to call him back.

Why had she only watched him that day, disappearing down the sidewalk? Why hadn't she called him back?

She should have thrown herself in front of the door, barred him from leaving, clung to him. She should have argued more, made him argue. They could have quarreled all day, until they were exhausted, hoarse, and tearful, then collapsed into bed together and made love and begged forgiveness from one another. She should have held him tight to her breast until he forgot the war, forgot that creature, let go of empty dreams of glory.

She should have done all that, should have found the bravery she discovered later, the courage of the survivor against all odds, the fortitude to believe whatever she needed to believe, all evidence to the contrary. Maybe he would have raised his fist, socked her hard for interfering. He'd never touched her before, but maybe he would have. And if he had, so what? She could have stood that, could have wrapped her arms around him like iron cables and held him, just held him, cried her love into his ear, used all her strength and will in that one moment when it counted most.

Instead she had watched him go, and awakened ten thousand mornings since smelling the sweet cherry aroma of his pipe and feeling the cruel blade of his absence.

5

Liam Royal walked the beach for an hour southwest and then turned back northeast into the stinging fresh breeze, retracing his steps. He did not feel old so much as ageless, a walking map of aching bones and sore muscles, all those years of hard work inside him now. He could not remember a time when his knees didn't grate and his back complain after the first mile, but he ignored all that. He had long ago learned to disregard hardship and hurt, the accumulated damage of a lengthy and arduous life.

The small pains reminded him that he was alive. His body sang its anthem of hard use and long labor, and he heard it vaguely, like the hum of a distant generator.

And carried a memory full of vivid impressions, hardly faded by all the years.

The faces of his lost brothers, forever young.

Wind and water, sky and sea.

The gray breakers limned by clouded stars. The clouds reeling across the sky, scudding past the low moon.

Flames on the horizon, towering orange spires bursting like skyrockets.

The slow-motion dream of a single violent night on the eve of war.

The war itself a series of moments when he was ambushed by the sudden weight of fatal knowledge, the in-between times a blur of vague, restless duty that accomplished nothing he was proud of.

All the anomalies of memory—a storm that laid waste to an island, sank ships and overturned airplanes, yet left behind undamaged a single carton of eggs.

He still had a sharp eye, saw the shapes of things far off, discerned detail and edge and nuances of color. Sometimes he fancied he could almost see to the far side of the water. He was not looking at the beach but at the waves, watching the state of the sea, the restless caps forming ridges at odds with the incoming wave trains.

Somewhere far offshore, the weather was confused, making up its mind. It was the season of storms, and all the forecasts for this one were bad.

Well, it's a wilderness out there, he thought. *Not a place for a man ever to be.*

6

Nick and Fannon passed the turnoff for the Bodie Island Light, glimpsed it spiking over the stunted maritime forest, black and white bands against the cloud-mottled blue sky. Almost at once, the long, high Bonner Bridge was under their wheels, narrow and steep. Far below, shrimp boats with their side-booms hung with nets picked their way through the twisting shoals of Oregon Inlet like bright paddling ducks. From the bridge, Nick could see the dark blue-black channel threading through the brown shallows, the breakers frothing on barely submerged sand bars.

At the apex of the span, Nick caught his breath—the roadway appeared to end in thin air. But it was just a trick of the eye. Soon enough, they were coasting down onto Hatteras Island, and he eased his right foot onto the brake. But they didn't slow down. The pedal flopped to the floor without resistance, and the Land Rover picked up speed. Nick slewed it out into the left lane to pass an RV as big as a city bus.

"Bloody hell, mate!" Fannon said. "You're going to flip us!"

"No brakes," Nick said, and gripped the wheel hard with both hands. He shoved the gearshift into low, but that hardly slowed them at all, just sent up a grinding racket from the engine.

A red minivan was blocking the left lane ahead, driving exactly beside a fuel truck. Nick leaned on the horn. The Land Rover flew toward the minivan, which at the last second swerved behind the fuel truck. The driver, a white-haired man in a golf cap, flipped them the bird as they rocketed by.

The road was clear now, but far down at the foot of the bridge was a tractor-trailer just starting its slow head-on climb. The bridge curved left, and Nick felt the tug of inertia leaning him toward Fannon, the Land Rover rocking dangerously. There was a break in the traffic on the right, and he dodged into it in time to avoid a school bus. The speedometer was at seventy and still edging up.

"Fuck's sake, put her in the sand!" Fannon said.

Nick saw it now, scrolling vividly onto the windshield in slow motion: Just past the guardrails of the bridge, as the road entered the flat, the shoulder turned to sand. A little ways back, beside a campground, a woman—probably a shrimper's wife—was selling fresh catch out of a big white cooler perched on the tailgate of an old red pickup truck.

He even thought of her that way, in that eternal moment—*a shrimper's wife*. She became the only other person in the world.

He felt a sickness in his stomach, a breathless terror, yet he could not stop noticing details. The world etched itself into his vision in painfully sharp images. The truck, the woman, the big cooler. Painted in shaky black letters, two plywood signs leaning against the fenders. *Fresh Shrimp—No Heads.* And the larger sign: *NO DRILL, NO SPILL! NORTHAM GO HOME!*

At the foot of the bridge, a camper hauling a boat slowed to turn into the marina and a yellow sports car zipped across in front of it and turned north with a squeal of rubber, narrowly missing the boat.

Nick had nowhere to go but into the sand, so he steered for it. The woman at the shrimp stand looked up wide-eyed at the Land Rover bearing down on her. At the last second, she tumbled heavily out of the way.

The Land Rover bumped into the sand, the tires plowing deep furrows. Nick lost the ability to steer. He tried to miss the red pickup, almost missed it, but the steering was so sluggish that the Land Rover's right front fender caught the edge of the tailgate. The pickup spun around, spraying shrimp onto the windshield, and then the Land Rover flipped onto its side.

The fall was surprisingly gentle.

Nick lay there a moment disoriented, crushed by Fannon's weight, listening to the engine tick and steam. His breath wouldn't come. Fannon squirmed off him and climbed toward the open passenger window, and Nick took a gulp of air. He clicked open his seat belt and touched his arms and legs. Nothing seemed broken, but his ribs were sore as hell from the steering wheel.

The shrimp lady staggered drunkenly toward them across the sand, slammed down her open hand on the upturned door, then spat on the NorthAm logo and kicked the roof of the overturned vehicle a couple of times.

"Jesus!" Nick said over and over, mostly to himself. His head felt heavy, as if full of water, and spun dizzyingly. His hands were limp, his body numb and shivering.

"Well, fuck all, there's our welcome committee," Fannon said hoarsely, heaving for breath himself. "Come on, mate, grab my hand."

7

By the time they climbed out of the wreck, a small crowd had gathered—tourists in shorts and T-shirts and a few grim locals wearing stained khakis. Fishermen, Nick guessed. He called to the shrimp lady, "Ma'am, are you all right?" His voice came back to him as a weird echo. She just turned and glared over her shoulder at him. The effort of speaking made his head hurt. "I'm sorry. . . . Hey, it's okay, the insurance—"

"What that old truck's worth won't buy me another!" she shouted.

"And I got two days' catch all over the road."

Fannon stepped up and held out a card. "You call that number, they'll fix you up."

She took the card and chewed the ends of her lank brown hair, eyes blazing.

Nick leaned on Fannon, shaky on his feet, the world rushing in his ears. He worked to find his balance. Everything was too loud, too fast, too vivid. He closed his eyes to stop his head from spinning and almost toppled over.

A white and blue Jeep pulled up without a siren, and a lanky sheriff stepped out and adjusted his straw hat. He ignored Fannon and Nick and talked to the shrimp lady, nodding solemnly. He patted her shoulder and then turned to Fannon. "Anybody hurt?"

"Nah," Fannon said. But he had a cut over his eye.

Nick opened his eyes, breathed deliberately, counting his breaths. "It was the brakes," he finally said. "The brakes went out."

The sheriff started writing on a pad. "Which one of you was driving?"

Nick said, "That would be me." He pulled out his driver's license and handed it to the sheriff, who copied his information.

Without looking up, the sheriff said, "You'll have a nice shiner by morning."

Nick touched his left eye and winced.

"Sure you're okay?"

Fannon nodded for both of them.

The sheriff handed Nick a citation.

"What's this?" Nick said.

The sheriff said, "Speeding and reckless driving. But you'll have your day in court." He handed Nick's license back and went to his car to use the radio.

A woman emerged from the crowd. She was wiry and dressed in men's overalls. Her salt-and-pepper hair was cropped stylishly short, and her face was tanned and wind-chapped. She folded her arms and said to nobody in particular, "Guess they'll want to put up a traffic light now."

"Last thing we need," a man agreed, again to nobody in particular.

"It's that damned bridge," another woman said. "I sure liked it better when there was just the ferry."

"Well, one thing's sure," the man said. "You can't keep parking a truck on its side like that. Sooner or later, it's bound to ruin the suspension." That got chuckles from the crowd.

The woman with the short-cropped hair stepped out of the crowd as the man went back to what he was doing. "You sure know how to make an entrance. Come on, then," she said to Nick. "Get your stuff."

"I'm Fannon—"

"I know who you are. I expect you need a vehicle."

"You are?"

"Caroline Dant. This is my place. Least, I run it."

Nick saw the big sign now: *Dant's Marina and Garage.*

Fannon rocked on unsteady legs. "Got to check on the payload, Nicky." He opened the tailgate door and ran his hands over the metal case. He opened it, peered inside, and quickly clasped it again.

"Everything okay?" Nick said, his voice sounding muffled, as if he were talking through a pillow.

"A bit banged up is all. Should be okay." Fannon shut the tailgate door.

They followed Caroline Dant across the gravel lot to the office. While Fannon found the restroom and Nick used the phone to report the accident to the company rep, Caroline Dant fished in a drawer and came up with a keychain made from a red and silver fishing spoon. "It's the yellow Scout over by the boat ramp."

Nick squinted out the window and saw a beat-up, rusted truck. "That one there?"

"Yeah, the yellow one. That would be its chief virtue."

Nick reached for his wallet. "Can you take American Express?"

"Nobody takes American Express," she said. "I know where you live. I assume you can drive a stick?"

Nick nodded as Fannon came out of the restroom rubbing a bruise on his arm.

She examined the bruise and Fannon's lacerated face and applied an adhesive bandage over his right eye. Then she said to Nick, "It works best with all four wheels on the ground."

"Thanks. And could you—"

"We'll tow it to the garage and find out what's broke."

"We lost our brakes."

"So you said."

"No, I mean, we lost them. There was nothing."

Caroline Dant nodded. "We'll look into it."

Nick said, "Our bags, the box of gear . . ."

She spoke with a cool certainty. "All taken care of."

As he and Nick walked toward the boat ramp, Fannon said, "Bit of an odd duck, that one."

Nick said, "Oh, I think we're just getting started."

They climbed aboard the Scout. The metal case and bags were tucked neatly in the bed behind the front seats. The NorthAm portfolio rested on the steel dash. Fannon flipped through it absently, making sure their papers were still there. He nodded.

Nick unzipped his canvas gig bag and checked the old New Yorker, plucked a couple of strings. Remarkably it seemed to be in one piece. "Good old box," he said, patting the guitar. He buckled his lap belt and took a couple of deep, slow breaths, which hurt his ribs. Then he ground the truck into gear, and they lurched back onto the highway, going south. He knew he shouldn't be driving, not with his head throbbing and his stomach sloshing with nausea, but he had grown used to shrugging off pain and stubbornly getting on with things. And he didn't need a hospital. What he needed was a stiff drink and some rest.

"I know what you're thinking, mate. Crossed my mind as well."

The company vehicles were meticulously maintained. "You don't lose brakes like that. You just don't."

Fannon lit a cig and shrugged with the air of a man who had seen it all and done it twice. "Well, apparently, sometimes you do."

8

The road passed through large swaths of pristine national seashore, miles of sand and sea oats deserted except for squadrons of gulls.

Nick said, "Must have been gorgeous before it was discovered."

"Yeah, as usual," Fannon said, unimpressed. He didn't have to say it out loud: *We're the people who do the discovering.*

Nick said, without turning his head, "Lot of ships have come to grief out there, from pirates on down."

"Pirates, eh?" Fannon said. "Guess it ain't safe out there, not like the fucking highway."

Nick laughed, and it hurt.

Beyond each clean patch of seashore rose a new village crammed with lavish vacation homes on stilts, gas stations, water parks, clusters of storefronts. The signs read, *Rodanthe, Waves, Salvo, Avon*—such odd names. Each seemed anchored by a large, gleaming office park with a *Royal Real Estate* sign featuring a faux coat of arms—a crossed fishing pole and oar under a crown. Most of the vacation homes bore smaller signs: *Royal Rentals.*

Nick recognized the name from the company brief. The family seemed to own every inch of real estate on the island. Still, he hadn't expected quite so many signs, so many properties. He was in a sour mood, and his ribs hurt. He wanted to have a big drink of bourbon and lie down.

When they passed another sign, Fannon observed, "The Royals, they're big cheeses around here. Own half of this whole sand bar."

"Who owns the other half?"

Fannon blew out smoke. "I'm not going to do all your work for you, am I? What is it you do again?"

"I make you the hero of the story."

Fannon laughed. "That's me all over."

They passed Littlejohn's Grocery and Tackle. Nick had seen one in each of the villages. Littlejohn. Another name from the brief. He had started reading it on the plane and quickly dozed off for the duration. Not like his own reports. If the writer had set out to make it dull and unreadable, he could hardly have done better. "There you go. It's always about the old families."

"Often enough."

Nick saw for the first time the NorthAm logo, crowning a white stanchion over the store's gas pumps. "Friendlies?"

Fannon laughed and patted his dark green golf shirt with the gold and blue logo over the left breast. He jabbed it with his finger and rubbed his thumb and index finger together in the sign for money. "Oh, they just love us."

A little farther on, a high-end development called Royal Harbour rose out of the sand dunes on the sound slide—cedar-shaked condominiums and a dozen homes styled as *palazzos* on concrete stilts.

"Who lives there, then, the bloody pope?" Fannon said.

"Patchett Builders," Nick read off the sign. "Same name as the mayor. He's on my list to see. And the marina—what was the name? Dant. Our benefactor."

"The Big Four," Fannon said. "Royal, Patchett, Dant, and Littlejohn."

Nick considered. Four families. He'd have to track them all down, find out who was who and what was what. Probably they had a kind of alliance among them. Probably their grandfathers and great-grandfathers had all been pals back in the day, divvying up the spoils of the island like feudal chieftains.

At least one was already on their side: Caroline Dant. At least he hoped so. She seemed like a down-to-earth person, someone he could have a conversation with. *Something in her eyes,* he thought. She struck him as honest, the kind of person who would have trouble telling a lie. The kind of person who might be fair and reasonable. She had a little bit of a crust, but that felt put-on. He had sensed a sweetness in her.

But then Fannon was always chiding him for being too naïve, too trusting. For expecting the best out of people, when he should be wary of their motives.

What kind of gas did Dant's Marina sell? Maybe he could get her a good deal on a franchise. The woman had done them a big favor. He could at least offer that.

Still, how had the four families divided things—property, provisions, fishing, construction—so neatly? Everything a person needed to live on the island for a week or a lifetime, from groceries and suntan lotion to gasoline and boat rentals and beach houses. The only commodity they had missed was transportation. Or maybe they hadn't. It was an island, after all, and Dant's Marina and Garage had plenty of boats and serviced plenty of cars.

Fannon smoked and watched out the window. "Wheels always turning, eh? You should switch it off for a while, just let the world go by, mate."

Nick smiled and began to relax. And with relaxing came soreness, his tense muscles letting go. He knew tomorrow would be a painful day.

They passed more developments—Royal Dunes and Royal Shores—and stopped at Buxton village, sheltered from the stiff ocean winds by maritime forest, beyond which rose the great black-over-white-striped Cape Hatteras Lighthouse. Buxton was just a small cluster of cottages, a little white church, and a Littlejohn's store—which would have the painkillers Nick wanted. Like the other stores, this one was a long bungalow with barn-sized doors and banks of broad windows open to the air. Inside, men in long-billed ball caps lounged on rocking chairs and talked fishing. One of them was a small, wiry man with a long reddish gray beard who squinted in Nick's direction, as if he recognized him. The others merely glanced Nick's way, sized him up, and ignored him as he paid for the medicine and a handful of postcards he grabbed off the rack near the checkout. He would send one off to Oma every day. She would wait for them each morning at eleven, sitting in the wing chair by the mailboxes in the lobby.

The young blond clerk said, "So you know Mister Littlejohn. He's got friends everywheres, I guess."

Nick said, "Mister Littlejohn?"

The clerk waved a hand toward the old fellow with the reddish gray beard. "My great-grandfather." She smiled big. "This is his favorite of all the stores. Best sun and breeze, he always says."

"I bet. A nice change from all that air conditioning."

"He can't be closed in," she said. "Sleeps on the screen porch all the year long."

"Thanks," Nick said, nodding, and walked over to where Littlejohn sat rocking. Nick extended his hand. "Pleased to meet you, Mister Littlejohn. I'm—"

"I know who you are," Littlejohn said, squinting one eye over a crooked smile. He shook Nick's hand, squeezing hard. "You haven't been around here before, have you?"

"No, sir, first time."

"Just call me Brick. Everybody does." He held on to Nick's hand.

"Quite a place you have."

"It's my place, that's all. Always a good thing for a man to know."

Nick nodded.

"That's big water out there, just so's you know."

"Yes, sir."

"A man is safest ashore. Learned that in the navy."

"Well, I'm a landlubber myself."

Littlejohn grinned. "Ain't we all." All the other men were looking at Nick now. "You take care now." He released Nick's hand. The other men went back to their business, and Littlejohn kept rocking, his eyes on Nick all the way to the door.

In the Scout, Fannon said, "Who was that character?"

"Littlejohn himself. In the flesh. Calls himself Brick."

"They're all coming out to play," Fannon said.

Nick ground the car into gear. A few hundred yards down the road, on a whim, he turned off the main road and followed the lane through Buxton Woods to the Hatteras Light.

The wind blew hard and steady out of the northeast, whipping sand into their faces. They got out to stretch their legs. Nick's bad right knee was stiff, and he tested it carefully before putting his weight on it. Then he stood and squinted through his Ray-Bans. The sea was thrashing against the jetty almost at the foot of the towering structure, spraying up in loud geysers with each wave. The place felt raw and remote, the far boundary of the land, and beyond it seethed a roiling wilderness.

They stood under the lighthouse. Up close, the structure was massive, tons of brick and stone rising so high that when Nick craned his head to look at the top, he was overcome by vertigo.

Offshore, the waves rolled in confusion, smashing into each other from at least three different directions. But no matter what their orientation, when they hit land they squared up and came in at close to a ninety-degree angle. It was one of those laws of physics Nick had never quite understood.

"It's awfully close to the breakers," he said.

"What, the lighthouse?" Fannon laughed shortly and stubbed out his cigarette in the sand. "You could always ask them to move it back a ways, yeah?"

Nick stared at a solitary figure far down the beach. The man's arms were akimbo, his back to the land.

9

Liam Royal's hearing was nothing like his eyesight.

His ears played tricks on him, masking conversations in the background hum of the world. He wore electronic aids in both ears, and sometimes they cocked him off-balance, as if he were walking on the pitching deck of a ship.

And sometimes he heard with astonishing clarity sounds that had been made long ago—voices arguing against a rising wind, the crack of gunfire, a radio news reader somberly reporting that casualties were lighter than expected, the worried voice of an incredulous Filipino gardener saying over and over, "Officer not dead?"

His wife's loving whisper in his ear in the dark. And then her awful silence.

Sometimes, more often these days, he heard the voice of conscience nagging him about his sharp dealing, all the islanders and neighbors he had bought out on the cheap. In the old days, he didn't give a damn, just plowed ahead with his plans, always building, always getting more. Never looking back or down or any way but forward, no regrets. But the regrets were creeping up on him, the faces of the dead more, not less, vivid so long after the war—a cruel trick of time and memory.

And just now, he was hearing voices in the sea, and they were no trick.

10

They drove out of Buxton and through Frisco, passed two more Littejohn's, then a small city of stilted cottages rising into the dunes—

Royal Watch—being roofed by Patchett Builders. Nick saw sign after sign for Royal Rentals.

And he spotted something else, something more disturbing. Staked into the lawns of cottages and hung in the windows of tackle shops and restaurants were other signs:

NO DRILL, NO SPILL!

NORTHAM GO HOME!

The signs were professionally printed. That meant organized resistance, unusual at this early stage. The lease had been activated only six weeks ago, according to Fannon.

"Just a few old hippies and fishermen, you said."

"So I lied." Fannon yawned.

Up ahead, in front of a small white clapboard church, a police car blocked the road, its lights flashing. "What have we got here?" Nick said. He slowed to a stop behind a green station wagon loaded with camping gear. From the sandy church parking lot, a white Cadillac hearse pulled onto the road, followed by a line of cars with headlights burning. A cop in a brown uniform stood in the highway waving them out.

"Funeral, looks like," Fannon said.

"Somebody important—look at all the cars." Nick noticed now that a crowd of pedestrians had spilled out of the cottages and lined the road, standing almost at attention. Many of the faces were black.

An attractive young black woman in a sundress stood near the Scout, one hand shading her brow, watching the funeral cortege. Nick said, "Excuse me, ma'am." She turned, looking puzzled at hearing a voice. "Can you tell me whose funeral that is?"

She walked closer to the car. "Not so loud," she said quietly. "There goes a godly man to his eternal rest." She flattened her hand over her heart. "Eighty-seven years on this earth, and every man a friend. The Reverend Isaac Abraham Lord."

"May he rest in peace," Nick said as reverently as he could, and the woman nodded and drifted away.

"Who the hell was he?" Fannon said.

"Not on my list," Nick said. "But it's not much of a list. I'll make a better one."

They followed the funeral procession for a mile or so until it turned down a rutted lane overgrown with wax myrtle and scrub oak. Soon they came upon Hatteras village, made up of a few shops and restaurants and a boat basin filled with charter fishing boats outfitted with tuna towers and outriggers.

"Drop me in the village," Fannon said. "I'm bunking on the boat."

"What about me?"

"Oh, you're living posh." Fanning nodded out the window toward the ocean. Down a long, sandy lane stood what appeared to be an old Coast Guard station. Nick slowed. The sign at the entrance to the lane read, *Lifeboat Station #17*. "That's your billet, mate—just you and some yokels from Ioway."

They continued around the bend. At Oman's Dock, the *Lady NorthAm* was tied to massive steel bollards that could have held an ocean liner. She stretched just under a hundred feet from her sharp, upswept bow to her low, flat fantail, not counting the work platform welded onto the transom. The company kept her immaculate: dark green waterline stripe, buff superstructure, a glint of brass here and there. The white hull showed as clean as a yacht's. The dark green funnel bore the gold compass rose and dark blue arrow of NorthAm. The *Lady* was part workboat, part office, part floating public-relations platform. Sometimes the company used it for schmooze parties with politicians and local bigshots. Depending on the job, Nick either stayed on the boat or found local accommodations. It was usually better for him to be off the boat, free to roam on shore, since occasionally the boat went out on site and might stay there for days at a time.

"The big stuff is already out there." Fannon gestured seaward with his cigarette.

Nick nodded. The anchored barges, the floating cranes, were prepping the site for the rig, which was being towed up the coast from Louisiana. "That was fast."

"Yeah, well. We had a heads-up, you might say."

"Thought I was coming in at the beginning."

Fannon grinned. "It begins whenever you start." He shouldered his duffel. "Nice and quiet. No sign of the *Rascal*." The *NorthAm Rascal*, a much smaller and faster boat, ferried workers and supplies to and from the site and handled any other errands. "Maybe I can have a lie-down. Christ, I'm beat."

11

Lifeboat Station #17 was just what it claimed to be—a former lifesaving station made over for the tourist trade. Up close, it was much larger and grander than it appeared from the main road—new cedar shakes, three stories high, with a spacious deck wrapped around each.

Behind the check-in counter, a tan teenaged boy in a powder-blue T-shirt and jeans with a thick mop of dark hair, his back to the entrance, was fussing with a printer. Clearly exasperated, he slapped closed the lid with a curse. Nick waited a beat, then set down his duffel, guitar, and portfolio. "Son, I can help you with that."

The boy whirled around to face him—not a teenaged boy at all but suddenly a slender young woman, her glossy, dark hair bobbed short. Twenty-five or -six, he guessed. Her brown eyes flashed at him, as if she had been caught at something naughty, and she was blushing crimson.

"Oh," he said, "I'm sorry, excuse me, I just thought, I mean . . ."

She let him stammer as her blush faded, then said, "Didn't hear you come in. I can never get that damned thing to work."

Nick stared, still getting over his surprise.

She had a brightness about her. Her dark eyes shone fiercely, and her whole manner radiated a kind of alert tension. He couldn't recall the last time he had met someone so . . . so *vivid.*

"What?" She canted her head and lifted a hand absently to smooth her hair.

"May I?" He slipped behind the counter and found the paper jam, and in a few seconds the machine was printing out reservations. "Happens at my office all the time."

"Lucky for me."

The hardwood-paneled wall behind the counter featured a large painting of a lifeboat on wheels being pulled toward the seething breakers by an enormous white horse and a clot of men in black oilskins, their faces hooded under black windblown sou'westers. They leaned forward into the weather like beasts of burden, heavy ropes strung taut across their shoulders.

On a shelf to one side stood a sleek wooden model of a sailboat flying a main, topsail, and jib. The brass plaque read, *Creef Shad Boat by Ham Fetterman.* He was impressed—Fetterman's models were famous, and nearly priceless. Cyrus Hanson had one—a lightship—mounted in the board room at NorthAm. He gestured at the craft. "That's a beautiful model."

She hardly glanced at it. "Yeah, Ham Fetterman. Used to set up shop at Littejohn's in Kinnakeet in the old days. Built a regular fleet of those things."

"Didn't realize he was a local."

"Everybody's a local someplace."

He flung a hand toward the gleaming wood and the oiled oak floor. "The owners must have sunk a fortune into this place."

She just stared at him. "You have a reservation with us?"

"Yes, ma'am."

"Your name, please?"

"Nicholas Wolf."

Something flashed across her eyes—he would have said recognition, except that they had never laid eyes on each other before. Then the look was gone, and her face took on a generic pleasantness, the habitual expression a waitress or bartender wore to keep the tourists at arm's length. She nodded slowly, unblinkingly, sizing him up. "Oh, of course." She wriggled past him and keyed him up on her computer screen. "So you've come for our oil."

He should not have been embarrassed, but she had caught him offguard, and he felt himself going hot in the face. He couldn't tell whether it was a reproach or just banter.

She cocked an eyebrow and leaned across the counter. "It's all right, Mister Wolf. Really."

"Nick." He held out his hand.

She took it. "Julia Royal."

Her hand was small and square and her grip firm. He held her hand, warm in his own, and she did not pull it away for a long moment. "Not—"

"Yeah," she said. "That Royal. I get that a lot. That's my great-grandfather in the painting there."

"Oh, Royal Real Estate, right?"

She sighed. "I wish they'd name all those stupid places after somebody else."

He hadn't thought about it that way—what it must be like to see your name staring back at you everywhere you went. How in the world could you ever have a private life? "I'm sorry," he said.

"Don't be sorry yet—you just got here. The reservation is open-ended. How long do you plan to stay?"

"All depends. But this will be home for a while."

"It's a direct bill, but I'll need a credit card for incidentals."

He handed over his NorthAm American Express.

She handed it back. "We don't take American Express. You got another card?"

He traded her for his Visa card.

She took it and then touched his face softly. "Hey, want some ice for that?"

His hand strayed to his swollen eye. "It's not what you think."

She laughed shortly, and he heard a slight edge. "Never is, is it? If you'll follow me . . ."

They climbed a wide wooden staircase, and she showed him to a second-floor room with an ocean view. He opened the French doors and stepped onto the deck. The sea breeze rushed around his ears, and he felt both exhilarated and suddenly very tired. At least his equilibrium was coming back. But his ribs were throbbing worse than ever with every breath.

Behind him, she said, "There's a reading room downstairs, and you have the run of the guest kitchen for snacks."

"Do I get a key?"

She gave him a look. "Nobody locks anything around here."

He had already gotten off on the wrong foot with her, and it seemed like everything he said made it worse. "Okay, then." It went against his grain, but this wasn't some Third World rathole. What little he had brought would be safe enough. *Relax*, he told himself. *Enjoy the view.* What Fannon had said: *Just let the world go by.* Anything happened, he'd know soon enough.

Below, snug among the dunes, stood an elongated white, black-roofed building that resembled a garage, except that it, like the house, was immaculate, blue curtains hanging at the windows. "What's that down there?"

"The old lifeboat house. Off-limits to guests."

He turned, and the wind suddenly stilled.

"My grandfather lives there. The Founder."

He didn't' get it. "The Founder?"

She shook her head and snickered. "You know, Scrooge? From Dickens? 'The Founder of the Feast'? It's a family joke—he's really very generous." She talked about her grandfather glibly, yet for just a beat there had been a catch in her voice.

"Right. Will I meet him?"

"Why?" She canted her head. Before he could answer, she said softly, "Oh, of course. That's your job."

"I only meant . . . Never mind." Talking with her was exhausting. He couldn't quite gauge her tone, whether she was being sly or merely polite. He was regaining his legs, but she kept him off-balance in another way.

"You like daiquiris?"

"Sure, if you'd like to—"

"Five o'clock. The lookout deck."

He glanced at his watch—quarter to. "Lookout deck?"

She glanced up, and so did Nick. He heard feet shuffling on the deck overhead, the clink of glasses. "Oh, right."

Nick watched her pirouette and disappear, like she was spinning loose from him.

12

The lookout deck was crowded mostly with paunchy middle-aged men in polo shirts and khaki shorts and shapeless women wearing loose, flowered cover-ups, all holding tall, colorful glasses from a bar set up at the south end. A young blond couple stood apart and stared out to sea—honeymooners, he guessed.

Julia Royal had changed into a rose-colored smock and made up her face—no mistaking her for a boy now. Her full lips were set in a slight, knowing smile, and her brown eyes were radiant. She slipped over to him with an older man on her arm. He was striking, taller than Nick, a shock of iron-gray hair combed back long and a thick black beard peppered with gray. Seventy or older, Nick guessed, but what a powerful upper body. In his prime, he must have been a bull. He wore faded blue jeans and boat mocs splotched with red paint and a chambray shirt with the sleeves rolled up to expose thick, scarred wrists. His complexion was the color of old brick. He squinted at Nick with faded blue eyes.

Julia looked small and fragile beside him. "May I present my grandfather, Liam Royal."

Nick offered his hand, and the old man leaned forward and wrapped it in his own two enormous mitts. Nick felt the strength in the fingers. *Jesus,* he thought, *who is this guy really?*

"Welcome to my home, Mister . . ."

"Nick Wolf."

"Wolf?" He cocked his head left and cupped a hand to his ear. "Wolf, you say?"

"From NorthAm, Paw Paw. I told you they were coming."

"Wolf. Mister Wolf."

The Founder gripped his hand tighter, and Nick had the odd notion that something was already terribly wrong. For just an instant, he feared this old giant was going to fling him right over the railing. Then, just as suddenly, the old man seemed to realize what he was doing and eased his grip, released Nick's hand as gently as letting go a fish.

"This used to be the lookout, you know." The old man turned and peered out to sea. Nick watched the blue shirt billowing around his broad back. "Those were the days. Things had a certain . . . a certain clarity."

"Paw Paw is a philosopher," Julia said. She took her grandfather's arm gently, her grip firm, still facing Nick.

"My father was a lifesaver," the Founder said in a voice that was a little too loud. "Used to put out to sea in a wooden boat powered by the old Armstrong engine." He coughed or laughed, Nick couldn't tell which.

"Can't say I've ever heard of that brand."

The old man held his free arm out from his side and flexed his thick bicep, smiling cannily. "*Armstrong*, you see?"

"Oh, right. Oars." Nick watched the wave trains rear up and slam onto the beach. "Well, I wouldn't try it in that surf."

"That? Phew. That's nothing." He flung out his heavy arm as if he were sweeping it all away. "Add a storm, seas like black mountains. Add a nor'east wind that freezes your bones and howls like the end of the world. Add fear, the kind that turns your guts to jelly. Add the blind darkness of a night with no moon, no stars. Add the worst—men dying just over the horizon." He paused and shuddered. "Oh, they would go out, all right. They always went out."

Abruptly he turned, but Nick couldn't read his eyes. The wind fluttered Julia's smock and blew her hair around her face in a feathery way that made him want to touch it.

The Founder said in a quiet baritone, "You won't find anything out there, you know. Everybody knows that."

Nick didn't know at first how to respond, so he just nodded. "Maybe not. It's always a gamble." He laughed to ease the tension. "Just like hunting for buried treasure."

"Buried treasure?" Liam Royal pulled himself erect, looking both disappointed and angry. He wagged a long, bent finger in Nick's face. "Don't be a fool, boy. There's no such thing. No such thing."

And suddenly Julia inserted herself between the old man and Nick, gently easing her grandfather away. He stood behind her for a long moment, eyes unblinking, then turned and went inside the house.

"You shouldn't get him so worked up," Julia said. "He's earned a little peace."

Nick said, "I was only listening."

She drew closer. "Well, now I'm listening. You really expect to find oil out there?"

"Not me," he said with a shrug. "The company." It wasn't the time to spell out Fannon's hopes of a big strike, the biggest since Prudhoe Bay.

"Well, they're wrong. Nobody's ever found it before."

"Maybe they didn't look in the right place."

"You ever been out there?"

Nick shook his head. "Other places, though. Lots of other places."

"Out there's not the place to be. The old-timers tell stories about hundred-foot waves. They come out of the deep ocean and trip on the shoals and break, and whatever they break over is gone. You ever seen that kind of water?"

"Can't say I have. But it's not my call. That's why we have bosses."

She smiled and shook her head, as if talking to an errant child. "You know what he was talking about, the Founder?"

"Iron men in wooden boats. Isn't that the phrase?"

She backed away. "This whole island used to make its living off two things: fishing and rescuing people from the sea. We had stations all up and down the coast, manned by islanders. Lifesavers, guys who were crazy-brave. Maybe a dozen men to a station. Corolla, Nags Head, Big Kinnakeet, Little Kinnakeet, Chicamacomico, Bodie Island, Hatteras. They each had a boat and a horse to haul it down to the water and just one job to do, twenty-four hours a day, every day of the year—just one. Rescuing people from out there." She swept her arm toward the breakers. "Exactly where you people plan to go. Now doesn't that give you pause?"

He stared across the beach toward the surf line, trains of rollers sweeping and breaking with a steady thunder along the beach. "They'll deal with it," he said. "They're professionals. They've been in rough water before."

She shook her head. "The storm season is coming on. Go out there one time and then tell me that." Her face was flushed, and her voice held an edge, surprising Nick with its passion. "That's not rough water," she said. "Out there, it's something else entirely."

"Your grandfather, the Founder—did *he* ever rescue anybody?"

She pressed her lips into a tight smile. "I'm being a rotten host. Let me freshen your drink."

13

After two daiquiris, Nick excused himself and went down to unpack. He eased open the door and for a second thought he had entered the wrong room—it was a mess. Then he recognized his old, scarred duffel upside down on the bed, his clothes and toiletries spilled out and scattered across the counterpane. The guitar was out of its canvas case and flung across the bed but undamaged. He rifled through the mess.

The computer was cocked open, the drive empty. The box of floppy disks was gone. No matter—they were all blank anyway.

The only other item missing was the one thing of value besides his guitar: his project journal. Leather cover, three and a half inches by five, half an inch thick, bound with a green rubber band—just the right size to fit into his pocket.

Hell, he'd been here all of an hour.

He took a couple of calming breaths, trying to remember what he had written in the journal. Some notes about the four families, a reminder to look into a franchise deal for Dant's, dates and deadlines for various reports, a list of local people to interview—the mayor, the head of the national seashore, the local Nature Conservancy person, names he had copied out of the company brief. A note to find out about the preacher whose funeral he and Fannon had passed. Tucked into the back sleeve was his citation for reckless driving. He would have to call the sheriff and explain he had lost it.

No use fuming, he told himself. In the course of his work for NorthAm, he'd been mugged and robbed at knife-point, once even thrown into a canal. It came with the territory, the sketchy places where the company set up shop. You didn't find oil in Manhattan or the Chicago Loop. But he hadn't expected that kind of trouble here. Though Hatteras was a sand bar miles out into the ocean, it was still America.

But already, he had almost been killed by brakes that shouldn't have failed, and now this. He sat on the corner of the bed. Should he tell Julia? No, not until he talked it over with Fannon. He felt in his pocket for the key to the Scout. *Use what you know to figure out what you don't know.*

But really, what did he know?

CHAPTER THREE

HATTERAS ISLAND, MAY 1942

1

The five of them hiked into the dunes south of the Light one last time together as the sun was sinking in a reddish blear at their backs. The sand was heaped unevenly, and in the twilight long swaths of darker flats showed where the sea had burst through in last winter's storms.

Liam Royal was the leader, son of Malcolm Royal, who was keeper and head of the lifesaving crew at the Light. Liam was nearly as large and powerful as his father and carried himself with the same air of assumed authority. He tramped toward the sea with a long stride and did not have to turn his head to know the other four were following like a patrol of infantry.

Liam was not handsome but formidable, with blunt features and a thick tangle of uncombed dark hair. He was no ladies' man—they found him too rough, too brooding, too hard to talk to. He'd rather be on the back marsh hunting ducks in any weather than sitting indoors with a girl, any girl. Heat or cold didn't bother him, nor any ordinary hardship.

Once he was guiding a hunting party from off, and one of the city fools discharged his shotgun by accident. Liam took half a dozen pellets of bird shot in the leg, wrapped it with a bandana, and stayed out for six more hours before he went looking for the doctor.

The other island boys knew better than to make him mad. When he was twelve, he beat up a grown man who came at him with a fish billy, accused him of poaching his crab pots on the sound. The man stood six foot three and was known as a rough customer who terrorized his wife and kids. Liam laid him out so bad the man couldn't work for a week.

The high-school team tried to recruit Liam to play football, but he considered football a silly game, an artificial way of finding excitement.

Now he was getting ready for something real—they all were.

Four of them carried rifles slung on their shoulders, and Liam held in his big hands a Remington double-barreled shotgun he used for market-hunting ducks in the fall over in the back marsh on Pamlico Sound. He shot ducks by the hundreds and sold them to a man who shipped them north to hotels in New York.

They threaded through the camelbacks and came out in a swale protected from the wind by a sand ridge but close enough to the ocean that they could peer over the top and watch the surf frothing onto the beach. The waves rose in great gray humps and then curled open and slammed onto the sand with a sound like rolling thunder.

"This'll do," Liam said, and squatted with his back to the wind. His loose chambray shirt fluttered and snapped like a flag.

"The sea's making up," Chance Royal said. His real name was Charles, but nobody had ever called him anything but Chance. It was a nickname that just sprang up full-blown, not anybody's invention but simply a natural sound like the wind. He was Liam's little brother by one year, just as tall but leaner and hard-muscled. He scissored down onto the sand next to Liam. He was the handsome boy, the charmer all the girls chased after—dark, soulful eyes, a sly, disarming smile, an easy, careless way of moving. He finger-combed his thick jet-black hair. Soon it would be shaved to crew-cut stubble.

Parvis Patchett, a head shorter than the Royal brothers and loose-limbed as a marionette, bobbed his head to see over the dune, then pointed a little south toward the water. "That's where we found him this morning, high up where the tide fetched him." He pronounced it "toide" like the others, and when they all got talking it was hard for off-islanders to follow their speech, a brogue that was full of old-fashioned local words and vowel sounds that hadn't been heard on the mainland since the days of Queen Elizabeth, and they enjoyed that. Sometimes they would camp it up just to baffle off-islanders.

Parvis shook his head and flipped his shaggy hair out of his eyes. He was much older than the others, nearly thirty. His straw-blond hair was already thinning. His face seemed to be made of spare parts—crooked beak of a nose, jug-handle ears, eyes set too close together and never focused on the same object. "The crabs a-been at him, you know? Poor bastard was covered in oil. I mean, just black as Sambo."

Liam said, "Goddamn Nazis."

It had become all too common to find bodies washed onto the beach after a night of U-boat attacks offshore. The boys came out here often, a kind of self-appointed home-guard patrol, and watched the flashes of gunfire and torpedo detonations on the horizon, out in the shipping lanes, the muffled concussions floating ashore long after the sudden flares of light. Sometimes they saw a towering plume of fire and knew a tanker had gotten hit and was dying hard on the sea.

A little north and east, the beam of the Light flashed along its arc and then went dark, as if turning its back on them.

They all recognized the Light as a blessing and a curse—a blessing to lost ships, a curse because the U-boats used it to hunt by.

Once, in the First War, Liam's uncle Jack had done the unthinkable, extinguishing the Light. But only briefly, until Liam's father, Malcolm, laid into him with his heavy fists and then relighted the lamp.

But Liam was not so sure his father had been right. Maybe what they needed now was the true dark of the island.

2

Back in the First War—the one called simply "the Great War," before the other one came along—Parvis's father had been killed in a strange battle with a U-boat, an event the locals still scratched their heads over twenty-four years later.

Peter Patchett was a genuine hero, and nobody could say otherwise. And though he had been a ne'er-do-well all his life—hardly able to scratch out a living as a beachcomber and salvage broker—in dying at sea, killed by the U-boat, he had given Parvis the greatest gift he could have bestowed: the gift of belonging. For in dying, his father had saved the lives of Alvin Dant and his son, Brian, grandfather and uncle, respectively, of the fourth boy, Tim Dant, who now sat beside Parvis, a heavy steel flashlight bulging in his pocket.

Tim was gangly and blond, the youngest of the crew. His eyes held a look of perpetual astonishment. Unless you counted his days on a fishing boat offshore, he'd been off the island only twice in his life, both times to Norfolk with his father, and he was eager to see the big world beyond. But it scared him, too. He wasn't physically powerful like Liam Royal, or handsome and self-assured like Chance. Whenever he looked in the mirror, he recalled what Valerie Oman had said when she refused to go out with him: "Your face doesn't have any character yet."

Well, he was a man now. And he was determined to get some character.

Because of what Parvis's father had done, Tim Dant regarded Parvis as a hero, too, and the two were inseparable. Parvis would never lack friends on the island. These boys had taken him into their gang as a kind of uncle who knew all the stories from the old days, when the island was inhabited by giants and strange, marvelous things happened almost every day.

And Parvis Patchett owned a car—a 1932 Packard Runabout. It was a sporty car for a man like him. Some rich dingbatter—what they called the tourists—had brought it across on the mailboat and raced it up and down the wide beach for a week before he got it stuck on a rising tide. Plenty of whiskey was involved, and a girl who was not his wife. The tide came in, and the rich dingbatter abandoned the car to the sea. Parvis came along with a good mule and hauled it out of the surf, then worked on the engine all winter, scrounging parts, until he had it humming like a dynamo.

The last boy was Jimmy "Brick" Littlejohn, nicknamed for his startling red hair. Brick was a born follower, a boy of no imagination who liked being among his pals. He knew his place with them, as he knew his place on the island. He wasn't sure if this new adventure they were hatching would turn out to be a good idea. He doubted it.

But they were his pals, and the plan was made, and he was all in.

He grunted and unshouldered a khaki rucksack and pulled out two Mason jars of white whiskey—moonshine his daddy had cooked up in a myrtle thicket behind the store in an ancient thirty-five-gallon copper still he had inherited from *his* daddy.

Every night, the boys expected invasion—the president had blacked out the entire eastern seaboard, warning of bomber raids—and they took their duty seriously. They had brought the 'shine only because it was a special night. Tomorrow they were all enlisting.

That was the plan. In the morning, they would go to Norfolk. They had waited for Tim Dant to turn seventeen, and he could now enlist so long as he had signed permission from his father.

Brick Littlejohn unscrewed the cap on the first jar. "Here's to killing Nazis!" he said, and took a long swig.

Parvis went next and then the Royal brothers, and finally Tim Dant took a timid pull.

"You feeling quamish, or just ain't never tasted good corn before?" Chance Royal said. "Drink up—it'll make you brave." He grinned like a movie poster.

"I guess I'm brave enough," Tim Dant said, and swiped a sleeve across his mouth.

"You'd better be," Chance Royal said. "Pretty soon, we'll be invading Fortress Europe, and it's going to be a bastard."

"Fortress what?" Parvis Patchett said.

"That's what they call it in the papers," Chance Royal said. "It's only one big goddamn pillbox about a thousand miles long."

"The whole coast," Liam agreed. "Nothing but Huns with guns."

They all drank again, and the jar was fast draining.

"I guess I'm going with the marines," Chance said. "Guts and glory."

Patchett said, "The marines are all out in the Pacific. That's the wrong damned ocean! What you want to go way out there for?"

Chance looked a little deflated. "Then I'll join whoever is going to do the invading, by God."

3

Liam figured that Chance was brooding about their oldest brother, Kevin, dead now for almost a month. He had served ten years in the Coast Guard before Pearl Harbor, then was assigned to the staff of some rear admiral in the Mediterranean.

Kevin was the boring brother, the steady, quiet one, like their old man, Malcolm. But unlike Malcolm, he did not have the breath of heroism about him. His gift was practical: He knew how to move things—food, ammunition, boats. What the military called "logistics." Even the word hinted at a kind of mathematical precision, an accountant's dream of neatly tabulated stores and the choreographed movement of many machines. That's what he did for the Coast Guard, and that's what he kept doing for the navy.

The admiral's plane left England for North Africa and never made it. That was all. Five days of search-and-rescue turned up nothing. No wreckage, no bodies, no flotsam. It might have been shot down or just gotten lost, or maybe a lightning strike jolted the aircraft out of the sky. Or maybe the engines just quit.

It had climbed into the blue sky on a clear day and just disappeared.

Chance was all torn up over it. Funny, Liam had never known the brothers to be close—one the hell-rake and the other the steady, somber ballast of the family. But you could never know what went on between two people, even your own brothers. Kevin's death had kindled a volatile anger inside Chance.

Maybe it was the sudden loss of certainty, the snuffing out of a life that had seemed as solid and predictable as the old brick lighthouse itself. That was Kevin, and then he was gone. It was worse that his fate was unknown. There was no body, no grave to visit and mark with a dated stone. No story to tell over whiskey and a smoke, and say, "Yeah, that was Kevin all over!" and laugh and take a drink.

Liam held his own anger close. But the void gnawed at him. How could a good man just disappear?

4

The light went fast, as it always did once the sun dipped below the horizon. There were no high places to keep its reflection, and the sky blackened like someone had shut the door to heaven. In the deepening dark, the surf pounded louder than before, a trick of the ear. Often the waves lay down at night, yet the sound of their breaking carried farther and bigger.

Tim Dant said to Parvis Patchett, "What about you?"

Patchett grabbed his friend's arm. "Navy. I'm thinking we'll be shipmates on a battle wagon. I figure they can always use a good mechanic."

Chance Royal said, just to needle him, "Oh, so you know a good mechanic?" And that got a laugh.

Liam said, "Come on, Par. You know they won't take you with those pipes."

It was true, Patchett had bad lungs. They had tacitly agreed not to mention it, but now the talk had turned to truth.

Tim Dant said quietly, "Maybe I've had enough of water. Maybe I'll just stay on land awhile longer."

Liam said, "What good is a battleship anymore?" His voice was low and grumbly and carried anger in its undertone. He had known anger all his life and was no good at hiding it. Tonight he meant the U-boats. They lurked and hid and used the sea itself for cover. How could you guard against the invisible? How could you fight what you couldn't see?

"You're right," Chance said. "But I bet you could drive a landing craft. You know, ferry me in so I can storm the beach!" He pointed his .30-06 over the dune and said, "I can shoot goddamn Nazis all day long." When he talked like that, with darkness in his voice, even Liam was a little afraid of him.

"It ain't going to be like that," Tim Dant said, too quietly for the others to pay attention. He was pretty sure none of them really knew.

Just that it would be bad. But it was something they must do. He felt the duty in him like a conscience. There was no other good reason to do this. All he really wanted in life was to go fishing. He understood the sea, loved the solitude of a boat on open water. He knew where to find crabs in the sound, how to gig flounder in the moonlight shallows, the best fishing grounds for tuna and mackerel. It was hard, honest outdoor work, and he was the boss of himself.

Once he joined up, he'd surely have plenty of bosses.

"The boy's right," Liam said. "Whatever you think it will be, you're wrong." He was sure of at least that much.

Chance went on, not listening, still sighting down the barrel of his rifle. "Just get me ashore, and I'll do the rest! Hell, if you boys can't drive a boat by now, what have you been doing here all your life?" He tossed the empty jar into the night.

Patchett said, "Hey, that's a nickel you just throwed away."

"Not one I'll be needing," Littlejohn said, already unscrewing the lid on the other jar.

Liam said, "Well, whatever we do, we're going to do it together. Ain't that the whole point?"

5

"Here's how, boys," Brick Littlejohn said. And then he passed the jar, and they all swigged the clear liquor, sweet in the front but burning at the back.

The boys were good and drunk when a burst of flame lit the horizon only a couple miles out. A few seconds later, the boom carried shoreward above the rumble of the surf.

Liam Royal gripped his shotgun and stood. The sudden eruption of fire had used up all his words. The boys stood automatically, suddenly sobered, as if in reverent tribute to the men who were dying out at sea.

Chance said, "Goddamn Nazis. I can't wait for a chance to shoot 'em like mallards."

Patchett said, "Yeah, but first you got to get 'em in your sights."

Chance said, “Oh, you just watch me.”

A burst of flame skyrocketed into the clouds.

Tim Dant said in wonderment, “Holy cow—it’s going up like the Fourth of July.”

They all watched the fire on the horizon, closer than they first thought.

CHAPTER FOUR

HATTERAS ISLAND, 1991

1

The seventy-foot *NorthAm Rascal* pounded through the rough seas, heading for the drilling site. Fannon was going out to inspect the project and coordinate the arrival of the drilling tower. Nick was along for the ride—and because he had made a promise never to write about a project he had not seen for himself. His golden rule, as close to an ethic as he allowed himself, because it served him in a practical way.

He was in the credibility business, and it helped if he could vouch for what he had seen with his own eyes. People could always tell. You could not tell the whole truth about a thing you had not seen, just as you could not lie about a thing you had seen. Or at least he could not—that was the naïve honesty Funderburke counted on. Nick was neither an advocate nor an opponent of any given policy, any operational decision. He was merely the witness.

Fannon and Funderburke and others like them shared the burden of decision, the risk of choice. Nick rarely had much to decide, and he liked it that way. He had known confident decision makers all his life, men and women who were always dead sure of the truth of things. And time and again, they got it wrong. Nick held a lifelong distrust of such people. His Opa had been a true believer, and he left behind a good woman sentenced to a lifetime of grieving uncertainty.

Most of whatever Nick thought he knew for sure about the world had vanished in that car crash in Door County. Now he watched the world with his eyes wide open and trusted only what he could see and touch and taste, and that was fine. He didn't need any Big Truth, any religion or philosophy of life. He understood basic fairness, and he took pride in his work. The world amazed him almost every day, and he felt no need to explain it, only to enjoy it.

Nick and Fannon stood in the cabin holding on to the stainless-steel grab rails on either side of the helm. The captain was not shy about slamming the bow into the building seas, the boat shouldering forward and lurching sideways at once, spray booming across the bow deck and sluicing the windshield. A knot of roughnecks filled the bench seats along the bulkheads and held on to hand straps, showing all the concern of commuters on a subway.

"Christ, I hope it calms down a mite," Fannon said. "This thing rolls like a pig when the sea gets up—too damned wide and shallow for deep water."

"Just give me a warning if you're about to hurl."

He shook his head. "I'm thinking about that bloody rig, the poor guys towing it up through this dirt. Until she's jacked and leveled, she's at the mercy."

"The outfit has never lost a rig—that's what you always say."

"Yeah, well. A lot of things never happened till they happen, yeah?"

They were about fifteen miles offshore with an equal distance to go. The sky was slate and low, and the wind sheared off the wave tops into sheets of spindrift so that it was sometimes hard to tell where sea left off and sky began.

The bow lifted on a wave and slammed into a trough, and the next wave exploded over the foredeck and broke so hard against the windshield that for a moment Nick had the sensation of being underwater. And the bow didn't rise as fast as before—the whole boat felt sluggish and heavy.

"What the hell?" Fannon asked the captain.

"She's handling like a brick," the captain said to his deckhand. "I don't get it. She's a good-enough sea boat. Check out the bilge."

"I got it," Fannon said, and shoved past the deckhand. He clawed his way from one handhold to the next with Nick right behind. He slipped down into the forward cabin into dirty water. "Shite!" Fannon said. He turned to the hatchway. "Turn on the pumps! We've got water down here!"

The captain throttled back to neutral, and the roar of the big Cummins diesel subsided to a rattling groan. The boat settled heavily and rolled on the high, steep seas. Fannon climbed back to the helm station. "Turn on the pumps, mate!"

"The pumps are already on!"

"What?"

The captain checked his console. "The main bilge pump is lit, Mister Fannon. Ditto the engine-room bilge pump. They went on automatically."

"Then she's got a hole in her." He turned to the roughnecks, who now were showing mild concern. "Get down below and find that hole before we swamp the engine!" He paired off the men and steered them to the engine room, the aft equipment lazarette, and the bow lockers. "Get on the radio," he told the captain. "Tell 'em where we are, and get a towboat out here pronto."

"No need to tell me my business," the captain said, and grabbed the mic.

"Come with me, Nicky."

They climbed back into the cabin and knelt facing aft. In the pitching sea, it took both of them to toggle open the lock-downs on the heavy inspection port and heft it up. Fannon secured it onto an eyebolt with a snap shackle so it would not drop on their heads. He snapped on a flashlight and shined it into the bilge. A stream of water gushed in from the pump. Nick could hear another gush farther aft, in the engine spaces.

Fannon slithered in through the oily water and reached the pump. "Nicky! Nicky, tell him to shut off all the pumps!"

Nick thought he hadn't heard right. "Shut them *off*?"

"Yeah! Shut the goddamn things off! Do it now!"

Nick clambered topside and told the captain, who flipped two toggle switches, and the rushing water stopped.

Fannon appeared in the forward hatchway, wet and filthy. "Cancel the towboat—we'll get back on our own."

The deckhand came up out of the engine room onto the after work deck. "We got water in the engine compartment, but it's stopped now."

"Of course it has." Fannon said to Nick, "Somebody reversed the bloody pumps."

"What do you mean?"

"I mean, instead of pumping water out of the boat, they're pumping water in."

"How in the world?"

"You've got a red wire and a white wire, right? All you do is reverse them. The impeller spins the wrong way. Sucks water in, instead of out." He turned to the men. "All right, guys. We're going to do this the old-fashioned way, with buckets."

They gathered every bucket and coffee can they could find and spent the next two hours relaying the water up onto the work deck, where they dumped it and watched it run out the scuppers.

When the *Rascal* was more or less dry below, Fannon said, "I guess we'll see the site tomorrow. Meantime we've got some wiring to sort out." And he went aft to get some fresh air on the fantail while the captain turned the boat back to the island. Nick settled heavily on the starboard bench, hugging his sore ribs.

2

The evening turned surprisingly mild. The weather had blown up the coast, leaving a clear sky studded with stars. Nick cleaned up in his room. The big house seemed deserted, so he wandered into the village looking for a drink and a meal.

Fannon would be on the phone half the night to headquarters, sorting out the events of the day. Some mechanic was going to catch hell, but that wasn't Nick's responsibility. His job was to mingle with the locals and find out what he could do to win them over. If the well hit, NorthAm might be here to stay. If not, no harm in establishing some goodwill. He might as well start finding his way around.

And maybe find out, too, who was behind the protest signs sprouting up all over the island. It was strange—there seemed no force behind the movement, just those showy signs. No town-hall meetings to demand concessions, no protests, no spokesperson. Just the damned signs.

Overlooking the boat basin on the sound side, he found a fish house called Lord's Manor. Inside, the cork walls were lined with old sepia photographs of lifesaving crews wearing dark, shapeless trousers and coats with brass buttons the size of coins. Among the photos was one of an all-black crew ranked in front of a station identified as Pea Island. That was up north, he remembered, near the other lighthouse. They had driven past it right after the accident.

He paused at the next photo, which depicted a strikingly handsome black man wearing a boxy cap emblazoned with *U.S.L.S.S.*—United States Life Saving Service. The man looked like an African prince, with fierce eyes and strong cheekbones that shadowed the light as in a charcoal portrait.

"They called him Chief Lord," Julia Royal said. She materialized at his elbow in jeans and a white smock that showed off her tanned arms and neck.

"So here you are." It wasn't exactly what he meant, just what he blurted out. What he meant but had no words for was how very present she seemed—somehow more vivid and sharply defined than everything around her, like the filmmaker's trick of focusing attention on a star surrounded by a crowd.

"Why, were you looking for me?" She had a look in her eyes he couldn't read—unblinking intensity, a kind of dare, but to do what?

"Nice to see a familiar face, that's all."

She canted her head, deciding whether or not she believed him. "I hear you people have as much trouble with boats as you do with cars. You've got to stop crossing your wires."

He was taken aback. "How . . . ?"

She shook her head as if explaining some simple fact to a child for the umpteenth time. "It's an island, you know? Everything goes round and round. All you have to do is listen for it."

He smiled tightly, still unsure what to make of her jibe. How in the world could she know NorthAm's business so quickly? Well, it would be the talk of the wharf, so maybe it was not such a mystery after all. Still, he had the sense she was showing off how much she could find out, and how quickly. "Just a foul-up, that's all."

She clucked her tongue, but her tone was serious, almost warning. "Lucky that's all it was. That's no place for trouble, not out there."

"So you keep telling me." He nodded toward the photos on the wall. "Guess that's why they had all those guys to come to the rescue, back in the day. That one, Lord, I know that name."

"It's an old island family," Julia said. "Goes back as far as any. Isaac Abraham Lord was our oldest living character. You probably passed his funeral on the way down here."

The white church. The godly man. He could still see that young black woman's earnest face, her hand over her heart, the respect she showed for the deceased. He made a mental note to find out more. "I wondered."

"Isaac Abraham was the son of Chief Lord."

"Chief? Why chief?"

She shrugged. "I don't know. Don't think anyone does. He took charge, I guess." She stared at the photograph as if she had never seen it before. "He was one of the heroes of the old days."

"That's exactly what he looks like, all right." Nick stood back and regarded Julia, how her dark hair caught the light and shimmered, how her eyes stared at him so fiercely, until—suddenly shy—she ducked her head. He said, "So this place is named in his honor?"

"He left a lot of descendants," she said, looking and nodding. For the first time, he noticed the young African American hostess, the black man in the flowered shirt behind the bar, other black faces at the booths and tables. Her eyes held him for a long moment. Again she looked away. "Chief Lord was one of the old giants."

"Giants?"

She laughed nervously, and he could tell he was making her ill at ease, but he had no idea why. And in truth, he didn't mind unsettling her.

"Like my great-grandfather Malcolm Royal, rest his soul. Larger than life, you know. The seas were bigger and the storms more terrible." She fluttered her hands theatrically. "In the old days, everybody was a hero." She laughed again, a musical little trill, and put a hand to her mouth to keep it in. "Even their horse was named Homer."

"Maybe they *were* heroes."

She tilted her head and chewed her lower lip. Again her eyes sparked and narrowed. "You're making fun of me."

He shook his head emphatically. "You're the one who was making fun. Me, I think we could use a few more heroes in the world."

She smiled, a flash of white teeth, then chewed her lip again.

"Hey, you know what?" he said. "Let me treat you to dinner." He touched her lightly on the arm, but she drew back. He felt repulsed, as if by an electrical charge. Her whole demeanor stiffened in an instant.

He stood for a moment, once more put off-balance by her. It seemed she had a genius for that. "Maybe another time then, okay?" he said. It had been a long day, and he was tired. His ribs ached, and he was bruised from the pitching and rolling of the workboat. He would enjoy having her company, but he wasn't chasing romance, and he didn't have it in him to work too hard to win her over.

But his face must have shown raw disappointment, for just when he had given up, she brightened and smiled. "Oh, what the hell. Come on." She hooked his arm and led him to a table by the window.

Outside, the boat basin glistened silver, pinked by the setting sun, and it was hard for him to remember that just a few hours ago he had been aboard a boat foundering in rough seas, and that he might have died by accident. Again.

3

"I was a third-grade teacher," she confided after dinner, as they sat finishing their wine.

Nick was feeling less achy and sore, more relaxed. "Off-island?"

She sipped and thought for a moment, nodded. "I got off for a little while. All the way to Charleston. Almost two whole years."

"You sound so disappointed." He thought about dreary Chicago in the heart of winter, a place he no longer regarded as home. Now it was just someplace else. "A lot of people would kill for the chance to live here on this island."

"Spoken like someone who just got here."

"Can't help that—I did just get here."

"Of course you like it. They all do. For a little while, it's paradise." She sipped her wine. "Stick around."

"How can you be so jaded? You're not old enough." He meant it lightly, but she frowned.

"I'm older than I look. Thirty-two, since April."

He shrugged. "That's not so old."

"Old enough."

He sighed. There was no use arguing. But he knew it was at least partly true: When you lived in a place long enough, you became dulled to its charms. In that one way, he was lucky, for he got to try on a new place every few months. He went in knowing the clock was ticking and that one day soon he'd leave and likely never come back. So he paid attention, let himself become infatuated. Sometimes it was as simple as getting up from his desk and looking out the window.

He was doing that now, looking at her. Memorizing the tilt of her delicate chin, the dark confusion in her eyes, as if she didn't know what to make of him. But there was more to it. He sensed that, for her, he was a problem, but he didn't understand exactly what kind, or even why. Maybe it was only about the drilling, the threat that might carry, the invasion of company workers that might follow—rough guys who liked to blow off steam after a hard turn on the rig. He'd seen the way the locals looked at them, frowning, when they'd assembled on the dock earlier to board the *Rascal*.

But he sensed something else was going on. The way he felt being here was like walking into a movie already in progress—the same dislocation he had felt in Chicago, now magnified.

He turned to the window.

It was pleasant looking out over the light-spangled water, and the wine was making him drowsy. He said, "I don't know how I like it yet. But it is the kind of place that catches you by surprise, you know?"

"Well, that much is true," she said softly.

He mused on the darkening harbor, the last light glazing the water. "You get it into your eyes and can't get it out again." He thought about all those lonely stretches of sand and waves among the crowded villages. The whole island must have looked like that, once upon a time. Beautiful in a stark, wind-swept way that could both thrill you and drive you mad.

She wagged a finger at him. "Careful—this island is a trap." Her tone was playful, but he also caught a note of true warning, and it puzzled him.

"So why did you come back?"

"It's home. Where else would I go?" She wrapped both hands around her wineglass and sat back from him. "The old, boring story. A bad marriage."

"I'm sorry."

"Don't be. I thought we were special. Thought he was Prince Charming, but he turned out to be just another lawyer. It wasn't even very dramatic." She looked down at the table. "Just kind of fizzled out."

"An islander, like you?"

She laughed sadly and looked up, holding her eyes on his. "You're an islander only if you have somebody buried in the graveyard." She sipped and held the wine in her mouth a moment before swallowing. Her eyes stared at the glass. "He didn't."

Across the room, he could hear the clink of forks and spoons, the low murmur of conversation. He expelled a breath and realized he had been holding it. "So you came home."

"Home is where they have to take you in, right?"

He couldn't name a place that was home, and it made him oddly embarrassed in front of her. She seemed so much a part of this island, as if it had been created just for her kind.

What did it feel like to belong body and soul, family and future?

To be able to look back at a string of photographs depicting all your people, generations of them, in the same landscape? To know with certainty that a hundred years from now, descendants bearing your name, your genes, would be walking the same ground under the same sky, maybe studying old photographs of you in that same landscape?

Some irrational part of him wanted to try it out, now, here in this place, with this woman. The impulse overwhelmed him with its force of surprise and longing at the back of his throat, mingled with the beginning of grief for his lovely grandmother, whom he knew was failing. He would lose her, too, before long, and then he would have lost everybody.

"And you?" she said.

He cleared his throat, shook off the melancholy. "Free as a bird." He meant to sound lighthearted, but it came out sorrowful and rehearsed.

"Ouch. A rocky divorce." She said it smugly, like she had him all figured out—just another person who thought she knew something and didn't know it at all.

He took a breath. "No, not exactly. I've just been on my own for, well, for a very long time."

She touched his hand reflexively, and for once her eyes did not look away.

He loved that she was looking at him that way, directly and with all her attention, but he hated why. He had a sense that she was seeing him as some kind of lonely misfit.

He found himself wanting to tell the rest of it, how he'd lost his parents when he was young, but he knew better. He did not want to become the object of her pity. Worse, she might think he was confiding in her just so he might win her over. His loss had value that belonged only to him, and he did not want to cheapen it. It belonged in a secret chamber of his heart, and he let himself think about it only on rare bad nights. He had already told her too much.

In a moment, she took back her hand. He waited for her to fill in her story, but she said nothing. So he asked, "Your parents?"

"Happy, healthy, and gone," she said. "Off the island."

"For good?"

She nodded. "Southern California, of all places." Another ocean.

"We talk, I see them holidays."

"I'm surprised. You know, the family business and all. Such deep roots here."

She hunched her shoulders and stared out the window. He waited for her to fill in the awkward silence. It was a trick he had learned as a newspaper reporter—stop talking and eventually the other person will say something to break the silence He didn't mean it as a trick now, but the habit was too deeply ingrained to turn off.

She said quietly, "My father had a falling out with the Founder. A real blowup."

"Sounds dramatic. What was it about?" He knew as soon as the words came out of his mouth that he had no right to ask—again, it was the reporter's obvious follow-up.

She stared at him, and he could see her shut down, utterly close off any avenue of revelation or trust. "I wasn't in the room for that conversation."

"Sorry, none of my business."

She nodded and waited a beat, looking past him. "It's all right. Anyhow, I'd see my parents more, but they never come here. Turns out I hate to travel. Airplanes make me claustrophobic—you know, strapped inside a big aluminum tube. And the West Coast, you know. So far."

"I guess it's all in how you measure it. If you think about the distance between two places, well, that's one thing. But if you just think of being in whatever place you're in at that moment, you don't much notice how far."

"You travel a lot, I guess. I'm afraid it would wear me out after a while."

"They send me all over the world. I get to see places most people have only read about in books."

"I'd be lost in translation," she said. "How do you manage it?"

He waved a hand dismissively. "Always had a thing for languages. German from my grandmother, a little French in college." He had also picked up a smattering of Dinka and Swahili and Russian. And anyway, government and business types usually spoke some bastard version of English. "You'd be surprised how far you can get in the Third World with Coca-Cola English and high-school French," he said. He leaned in, as if to share a secret.

"Do you always do that?" she asked.

"Always do what?"

"Tell something about yourself without actually telling anything about yourself."

He sat back. "Not sure what you mean. I'm an open book."

She shook her head. "You're doing it again." She smiled, and he could not tell what she meant by it. "Tell me something true about yourself. In the present."

"Okay," he said, and thought a moment. "I have actually been to Timbuktu."

"There! See what I mean?"

"Come on, you don't understand. It's on the edge of nowhere. Beyond it, nothing but desert for thousands of miles. I mean, it's the last stop." He heard the enthusiasm in his voice, trying to convey the thrill he had felt. It wasn't about the place but about him—if she would only listen.

She laughed and then caught herself. "There's actually a Timbuktu? I thought it was just a figure of speech. What could possibly take you to Timbuktu?"

He smiled. "Same thing that took me to the Gobi Desert and the Andaman Islands."

She sagged in her chair and set down the wineglass. "Yeah, I guess that's a sore point around here. We like our oil safe under the water, not all over the beaches."

"Come on, don't be like that. It's just an exploratory well." He held up his index finger. "One well."

"I went to Gulfport once. It was a business trip with the lawyer. I saw what one oil well turns into. And besides, there's never only one. Not if you find what you're looking to find."

"Let's talk about something else, okay?"

"Why? So we don't get into an argument? You're the one who brought up the job." She folded her napkin, opened it, and folded it again.

"I'll tell you all about myself, anything you want to know."

"I doubt it." Her eyes flashed, and the way she tossed her head made her hair bounce.

Nick said, "Look, my ribs are sore as hell. It's been a long day. And I really don't want to argue with you, okay?"

"You want to be liked," she said evenly. "You think they'll all like you." Her voice held a tinge of disappointment.

"What's so wrong with that?"

"Nothing, nothing at all. Unless you want it too much." She poured more wine.

"I'm not following you. It's not okay, wanting people to like you?"

"Not if you want it so much you can't be yourself. You have to be what you think they want you to be. What you think they'll like. You have to hide the other parts."

He couldn't tell whether she was talking about him or her own failed marriage.

"After a while, you get used to hiding. After a while longer, you lose yourself." She had been talking fast, and now she paused and took a long sip of wine but kept her eyes steady on him. "Do you want it too much?"

Maybe, he thought. *Maybe what she says is true.* He sure wanted Julia to like him. But why the hell did he care what she thought? Well, he did, and it irritated him. She made him out to be some kind of sleazy grifter.

He had always been the good guy, the one people liked, even when he couldn't speak their language—in Thailand, Indonesia, Irkutsk, Venezuela. Oil meant jobs. Oil paid for schools and roads and medicine. And when he worked in the U.S., he was usually promoting a wildlife refuge, a new double-hulled tanker for minimizing spills, a state-of-the-art skimmer boat to clean up spills, bacteria that digested oil slicks. When he wasn't doing research or writing reports, he gave slide talks to the Rotary and the Lions Club, and afterward they shook his hand and he felt proud to be doing his part. There was nothing fake about it.

Now Julia was making him feel like a phony, a threat, *persona non grata*. It shook him up. All at once, he felt a flutter of doubt. Maybe he *was* a grifter. Maybe he was a fake. Maybe she was right not to fall for his easy words, not to be charmed by his smile. Could he be sincere and still be a fake? He wondered. Was it just the job she hated? A man was more than his job—didn't she know that?

Or was it some glaring flaw that was as apparent to her as a grease stain on his shirt?

She kept on. "Why do you care what a bunch of strangers think about you?"

"I don't know. Maybe because it's my business to care."

"Right, business. Not personal."

"That's not what I meant."

"It's what you said. What is it you want? I mean, really want?"

He raised his hand like a flag, palm out. "Just to do my job, I guess." True enough, he knew, as far as it went. But it didn't go very far. But what else could he say—*I want to go home*? Which was nowhere. His job was all the home he had. There just was no use going into it, not with her, not now. Like as not, she'd make a mean joke out of it. He said, "So what about you? What do you want?"

"It's not about me."

He shook his head and said quietly, "Maybe you just don't know yet."

But she knew, all right. Escape, that's what she wanted. To get off the island, to get out from under her heavy name—even though she loved with all her heart the old man who had given such weight to it. She said, "What are you like when nobody's looking?"

"Me?" he said. "The same person you see now, I guess."

"Really?" She sipped her wine, and he could see the flush in her cheeks. "When's the last time you got angry at something? At somebody? You won't even let yourself get angry at me for being rude to you! Or maybe you'll just blow off steam behind my back."

"I'm not angry at you. Why would I be angry at you?" But even as he said it, he could hear the edge in his voice.

"Never mind." She balled up her napkin and set it beside her place. "It's about what you stand for."

"And what's that?"

She pursed her lips and looked at the table. "Everything that's gone wrong on this island."

He had no idea what to say to that. He sipped his wine, which suddenly tasted acid in his mouth. He was oddly embarrassed, the way he had felt calling up a girl in high school to ask her on a date and then waiting through the long pause before she made some lame excuse, some lazy lie, about why she couldn't go out. "I wouldn't know anything about that. Like I said, I just got here."

"You could fill a book with everything you don't know."

"No argument there. That's my job."

"Just what is your job, exactly?"

He steepled his hands. "I find out stuff. Pay attention to things." She wasn't getting it. "I talk to people."

"So you don't *do*—you *talk*."

He opened his hands and laid them flat on the tablecloth. "Mostly I watch and listen. Then I write stories about it."

"You're a reporter?"

Company storyteller, he thought. "In a manner of speaking."

She took it in for a moment. "And you report to . . ." She backed away, held up her hands, palms out, as if to push away the idea of him. "My God, I'm a *source*."

He shrugged. "No, come on. I mean, yes, I guess everybody's a source. But that's not why . . ." He couldn't even finish the sentence, just smiled weakly.

He was always around people but never exactly *with* them. In that moment, he saw himself suddenly through her eyes—as a Fannon character, someone without *der kern*, speaking in an accent that came from everywhere and nowhere, inscrutable, guileless and deceptive at once, acting out of no larger motive than to pass as one of them and not be found out. Even his clothes were a kind of disguise. At least Fannon wore the company logo, announced his allegiance.

With Julia—here, now—he felt like an enemy spy. Which was as crazy as it was true.

She smiled tightly. "My heavens, but you're charming. You should be in sales." Her eyes widened in mock surprise. "Wait—you are!"

"Aw, come on, that's not fair."

The waitress materialized at their table—a slim, young black woman with a glowing smile, a college kid home for the summer. Her name tag read, *Rosa Lord*. "Is everything all right?" she asked. He saw that Julia was ready to bolt and Rosa Lord was blocking her in her seat.

"Sure," Nick said. "Hey, that name—*Lord*."

She glanced down self-consciously at her nametag. "Right. This is my uncle's place. You one of the oil guys?"

He nodded. "Then the funeral procession—"

"He was my great-great-grandfather."

"A good man, I hear," Nick said. "You have my condolences for your loss."

"The best there was," she said with obvious pride.

Julia was still trying to edge out of her seat.

Nick nodded sympathetically. "So what do you study at college?"

Rosa Lord smiled. "Is it that obvious? History. I study history."

"History's a good thing to know, all right." He was stalling, giving Julia a few moments to calm down. Maybe she would stay a little while longer. "My dad was a history teacher."

"Really? I want to teach someday, too, you know, help people figure out how we got here and where to go next."

"Got to admire that," Nick said. "But you make it sound so simple. So logical."

Rosa Lord threw back her head and laughed. "My professor says history is just one damned thing after another."

"I have to get back," Julia said. "I still have chores to do." She was already pushing away from the table. The young waitress moved away, puzzled concern in her eyes.

Nick put a hand over Julia's as gently as he could, felt its tense warmth. "I'm sorry," he said. "Whatever I said, whatever I did."

"Stop being sorry, for God's sake," she said. "It's not about you. I'm sorry."

"Why do you stay here if you hate it so much?"

"You don't get to ask me that."

"All I meant was, maybe you're working too hard, up at dawn, serving guests all day long."

Julia straightened, jerked her head and flipped her hair. "You mean because I'm a Royal."

"No, I only meant—"

She threw down her napkin. "You haven't got a clue. In the Royal family, everybody works. We're all in this together." Her eyes flashed, and he could see her physically drawing away from him.

"I'll walk you."

"No, stay and finish your wine. And remember something: You're from off."

He felt his neck flush. And she was gone before he could think of what to say next.

Rosa Lord stared open-mouthed at Julia as she departed, turned toward Nick and shrugged sympathetically, then retreated to the beverage station and watched him, her mouth pursed, as if she wanted to ask him something. Then she disappeared into the kitchen. Through the serving window, he saw her gesture toward him and say something to the old black cook, to which the cook nodded somberly.

4

Nick strolled along the harbor basin before heading home, trying to let the day settle. Julia infuriated him, yet he was drawn to her in a way he had not felt toward a woman in years—or maybe never felt. She was at once completely who she was, no pretenses, and impossible to read. He had just met her, yet she had gotten into his head, spun him around as if they'd been sparring for years.

He had no idea what she might do next, or even how she felt about him. Some moments, she seemed to like him, and then without warning she would turn on him, full of accusation and judgment. And all he wanted was to do his job well and do right by the company and everybody else.

Maybe that was the sticking point—could he do right by the company and the islanders at the same time? Why was this place so different from all the others he had worked, each time balancing his loyalty to the project with his integrity?

Something surely was different. Maybe the curse of his Opa, the very name of the island his epitaph. It was as if Julia knew some troubling secret about him that even he didn't know.

Back at Lifeboat Station #17, Nick stopped in the foyer and listened to the silence. Far down the corridor, a sliver of light showed beneath the door to Julia's suite. He hesitated—no, he'd better not disturb her.

He slipped up the stairs. He could hear a murmured argument in one of the guest rooms—the honeymoon couple—and kept going, vaguely uneasy without knowing why. He opened his door and immediately had the sense that someone had been in there. The bed was newly made, and a spray of fresh daisies stood in a blue vase on his dresser. The housekeeper, he figured.

Or maybe Julia Royal, a peace offering.

A folded note was on the pillow. He opened it. It was a page torn from a spiral notebook, and on it, in block letters, was printed a single word: *GOLIATH.*

He studied the paper, turned it over, held it to the light, but no other mark was visible. "What the hell?" he said out loud.

5

At breakfast on the back deck, Nick sat alone and nursed his coffee. The local weekly newspaper had been waiting outside his door, and the front page was full of Isaac Abraham Lord. Captain of the mailboat during the years before reliable ferries and bridges. Preacher of the gospel. Friend to the downtrodden and unlucky. Patriarch of a large family, one of whom was a doctor. Another of whom was a waitress home from college.

He checked out the masthead. The editor was listed as Sallie Lord. The publisher was Diogenes Lord. Pretty soon, he'd want to meet them both.

Families, Nick mused. *It always comes back to families down here.*

The honeymoon couple sat at the next table jabbering like tropical birds, their spat apparently behind them, and a large, overweight family was camped at the end of the deck sharing a long table piled with plates of sausages and eggs and fruit. Out of the corner of his eye, he caught sight of Julia pouring coffee for the honeymooners. *Let her be,* he told himself. *Stick to business.* His ribs ached like hell this morning—he had tossed and turned all night. He took the note out of his breast pocket and studied it again.

Julia said, "You ready for a refill, cowboy?" Her voice was soft and throaty, full of gentle hospitality. He could hardly believe she was the same person who had left him at the restaurant last night. *You're from off.* That still stung. He'd never felt more an outsider anywhere than here.

He smiled. "Yeah, thanks." He watched her hands—small and squarish, the unpainted nails trimmed short—as she poured. "You were up late," he said. "I saw the light on."

"Going over the books," she said. "No fun at all. Got to do it at night when the house quiets down." She poured him coffee.

"Yeah, I had homework of my own."

"Was I as bitchy to you last night as I remember?"

"Forget it," he said. "I hate apologies."

"I wasn't apologizing. You're the one who bought the bottle of wine." She smiled, and he felt a flutter in his chest. She was a woman he could fall into and get lost for years.

She was also driving him crazy. Nothing she might do would surprise him. But just once, he'd love a straight answer. "Know anybody around here called Goliath?"

She looked him in the eye but paused before answering. "What, like in the Bible?" Her face gave away nothing.

He turned his palms up. "I have no idea. A friend said to ask, said it had some local meaning." It was only a small, harmless lie, but still a lie, and still to her.

"Really?" She waited a beat. "Well, I'm not big on the Bible."

A heavy tread shook the deck. Liam Royal, the Founder, leaned on the table, and Nick practically felt the weight on his own chest. "That's what Par Patchett used to call my old man, Goliath," he said, as if speaking to no one in particular, and laughed a deep, throaty laugh. "A titan of a man, that was Malcolm," he went on. "Old Par Patchett, now he was sommat of a prowser, always haunting the beach at night, like his crippled dad, Patch. Patch died a hero in the First War, oddest damned thing you could imagine. Rescued Alvin Dant's boat from a submarine attack and sank his own."

He stood staring off at nothing, as if still pondering the oddity of it all these years later, then suddenly barked out, "Unlucky or brave, take your pick." He leaned closer and stuck a big finger right in Nick's face. "He had a stove-up leg from a fishing accident, but he went out anyway. You understand me?" He said it again, emphasizing every word with his finger: "*He went out anyway.*" As if that settled something.

Nick stared at the mottled, rough hand inches from his nose. What the hell was the old guy rambling on about? "Yes, sir, I think I do." He let a moment go by. "So old Patchett is dead now?"

The Founder looked at him oddly. "Old Parvis? Hell, no, not so I've heard. You heard something I ain't?"

"No, sir, I just thought, the way you talk about him . . ."

"Sometimes I think that old crab won't niver die. The Good Lord won't have him, and the devil don't want him." The Founder backed off and stood up straight. "Do you know what war fever is?"

"Patriotism, I guess." Nick had seen people get worked up over the Gulf War.

"Not the same thing at all. What do you know? That little war in the desert? I'm talking about war right up close, right in your backyard—flames all night long on the horizon, burned bodies on the beach at dawn." He flung his arm toward the sea. "I'm talking about island men who leave and don't niver come back."

Nick thought, *Which war is he even talking about? The First World War, the Second World War—all of them?* He wasn't making a lot of sense. But he had been around in the old days, and maybe of all the people here he could shed some light on what happened to his Opa, out there on the water.

Julia stepped in and touched the old man's shoulder. "Paw Paw, can I fix you an omelet?"

Liam Royal was winding up to say more, but he caught himself and bowed his head briefly, as if embarrassed. "I get to talking," he explained, and smiled crookedly. "The old days, you know."

"I love the stories," Nick said. "In fact, I wanted to ask—"

"Stories." He grunted. "Stories never happened—they're just make-believe. Storytellers are just damned liars. What I'm telling, it happened just that way."

The Founder filled a heavy blue mug with coffee and wandered out across the sand to his boathouse.

"I'll bring down your breakfast!" Julia called after him.

Nick said, "He was in the war?"

"Yes," she said shortly. "Wasn't everybody?"

"What did I say now? All I said was about Goliath."

"Nothing," she said. "Absolutely nothing. He just gets . . . I just get . . . Never mind."

"That's okay," he said, unwilling to let her go. "What's the story with Rosa Lord?"

"The girl who waited on us last night? What do you want to know about her for?"

"Just curious."

"I don't know, just a smart college kid. Seems really sweet. Great-great-granddaughter of Chief Lord."

"The guy in the picture."

"Yeah, that's him. One of the giants."

Maybe *he* was Goliath. "The Lord family, they do okay?"

"What is this, the third degree?" She pursed her lips, weighing her words, Nick saw. "They do fine now."

"Now? But they're an old family, you said."

"They hit a rocky patch just after the war. Lost some land, you know how it goes." She didn't sound convinced. "At least, so they say."

"But that was boom times. I thought everybody got rich."

"Not around here. A lot of men went to fight, and only a few came back, and they kind of got pushed aside by, well, by other people. Some had big debt and lost land over it." She was saying more than she intended.

Nick didn't say it, but they both knew what he was thinking: *Pushed aside by men like her grandfather.*

6

Fannon was poring over sea charts in the main saloon of the *Lady NorthAm*. "That dirty weather put us behind by a day, mate," he said. "The tower will be on site tomorrow. Knock wood." He knuckled the paneling.

"Good." Nick couldn't wait to see the rig, to witness the reality of it. He never got tired of watching big machinery doing its work. And that would make the job come to life. Right now, the test well was just an idea, a plan. Soon it would be a massive, real thing in action.

"How's your end coming?"

"We're not in Kansas anymore." Nick flipped the paper onto the chart table.

"What's this, then?"

"Fan mail from a secret admirer."

Fannon looked at it and scratched his head. "Fucking Goliath? You're kidding, right? That's all? The giant wanker that got killed by the slingshot? Means fuck-all to me, mate." He flicked the paper aside, and Nick retrieved it.

"Maybe they mean the company. Big and powerful, and they're the little guy, little David," Nick said. "You know, I was thinking about our little boat ride."

Fannon had his head in the chart. "Yeah, well. About that. Seems they had a bit of routine maintenance done on the old *Rascal*."

"The company mechanic?" Nick had a hard time believing it.

Fannon shook his head. "Local guy. Ours was tied up with the *Lady*. So they called around and found some local talent." He checked a clipboard. "Guy named Gandil. Charles Gandil. Seems to have vanished. Our people are trying to track him down now."

Nick said, "Gandil? Think that's his real name?"

Fannon shrugged. "Probably not. Maybe the same guy who did the Rover."

"Well, if he did, he sure gets around."

Fannon said, "I don't mind telling you, it spooks the shite out of me.

Fucking bull's-eye on my back, yeah?" He punched Nick lightly on the arm. "Yours, too."

Nick wanted to find out what was what. He didn't like looking over his shoulder all the time, wondering whom to trust. It was a new thing—having someone out to get him. That's what it felt like—personal, targeted. Creepy. "I'm driving up to see about it. Want to come along?"

"Nah, you go," Fannon said. "I'm buried here."

On the dock, a dozen protesters waved signs at Nick as he stepped off the gangplank: *NO DRILL, NO SPILL!* Again the signs were professionally printed. He would have to find out who was behind the protests—some local activist group. Or were these people being coached by an outside organization? The protesters seemed friendly, half-hearted, not the rabid environmentalists he was used to encountering. The whole scene struck him as odd and stagy, as if the rowdy mob were a bunch of extras in a movie, just background noise against which the main characters would play out their drama.

He nodded pleasantly and got into the Scout, but they crowded around. He ground it into gear and eased off the dock, and the crowd slowly parted, slapping the sides as he passed. On the sheet-steel fenders, the hands sounded like hail rattling a tin roof.

7

At Dant's Marina, they stood in the shade of the garage next to the boat shed and stared at the crumpled Land Rover.

Caroline Dant shook her head and declared, "Frame's bent. You may as well have it hauled off to the junkyard." Standing beside her, he felt tall. She squinted as she talked. The double overhead doors were open, and a breeze wafted in, smelling of salt and hot asphalt.

The wrecked car was the insurance company's problem, and as far as Nick was concerned it could do whatever it wanted with the Rover. "What about the brakes?"

To a darkly tanned, lean youth in coveralls, she said, "Henry, pop the hood." To Nick, she said, "My favorite nephew. He studies nights at the community college. Works here days."

Henry opened the bent hood and said, "The master cylinder is dry as a popcorn fart."

Caroline Dant squinted and said, "Henry's learning metaphors in English literature."

"Well, it is," Henry said.

"Just say it plain." She had a way of smiling that made her eyes crinkle and a loveliness come across her face that was missing in her expression at rest, when she thought no one was watching. That face held a sadness, a memory of pain. But whenever she smiled, she looked like the young, pretty woman she had not been in years.

"Well, like I said, there's not a drop of brake fluid in the master cylinder. It's been bled out," Henry said.

"Leak?" Nick said.

"Couldn't find no leak. But it's dry. You got nothing in your lines but air." He pronounced it *arr*, shook his head so his blond curls bobbed. "Arr won't stop two tons of steel rollin' down that bridge."

"So if it didn't leak, what happened to the brake fluid?"

Caroline said, "He told you—somebody bled the brakes."

So it was a riddle. "How? And who?"

Henry grinned, showing off buckteeth. He leaned down at the back wheel and said, "You did, Mister Wolf. Every time you stomped on the pedal." He pointed. "See? These two metal parts joined by flex hose? It's the wrong size—too loose."

Caroline Dant said, "You should fire your mechanic."

"That would be the same guy who fixes bilge pumps."

"Yeah, heard all about that."

Nick said, "Can you tell if it was done on purpose?"

She shrugged. "I don't see how."

He nodded, resigned to the uncertainty. "Just bad luck then, I guess."

Caroline Dant said, "You know any other kind?"

"Thanks," Nick said. "As for the bill—"

"Already taken care of," she said.

"Good. What about that poor woman we almost ran over?"

"Almost?" Caroline Dant said. "You did sort of run over her."

Henry laughed.

Nick held that frozen moment in his mind's eye, shrimp spattering across the windshield, the woman cursing him and spitting. "We owe her for a lot of spoiled shrimp."

"All covered by the insurance check, I promise. Getting run over by you guys was the best thing that happened to her all year."

"All the same, I'd like to apologize in person."

She wagged a finger at him playfully. "Let sleeping dogs lie, hon." She smiled warmly. "You'd better get back."

As he turned to go, she stopped him with a gentle hand on his arm. "By the way, don't worry about the summons you got from that sheriff."

"Good thing—I lost it."

"I talked to the magistrate."

"You must have lots of pull around here."

She smiled again. "No, just lots of cousins."

The bridge glinted in the high sun as a steady stream of cars and campers slid down its curving slope onto the island. A yellow dump truck bearing a big, scripted *P* on its door for Patchett Builders rumbled down and pulled in next to the gas pumps. The young driver swung down. He was wearing a red, white, and blue Chicago White Sox baseball cap.

"Hey," Nick said. "Think the Sox got a shot this year?"

"You tell me," the driver said. "I never get my hopes up. You know how they always fold."

Nick crossed his fingers and held them up.

8

Nick had an appointment with the head of the local Nature Conservancy, so on his way back south he looked for the turnoff in a patch of scrub pine, marked by a rectangular blue sign. He drove down the sandy lane on the sound side to the trailer that served as her office. He knocked on the aluminum door, but no one answered. An air conditioner buzzed in the side window.

This took him aback. The environmental people always kept their meetings—they lived for meetings. They spent half their time angling for a seat at the table, and she wasn't about to blow off the one guy who could put her there.

Still, she was nowhere to be found.

He checked his watch. Right on time.

He waited half an hour, pacing and drinking in the sultry stillness.

He walked around the clearing, feeling at a loss, slapping mosquitoes off his bare arms. Overhead, laughing gulls cackled.

He approached the trailer one more time, intending to leave a note. He pressed his face against the cloudy window and peered into an office full of cardboard boxes, stacks of papers, and a cluster of signs leaning against the far wall: *NO DRILL, NO SPILL!*

She'd clearly blown off the meeting, was just wasting his time.

He left her a note anyway.

CHAPTER FIVE

HATTERAS ISLAND, 1991

1

From the pitching deck of the *NorthAm Rascal,* it was something to watch. The lead towboat churned through the water, throwing up a frothy commotion in its wake as it labored to drag the tower into position beside an anchored barge. Four other ocean-going tugs hauled along the flanks. There was raw power in their motion, an inexorable unity of purpose that Nick found inspiring.

The rig consisted of a triangular orange platform with a high white house and heliport, above which rose a derrick. The whole thing looked like it had been constructed from a gigantic Erector Set like the one he'd played with as a child. On each side, a steel jackleg rose seventy-five feet into the air from a triangular socket. Ten more feet of jackleg were already invisible underwater.

The tugs drew the ungainly floating monster into position, and deckhands on the rig threw out messenger lines attached to thick mooring hawsers. The tug crews caught the messenger lines and hauled the mooring hawsers, each as thick as a man's arm, across the gap between the vessels and secured them to massive bollards on the barge.

Nick marveled at the sheer muscle power. The most sophisticated drilling machine on the planet, and it still required good men with strong arms to muscle it into place.

Now that the rig was steadied, the rig master and his crew began the slow process of lowering the jacklegs through their sockets fifty feet onto the ocean floor. The jacklegs were three-sided geometric vertical frames. The telescoping interior legs were cranked down deep into the sandy bottom. Then the men jacked the whole platform out of the water twenty-five feet. It rose with a screech of metal on metal, the booms and bangs of the ratchets hammering at the sky like cannon fire.

Even two hundred yards away on the deck of the *Rascal*, Nick covered his ears and watched the deck rise exactly the way a heavy car is lifted on a skinny bumper jack.

But this wasn't some old Chevy weighing a couple of tons—the rig was more than twenty-five thousand tons. It was a glorious monstrosity, naked girders spiking out from the top and sides, a thicket of yellow, black, and orange pipes snaking across the deck. At night, it would glow with hundreds of work lights and be visible to the naked eye from twenty miles—and have the atmospheric glow of a small city from twice that distance, from far off over the horizon, beyond the curve of the earth.

2

Nick stood captivated.

The rig was a hideously unnatural blight on the gray swell of the sea. It was also an engineering marvel, a thing of stunning beauty.

He had seen rigs like this one many times, watched them take up their stations as men swarmed over them in apparent chaos, each one doing a specific job with remarkable skill and precise timing to get the great machine on line.

Yet he never got over the sight.

The rigs reminded him of those Martian death-ray machines in that old movie *The War of the Worlds*—powerful and ingenious. Awesome in an exact sense.

He was infatuated with complicated machines, the bigger the better.

He had watched dump trucks with tires taller than a man hauling ore from an open pit mine in the Iron Range of Minnesota, and his body had vibrated to the thrum of the great turbines inside the Hoover Dam. As a kid in Chicago, he used to go to the Museum of Science and Industry to sit in the cab of the massive Baldwin steam locomotive and, best of all, crawl through the claustrophobic steel maze of the U-505, a captured German U-boat towed through the St. Lawrence Seaway and four of the five Great Lakes to a permanent dry dock.

This fascination with machines made him a kind of throwback, he knew, to an earlier age when every problem was one of want and power, and every solution was a machine to get what was wanted faster, in larger quantities, with more force, across greater distances.

He did not have a clue where this fascination came from, for he had no particular aptitude for engines or mechanical apparatus. True, his grandfather Nicholas had been a machinist who built turbines and dynamos and railroad carriages with sure, clever hands, so maybe he had inherited this strange infatuation without any of the skill to act on it. But his father had taught high-school history, his mother algebra. They had lived in books, not machinery. His father couldn't even change the oil in their family station wagon.

Whatever the reason, Nick loved machines. Fire engines and aircraft, freight trains and big rigs, machines that dug and reaped and lifted and elevated, and especially these great rigs that rose like industrial castles out of the sea. They testified to the inexorable logic of physics, of leverage and torque, how mass was lifted and twisted and spun, momentum achieved, driving power made.

There was something reassuring in that logic, in the way machines performed the same physical work over and over again, exactly the same way, pistons driving in and out, wheels turning in precise circles, shafts spinning, lever arms lifting and pulling. Life was always slightly out of control, people always a question mark, their motives obscure, their actions unpredictable. But you could count on machines. And the great ones stood like wonders of the world, colossal kinetic sculptures, artistic and awe-inspiring. Nick had been the little boy who could watch the steam shovel work all day long and never tire of its relentless, repetitive motion. Maybe he still was.

Fannon understood this and used it, and Nick did not mind that he used it. He wondered how Funderburke felt about it all, ensconced in his glass cube twenty-eight floors above a city a thousand miles away. Did he understand the adventure of it? The majesty? Did the whole audacious, gargantuan enterprise make pictures in the man's head? Or was it all, finally, just columns of numbers on a spreadsheet?

Nick would have to ask him someday—if he ever saw him again. Retired guys tended to go away for good. But maybe Funderburke was different. He was one of a kind in the company, back to the old days. He was the memory and the conscience of the whole organization, the fiduciary soul of the enterprise. Nick couldn't imagine he would ever really just walk away from it.

Nick's allegiance to the industry, to NorthAm, was visceral, an infatuation with technology and machines. Technology had an amoral purity that lay beyond argument, a precision that lent a reassuring certainty to a jumbled, unreasonable world.

It made him a believer, whether he wanted to believe or not.

Even the company logo reassured him, the compass another reliable machine doing its job, the arrow always pointing true north.

3

Within a few hours, the whole rig was poised above the waves, humming with winches and motors and the noise of shouted orders. The roughnecks would work in continuous shifts from now on—the rig would never be idle. The tool pushers would finish assembling it in the next couple of days and then get down to business sinking eight-inch drill pipe into the ocean floor as deep as they had to.

The geologists were betting this would be a shallow reservoir, maybe eleven or twelve hundred feet below the sea bed. They'd be pulling up core samples in a matter of days, looking for the telltale grit of shale. They knew exactly what they were after, the striation pattern and density and chemical composition, and they'd recognize it quick when they found it.

That's what Fannon had told Nick. All of it was fast-tracked: Get in, find the goods, make the venture pay off, beat the weather.

Nick stood on the rolling deck wearing a yellow sou'wester, balancing reflexively by long practice. Tonight he'd be sore from the continuous effort of compensating for the shifting deck. He couldn't take his eyes off the rig. Closer now, he could see the jacklegs were scabbed with rust and one was badly creased, as though some great vessel had collided with it. He wondered if the crew would be able to level the working decks.

Meanwhile the weather was kicking up again. Nick was beginning to see that what was unusual everywhere else was normal out here. Julia had a point: The dirt could blow up in a matter of minutes, a full gale, and it could evaporate just as fast.

The flag at the jack staff snapped, and the cables anchoring the antenna mast sang with the wind. The rig stood motionless in the midst of the tumult of water, scalloped waves creaming white against the bright orange steel jacklegs. The waves advanced from two directions forty-five degrees apart and met in a ridge of water that piled up like a seam directly under the rig and went all the way to the horizon in either direction.

It was something Nick had not seen before. He grabbed Fannon's shoulder. "Check it out," he said.

"What?" Fannon stared off one way, then the other, until he saw it. He said, "Oh, shite. That can't be good news."

The ridge of water rippled and flashed white. To the south of the ridge line, it shimmered blue. To the north, it was gray and dimpled as hammered tin.

The *Rascal* powered across the maelstrom, moved in to dock at the rig.

"Give it time to settle down!" the captain called from the pilothouse. "Don't try to get off while she's rockin' and rollin."

The boat pitched violently, the tire bumpers compressing against the orange steel legs as the waves pinned the *Rascal* against them. At last, Nick saw his chance and leaped onto the narrow ladder, the deck disappearing under him. He scrambled up as another wave caught the boat and flung it upward, nearly crushing him.

Fannon made the leap a few moments later, and they were both thoroughly drenched by spray by the time they reached the hatchway.

4

They stood, toweling their necks and faces, around a steel conference table in the rig master's office, a kind of penthouse with a gallery of windows leaning outward as on the bridge of a ship. They had already got through all the hand shaking—Fannon and Nick and Bucky Malagordo, the drilling foreman, and Cal Root, the rig master, who was God on his platform.

Bucky Malagordo was a small, alert, squared-off man dressed in khaki work clothes. A bright red and yellow ball cap covered his bald head. His right hand had only two fingers and a thumb. He had been in this business since high school, when Eisenhower was president, and it had entered his body as scars and missing pieces.

Cal Root was tall and had once been lean, but now a paunch overhung his Western-tooled concho belt. He stooped a little—he had broken his back years ago in a fall from an inspection ladder. He slugged down half a cup of coffee and tossed his white hard hat onto the table. "Goddamn piece of junk they give me," he said. "This the best they can do?"

Fannon said to Nick, "Rig weathered a hurricane in the Gulf last year."

"Weathered a goddamn barge crashing into it, you mean," Cal Root said.

So, Nick thought, *that's what put the crease in the leg.*

Bucky Malagordo said, "Come on, boss. You know as well as I do there's not more than a hundred fifty of these rigs in the whole world. We take what we can get."

"Then give me one of the other hundred forty-nine," Cal Root said.

"How I'm s'posed to work with a junk rig?"

Bucky Malagordo said, "Cal, it only has to hold up a little while. This is a short job, corporate keeps saying."

"No such thing as a short job. Never was, never will be."

"I know the routine, boss," Bucky Malagordo said, grinning. "Every job takes longer than you think."

Cal Root broke in, "And every job is harder than it looks. And every job costs more than it's s'posed to."

Bucky Malagordo laughed and shook his head. "Not this one. This one is in and out. Quick and dirty—slam, bam, and thank you, ma'am."

"Keep talkin."

"It's your circus now, all I'm saying. Make it happen, boss."

Cal Root nodded and looked at the deck, ran fingers through his thinning sandy hair.

Nick walked to the glass and watched the weather purpling the sky to the east, and when he looked down he could see the rain sweep across the platform in gray sheets, lashing the men far below. He admired how they just kept at it, in any weather. They made good money on the rig, he knew that. But he also knew it wasn't really about money. These were the kind of men who would be lost without a world that required toughness. Out here, they had no choice—every job was hard, every movement dangerous, every other man just as hard-headed. Out here, they could be exactly who they were.

From this high up, the men were just blurry yellow and orange forms half-obscured by the driving rain. They kept right on working at the same steady pace as before, oblivious.

It dawned on him that these men were just as much mariners in their way as were the old-time sailors. In any direction as far as the horizon, all that was visible were gray, roiling seas. Between the wind and the racket of tools, the men could not hear spoken commands, so the foremen wore radio headsets like football coaches and relayed orders by hand gestures to the roughnecks and tool pushers. They were alone out here, day after day, for weeks at a time. They could not even maneuver their vessel to face the weather sweeping over them, or to outrun it.

Whatever direction it came from, they had to endure it.

On any given day, seventy-five men, give or take, worked on the platform. They had only each other for company. In case of catastrophic failure, they had two lifecars, bullet-shaped orange vessels each the size of a school bus, capable of holding forty-two souls. The lifecars sat poised at a steep downward angle on tracks fifty feet above the waves, accessible by steel catwalks. Nick imagined them crammed full of men in coveralls, the hatches clanging shut and being dogged from the inside, the lifecars sliding fast down the tracks, gaining momentum, splashing like fat rockets into the gray water, submerged for a long moment, then breaching like whales. They were motorized, packed with food and water and first-aid gear.

It would be quite a ride—bone-jarring and whiplashing, with all the terror of an amusement ride gone off the rails into thin air, the stomach-clenching fall toward what would seem like certain death, before the smashing impact.

But not today. Today was routine. Inside the office, the noise of weather and machinery was muted into a general hum like that of a city—a weird live murmur of engines and cooling fans and thousands of invisible moving parts.

Then Nick was aware of another sound—the sporadic creak and groan of metal.

He had heard it before on other jobs but never got used to it. A small lurch in the floor made him reach out a hand for balance, and he felt the whole structure swaying ever so slightly under him, causing a sensation like drunkenness. The rig was settling, like a big dog tamping down its bed before lying quiet—except that it would never truly lie quiet.

"She's trying to find her spot," Bucky Malagordo said. "She'll settle down by and by."

But Nick knew better. Even weeks from now, the rig would still shift and shimmy, would never really be still. It would continue to move like a restless sleeper. Some guys never got used to it, just simply couldn't work out here—it spooked them too bad. They went a little crazy, had to be taken off before they jumped.

The girders swelled and contracted with temperature changes, and the steel popped like great knuckles cracking. Waves shoved against the jacklegs, and the rig twisted ever so slightly. Wind pushed at the sheer walls of the workhouse, which leaned just enough to slosh your coffee.

The rig perched on three skinny legs. It was designed for temporary siting, after all.

The permanent platforms would be anchored with caissons filled with ballast stone. But not this one. After the crew discovered whatever was to be discovered here, it would cap the wellhead, then crank the jacklegs back up, and the platform would gradually settle on the water, and the bluff-bowed seagoing towboats with their monster diesel engines would tow her away, just like that, and it would be as if she'd never even been here at all—a clean getaway.

Cal Root said, "I don't like this water much, I can tell you."

Bucky Malagordo said, "We don't have to like it."

"I've been around, all I'm saying. There's too much going on out here."

Below, Nick could see the ridge of black water cutting right into the rig like the wake of a torpedo.

Cal Root shook his head and pointed to the water. "It's a fucking permanent wave. Look how it stands right up, all jagged and stiff. It's got a goddamn ridge back."

"They call it 'the Point,' Cal. Labrador Current meets Gulf Stream. Good fishin,' I hear."

"Yeah, if you like fishin'," Cal Root said. "Me, I'm huntin' dinosaur blood."

Bucky folded his thick arms. "Look, we expect to hit shallow, so we'll get our first cores in no time flat. Then we'll see where we stand. You tell me what to do and I do it, boss, same as always."

Cal Root grinned for the first time. "When did you ever do that?"

"Well, then, let's get her done." Bucky Malagordo turned to Nick. "You want to watch the first pipe go down?"

"Sure, why not?"

Bucky grinned. "Then grab a hard hat and hold on to your balls, 'cause we're going drillin'."

5

On the trip home to the dock, they were ambushed by a storm. It came out of nowhere and caught the *Rascal* on the port stern quarter with a steep wave much larger than the wave train around them. The boat slewed and rolled, and Nick banged against the bulkhead, bruising his ribs all over again. He cursed, and Fannon looked up from the GPS chart-plotter screen.

"Yeah, we just got spanked," Fannon said. "Bloody weather—never seen anything like it. All calm as a millpond one minute, the next it's a fuckin' Mixmaster."

Just then, lightning arced across the sky ahead and a terrific boom rattled the boat. Then the lightning was all around them, blue and orange threads binding sky and sea. Then it eased just as suddenly.

Nick let out a held breath. "Just a microburst," he said. "I've seen it before."

Fannon grinned, but he was not happy. "Yeah? I've seen salties before, and I still don't like 'em sneaking up on me."

Nick laughed. "What the hell's a saltie?"

"Crocodile, mate—the Aussie kind." Fannon chomped his big white teeth. "Eat you right up."

The captain got the vessel under control and back on course, but his hands gripped the joysticks that controlled the jet drives too hard. "Relax!" Nick shouted above the roar of engines and weather, and the man grinned tightly. Nick remembered the black ridge of water splitting the sea beneath the rig, and Cal Root's words: *I don't like this water much.*

As suddenly as it had hit, the storm was gone. They watched the big, dark cell move north, raking the sea into froth. All ahead of them was calm blue water.

6

Nick spent an hour typing up notes at Fannon's floating office as other company men came and went. The steward, a Filipino named Aguinaldo, was setting up a reception for some senior engineers who would stay aboard the *Lady NorthAm* tonight and be choppered out to the rig in the morning to conduct inspections.

"You're welcome to stay," Fannon said.

"And talk to engineers? I'll pass."

The radio whistled and buzzed in a pattern that signaled an urgent message. Fannon keyed the mic, signed on, grabbed the headset, and listened. "Roger and out," he said. He racked the mic. "Fuck all."

"What?" Nick asked.

Fannon looked at the radio. "They just had to chopper one of the tool pushers to Norfolk," he said quietly. "Mangled his goddamn hand in the chains."

"An accident? Already?" He thought of the bilge pump, the brake line, the theft from his room. "You don't think—"

"Nah, just bad luck." Fannon reached for a bottle of Johnnie Walker. "Green crew, is all. Everybody in too much of a fucking hurry. Bloody hell."

Nick couldn't help remembering Caroline Dant's remark regarding bad luck: *You know any other kind?*

7

The sky was settling into a bloody dusk when Nick stopped at Lord's Manor on his way home, hoping to run into Julia—or maybe not, he couldn't decide which. But he could use a cold beer, and he wanted to be around people. It would be lonely in his room.

The place was subdued, only half a dozen tourists lounging at the bar, the restaurant nearly empty. He stood at the entrance to the dining room still swaying, feeling the sea in his legs, then followed the hostess to a table.

He polished off a plate of fried oysters and a pint of beer and signaled for the check. The waitress, a stranger to him, brought it in a leather case, and when he opened it he saw the receipt was marked *PAID* in block letters. And there was another word, printed just as carefully under it: *CHANCE.*

He followed the waitress to the silverware station. "Excuse me, do you know who paid this?" He held up the check.

She smiled. "Shug, that's how I found it in my apron pocket." She winked and disappeared into the kitchen.

Chance at what? To do what? Random happenstance? What did that have to do with anything? Everything about this job was creepy. The weather turning all weird and unpredictable. People ducking appointments. Now secret notes in some kind of stupid code.

One more odd thing to put in his report tonight. *CHANCE. GOLIATH.* Luck and a biblical giant killed by a slingshot. Or maybe somebody was just messing with him, trying to keep him off-balance. But why? He wasn't in charge of anything—that was Fannon's job. And nobody seemed to be messing with Fannon.

True, Fannon had been in the Rover and aboard the boat. But what did that have to do with this?

He sat up awhile, fingering chords on his Martin New Yorker. He wasn't much of a player, but he loved putting his fingers on the old frets, worn into the shapes of forgotten chords once played by his grandfather. The guitar was a tool for focusing, for calming his restlessness, for working out a problem slantwise. Whenever he touched the fingerboard, it felt as if he were slipping on the clever hands of his namesake like a pair of gloves.

His Oma loved to tell him how her Nicky would play for her the old folk songs of her youth in the Schwarzwald, the Black Forest. Her favorite was a children's song, "*Alle Leut, alle Leut gehen jetzt nach Haus!*"

"He had a wonderful baritone voice," she would say, the same words each time, as if she were only at that moment remembering. "A woman could fall in love just to hear it." Her eyes would drift far away, reliving all the moments of her marriage before his grandfather left. He had a sense that she remembered every second of her time with him, that each minute was a jewel she kept in a secret place. She remembered her life with him in such minute detail—a fact that was either touching or unutterably sad, or maybe both.

She would sing it to Nick when he was a little boy, first in German, then in her heavily accented English: "Everyone, everyone is going home. Everyone, everyone is going home. Big people, little people, fat people, thin people, loud people, quiet people—everyone, everyone is going home."

Sometimes at the finish, her voice would falter, her eyes would well with tears, she would go silent and still and just let the tears track down her cheeks, not bothering to wipe them, as if he were not even in the room.

He played it softly now, the simple chords part of the muscle memory in his fingers. For a small-bodied instrument, the New Yorker had a lot of bottom. When he held it close and strummed a big open chord, he could feel the vibration of the wood in his chest, the reassuring hum of the soundbox against his ribs, as if the music were entering him physically, the spirit of his grandfather settling inside him, the eyes of his Oma looking on in approval and, yes, love.

And he wanted to ask the old man, *Why did you leave her? Why did you leave the love of your heart's heart?* For the one thing that would let her die happy was to be reunited with him— what she had waited for all these decades, the one thing that was clearly impossible, as impossible as dying for two different countries at war with one another.

He strummed the chords softly and sang the words to himself: "Everyone is going home." And before he realized what was happening, his own eyes were blearing and the voice in his head was saying, *Not me. Everyone else, but not me.*

CHAPTER SIX

HATTERAS ISLAND, 1991

1

In the morning, Nick stood on his balcony looking out over the gray swells. He had gone to bed teary-eyed, ambushed by emotions he couldn't name, and slept fitfully, his dreams full of strangers and traveling, the world moving under him, unsteady and shifting, voices talking past him. He awoke unsure of where he was and took several moments to get his bearings.

Now he sipped strong coffee, heavily sugared, trying to wake up.

Later he would meet Fannon on the boat and get a progress report, and after lunch he was supposed to have coffee with the mayor. He had not spoken to the man himself, only to an assistant whose tone had been abrupt and anything but friendly. They had broken three appointments so far, and Nick was not hopeful of the fourth try.

Despite repeated calls, the Nature Conservancy woman had never called him back.

Liam Royal was off-limits, so insisted Julia. She ranged around him like a shepherd dog, protecting him—but from what? What was she so afraid of for him? The old guy could surely take care of himself.

Nick had called a dozen people yesterday—city councilmen, the newspaper editor, the head of the chamber of commerce—and spoken to exactly one, the rude assistant to the mayor. Nobody wanted to talk to him. Yet somebody was sending him cryptic notes. And somebody else apparently had it in for him. It was like being in a foreign country without a fixer, he thought—everybody else but you understood what was being said, even when you were part of the conversation, or thought you were. And if you didn't comprehend the language, it was hard to figure out what was going on.

He had been up until well past midnight making notes, trying to connect the dots between the strange notes and the sabotage—if that's what it was.

He hadn't gotten far. Something was going on, but whatever it was seemed random and unfocused. Had he and Fannon died in the crash of the out-of-control Rover, there would have been an investigation and all kinds of trouble for whichever locals were involved. And it wouldn't have stopped the drilling, any more than would sinking a seagoing tender full of workingmen. Either calamity would have turned the protesters into killers and lost them the moral high ground, if there was any moral high ground. The drilling would proceed on schedule.

Nick had no power over the process, so why was he the target? For him, it was just about doing a job that needed to be done, and doing it right.

So who was the someone trying to harm him, and why? Or was it just incidental that he happened to be in the Rover and on the boat, too? Was the company the target? Or was it somehow more personal? He couldn't understand the pattern, and without a clear pattern there was no way of knowing. Just how much danger was he really in? Enough, he figured.

There was no danger here, at this moment. For now, he had the morning to himself. The sky was bright, and the breeze riffled the decorative red, white, and blue flags at the corners of the deck. Down below, Liam Royal, the old Founder, emerged from the boathouse. Royal stood arms akimbo, head cocked to one side, staring at him, then waved his arm in a roundhouse motion, beckoning Nick to come and join him.

Nick carried his coffee mug down two flights and stepped onto the boardwalk leading to the boathouse, but there was no sign of the old man.

2

Julia Royal slipped out of the doorway of the house holding a dish-towel and a platter, like a girl in a Dutch painting. "Where do you think you're going?"

Nick turned, felt caught at something naughty. She stared at him accusingly. All he could think of was how soft her dark hair looked in the lifting breeze, how the cornflower-blue dirndl skirt fluttered around her brown legs. Somehow she always seemed to be in motion. "Your grandfather, he—"

"I told you, the boathouse is off-limits." Her tone was scolding.

"He asked me to join him."

"Asked you?" She looked beyond him at the empty boardwalk. The door to the boathouse was closed. Her eyes flashed with a kind of fierce accusation.

"Not exactly. He, you know . . ." He mimed a wave.

"Well he's not waving now."

Nick shook his head. He was beginning to lose patience with her. "What's the big secret?"

She folded her arms. "Just show some manners."

"What does he keep in that boathouse?"

"The Founder is a very private man. Don't bother him, that's all. I mean it." She turned to go back into the house. The sun felt suddenly hot on his neck.

3

When Nick had gone, Julia walked down the salt-bleached wooden stairs to the boathouse, the rough gray boards already warm under her bare feet. She paused and listened at the bottom and heard only the soughing wind across the beach.

She knocked at the side door and then quietly eased it open. Beyond the boat on its trailer, which took up a big space of the floor, there was her grandfather, seated heavily in a worn rattan chair, a mug of coffee steaming on its broad arm. He sat very still, staring straight ahead, his features set.

She caught her breath. She had always wondered how she would find him, when his time was up. Never doubted that she would be the one. But he wasn't so old, not yet. He was still vigorous, full of opinions, and able to work hard. He roamed the beach for miles every day in any weather, a figure larger than life with purpose in every stride.

His voice startled her. "Don't worry, Bug, I ain't dead just yet." He alone called her Bug, a nickname from earliest childhood, and only when they were alone, like it was their secret code.

She flushed and smiled. "I just—"

"Came to check on me. I know. Do me a favor?"

She cocked her head, waiting.

"Swing open those big doors. I want to watch the ocean."

She walked past him to the big double sea-facing doors suspended on tracks. With just a nudge, they rolled easily open, like the doors on a boxcar. A sudden wind gusted in and scattered some papers on the old rolltop desk, but Liam didn't move. Her grandfather had been retired for years now—at least officially. That didn't stop him from visiting job sites, meeting with bankers, keeping his hand in. But the day-to-day management was handled by his nephew Billy Royal, just one year old when his father, Kevin, Liam's brother, disappeared in the war. But Julia was chairman of the board. All the big decisions finally came to her at the quarterly meetings and the monthly executive-committee meetings in between—even though most people knew her only as the manager of a bed-and-breakfast.

Liam tilted his shaggy head back and inhaled a deep, bracing breath. "That's more like it," he said. "Come, sit awhile, Bug."

"You know I have chores."

"I guess I'm your most difficult one, eh, Bug?"

“Oh, hush. Your coffee must be cold by now. Here.” She grabbed up the mug and went to the sink and poured it out, then from the pot on the broad slab of oak that served as a counter poured him another, and one for herself. She spooned a healthy dollop of sugar into his but left hers black.

When he tasted it, he said, “Strong and sweet—just like a good woman.” He winked.

“I bet you say that to all the girls.” She settled into a chair beside him and sipped the strong coffee.

“Your grandmother was all that and more,” he said. “Sometimes I can’t believe she’s been gone so long.” She had died suddenly almost ten years ago now, a heart attack in her sleep. A gentle way to go, he had always thought, but then the memory of waking beside her and realizing she had left him in the night would stab him in the gut. He had heard nothing, had awakened at daylight as he did every morning, surprised she was not already in the kitchen. In bed, she looked small and weightless. He had whispered her name—*Julia*—over and over. “Have you spoken to your father?” *My boy, Malcolm,* he thought, a heaviness in his chest.

“Last week, on the phone. Didn’t have much to say, as usual. We talked about the weather.”

“Well, the weather is something. Some days, that’s all anybody around here talks about.”

She smiled. “You know what I mean.” Then she said, “Why don’t you ever call him?”

He shook his head firmly. “Couldn’t do that. He don’t want to hear from the old man.”

She leaned over and took Liam’s big, mottled hand in her two small ones. “You don’t have forever, Paw Paw. Nobody does. You should call.”

“He made his choice, and I’ve made my peace.”

She didn’t speak for a few minutes. The night before her father had left for good, the two men had shouted hard words at one another, words that would be difficult to take back. She caught only the gist, listening outside the boathouse. Her grandmother was still alive, and Liam didn’t yet live in the boathouse, used it only as an office and workshop. Whatever was said, her father stormed out and past her without a word. She wasn't sure he had even noticed her standing there in the circle of wax myrtle.

After that night, her father was out of the business.

Now, when the Founder passed, she would inherit everything.

To her mind, when that day came, a heavy and dark burden would fall upon her from which there would be no escape. She would be shackled to the island for life. All those assorted cousins and all those working people who depended on the Royal company for their livelihoods would then depend on her personally. She would have all that land to manage, all those accounts to keep straight, the foundation to lead. She would own the name and all that went with it—real estate and businesses and investments, but also responsibility and reputation and history.

If she thought about it too hard, she would flee the island for good.

But she couldn't leave her grandfather, not now. Not anymore.

Julia was the only child of his only child, and from the earliest days he had taken her as his own. When she was just five, she caught her first bluefish in the surf below the boathouse, her grandfather's sturdy arms helping her land the aggressive fish that was almost as big as she was. Together they had dragged it thrashing onto the sand, and later he grilled it for her over a driftwood fire, seasoned with black pepper and sea salt and rubbed with limes and olive oil. They ate it off cedar shingles from the woodpile and then threw them onto the fire, where they popped and flamed like sparklers.

Other times, they grilled rock lobsters that had found their way into the fishermen's nets. They called them "bugs." She loved the briny taste, the rich, juicy meat slathered in garlicky butter. "You eat enough of those, you're going to turn into a bug yourself," her grandfather said. And the nickname stuck. Whenever he said it, the name made her feel special. It brought back everything from those days—most of all that wonderful protected feeling of being her grandfather's special pal.

Her grandmother, her namesake, was wise enough just to let them be.

As she grew older, Julia had no interest in girls' things. She roamed the beach with Liam, rode to job sites in his old Chevy pickup during summer months. From him, she learned how to tear down and rebuild a marine engine. She could handle a small boat and tune up the Chevy, saw a board straight and hammer a nail true. He taught her to throw a baseball overhand like a boy, and she played a few seasons as the only girl in Little League.

She even dressed like her grandfather—in weathered work shirts and paint-stained khakis. For years, she wore her hair in a practical ponytail under a faded blue Evinrude ball cap. Then, in college, she simply cut her hair and wore it short. She hardly ever bothered with makeup or dresses and didn't own a pair of high heels until she was married.

It was a small—and unfortunate—miracle that she had ever gotten married.

His name was Richard. Not Rich or Rick—he insisted on that. They met at the Fourth of July picnic at the firehouse the summer she graduated from Old Dominion. He was down from Richmond, renting a cottage for the week, handsome in a buttoned-down way, funny and thoughtful, five years older than she, a rising star in his corporate law firm. Somehow he never believed she was exactly who she said she was—a tomboy with a quick temper, who spoke her mind without invitation from anybody, who would rather fuss with an outboard engine than make a casserole. Maybe because that day she was wearing that powder-blue sundress, and they both got slightly drunk on a jar of moonshine the Littlejohns were passing around, and went back to his cottage.

But it didn't explain why she had fallen for him.

Maybe, she figured, she had just wanted off the island. She had been away to college, but that was only as far as Norfolk, and she could drive home almost every weekend. She came home to a row between her father and the Founder, and then her parents were packing up to leave—almost as if her father had waited till she was all grown up before he made his own escape.

Maybe it was getting to know him out of context, relaxing in a hot tub together, taking long walks on the beach at sunset—vacation stuff. Real life for him was a monogrammed shirt, tassled loafers, a suit and tie, long days at the office, weekend trips to boring cities where depositions waited. The divorce had been a mercy to them both.

When it happened, she felt both relief and shame. Her parents had warned her that she was rushing into marriage, but she'd brushed aside their counsel. Now they were both full of I-told-you-sos. They didn't say as much, but she could hear it in the pitying words they spoke over the telephone, the judgment in their voices. *We were afraid this would happen. It was bound to. You went into this whole thing way too fast.*

Her off-island friends were all couples, and with the divorce she found herself suddenly alone and, for the first time in her life, lonely.

Since the breakup happened at the start of summer vacation, she had no teaching duties to keep her focused. She slid into depression, staying behind closed blinds, watching mindless daytime television—something she had never done. Some days, she forgot to shower. She almost never went out, grew pale and listless. When the food in her fridge ran out, she lived on stale crackers and coffee and lost weight.

When the new school year started, she simply stayed home. She didn't answer her phone, and after a while it stopped ringing. She had plenty of money from the settlement. It might have been better if she had been forced to fend for herself. Instead she folded her wings around her and did nothing.

She was as baffled as she was depressed—surely Richard hadn't meant that much to her. Was it just her pride that was injured? After all, he had been the first one to say it out loud: *This just isn't working out. I've found somebody else.*

The voice in her head screamed, *This is all my fault!* And maybe it was.

Maybe she had been a fool to believe she could ever be the kind of wife a man like Richard would want. Maybe she was a fool to believe she'd make a wife for any man, that she even wanted to. She was hard-headed, independent, impatient, impulsive, smart, self-confident—or had been all those things. Maybe all the qualities her grandfather had encouraged in her were toxic, when it came to love and romance.

Or maybe it was just that she had come to a horizon line in her life and could not see beyond it to what was supposed to come next. She had never known what it was to need something so bad she couldn't function without it. If it wasn't Richard, what was it? What was supposed to come next?

She waited, frozen in the limbo of her life, sinking deep into a place where she did not recognize herself.

Then, one day without notice, her grandfather showed up at her apartment in Richmond. She heard the knock at the door and felt her heart quicken in panic. Who could be out there? What had she done wrong now? Cautiously she peered through the spy hole, and there was his big, wind-burned face—unkempt white whiskers, squinty blue eyes—peering back at her, comically magnified.

She had never felt so happy to see anyone in her whole life.

She opened the door, and he swallowed her up in his big embrace. She breathed in his smell of turpentine and Old Spice and burley pipe tobacco and dissolved in throat-burning tears. And he held her with all the strength in the world.

He never mentioned Richard or the divorce. Never commented on her ragged, emaciated appearance. Did not tell her to stop crying or go clean herself up. He didn't tell her to come home, or even ask her. He didn't say a word about how her grandmother was gone. That came later. They sat at her kitchen table, looking onto a view of an autumn courtyard with bare-limbed elm trees raking the light into long shadows, and drank the strong coffee they always drank together.

And all he said was, "I need your help, Bug."

It was a way of releasing her from obligation, of allowing her to be the one who was generous. He had already moved into the boathouse. He had plans to renovate the old lifesaving station, which he had owned for years, into a bed-and-breakfast. His late wife had dreamed of such a place but did not live to see it come true. He would do it in her memory. He knew how to do the building part, and he had all the money necessary to make it happen, but he had no clue how to outfit such a place and no desire to run it himself. His wife had planned to do all that.

She listened to his big plans and felt his strength flowing into her body. She finished her coffee and showered quickly. And then her grandfather took her out for a thick ribeye steak, and they drank a bottle of Cabernet together, and that night she slept without dreams and woke to find the old man making coffee. She packed only what she could carry and left everything else behind.

First there was a funeral to arrange. Julia handled it, and her own sorrows suddenly seemed small.

So she came home, but it was a new home, and somehow that made it easier.

She busied herself with plans and budgets, helped her grandfather and his architect design the new interior, shopped for fixtures and furniture, and finally spent a couple of nights living in every room in the place to make sure each was comfortable, properly lighted, and contained anything a guest might reasonably want.

Months went by, and one day, sipping wine on the high deck, tired and sore from lifting and moving furniture, she felt a profound sense of peace as she watched her grandfather stride up the beach, home from one of his walks. She had moved past her other life and found a new, good place, if only for a while. The old Founder had rescued her as surely as if he had plucked her from the stormy sea.

But truth to tell, she also felt caught.

Her grandfather said now, "Out of everybody, Bug, you're the one who stayed with me. You came back to me. You're my Bug."

"I'm not going anywhere, Paw Paw," she said.

The world beyond the open doors of the boathouse was framed in a blaze of sunlight, like a movie screen, but real.

4

Nick waited more than an hour for the mayor to show up, but again no dice. The assistant said she had no idea where he'd gone, and would Nick like to make another appointment?

"Sure, why not?" he told her, with no expectation that the mayor was going to keep it. He wasn't giving up—that was not his habit.

Since then, Nick had been hiking all over the village, along the sand-dusted roadway that led ultimately to the ferry landing for Ocracoke Island, to the south.

It was one of his habits in a new place, to walk it. He could not understand a place from inside an air-conditioned car, breezing along at speed. And if he could not understand the place, he could not begin to know its people. And then he could not do his job.

Walking gave him a sense of scale, of distance and proximity. The motion of his legs created an exact map in his head. In a car, he routinely got lost, but if he walked someplace he could always find his way back, and could always find that place again.

And there was the other thing: his own lack of a place. "A landscape of the soul," his Oma called it, the place where you lived in your deepest memories. For her, whenever she closed her eyes, it was a run-down urban neighborhood in Chicago that opened magically onto a clearing in the Black Forest, where she had spent her girlhood. Her body was imprisoned inside an assisted-living home, and she could bear it only because, in her heart and dreams, she lived elsewhere—in a land of towering shade trees and deep grottoes, hilltop meadows and bold, rocky streams, ferny glades echoing with bird song, redolent with damp moss and wood smoke.

But Nick had no such grounding.

Whenever he walked a new place, he felt it enter his body, map itself onto the muscles of his legs, imprint itself on the lenses of his eyes. He walked the place like a cautious swimmer entering water, wading deeper, feeling its fluid weight surround and overtake him.

It was a good feeling, in the main, conferred a sense of being completely there, aware of the landscape in three dimensions—aware, too, of its history and future, of himself as a sentient being moving through time and space. It was not belonging, exactly, but its close cousin. Often it felt as if he'd stepped inside a museum diorama—a historic mock-up of a Pilgrim village or a Wild West cow town, full of props and false fronts, doors that opened onto empty lots behind the façades.

But one day, he expected to walk into a landscape, step beyond the façade, and stay, captured by the place for good and all, home at last.

He passed a couple of fishermen stacking crab pots into the bed of an ancient melon-green pickup truck. They worked slowly, methodically, not a word between them. A father and son, by their looks—one gray-bearded, the other fresh-faced and wiry, both their faces and forearms the color of brick. He nodded, and they nodded back and kept working, no sound but the occasional grunt.

Then, as he passed, the father said something to the son in a queer and impenetrable accent. Nick couldn't make out the sense of it. He had worked a stint in northern Scotland, and the fisherman's words reminded him of pub talk, of how the meaning never quite reached him.

From a kitchen window up the lane drifted the tinny sound of a radio playing a song, a woman's plaintive, reedy voice singing along. A breathy, off-key voice.

His Oma had a sweet, clear voice, even if her English words sounded foreign. Nick listened a moment too long.

5

He passed one of the new tourist developments, tall, stilted wooden castles painted in bright candy flavors with decks on every story, railings hung with bright beach towels, boxy SUVs tucked underneath. He ventured off the main road into a neighborhood of older, wind-scabbed white clapboard homes, many with swaybacked roofs and porches crowded with old furniture.

He turned onto a narrow lane shaded by wax myrtle and salt-twisted yaupon holly trees and lined by waist-high iron fences, some going to rust. The fences ran back from the road, dividing the property into small rectangular lots. Some were heavily overgrown, untended for months, years. He stopped and studied one lot, noting lumps of stone in the high grass.

The stones struck him as queer, orderly but not quite. Then he recognized them for what they were: tombstones.

It was a little graveyard.

The whole neighborhood on that side of the road was a row of graveyards. Each one, fenced off from its neighbors with no apparent gate, was big enough to hold half a dozen graves. *Strange,* he thought, *no gates.* Did they want to make sure the dead stayed inside, or keep the living out of sacred ground? The fences were low enough to step over easily. They were a formality, he guessed, a gesture toward probity.

He stopped and squinted at a row of headstones. One was substantial and bore legible lettering: *Peter Patchett, b. Feb. 14, 1883, d. July 23, 1918. "When the sea shall give up her dead."*

Patchett—he knew that name. The mayor was named Patchett. Julia's grandfather had told a story about this one.

A familiar voice behind him said quietly, "Nobody is buried under that stone."

He turned: Julia Royal. He smiled and shook his head. "Scared the devil out of me, lady."

She half-smiled, biting her lip, and touched his arm. "I had an errand in the neighborhood."

He didn't believe that for a second. "Of course." How long had she been following him? Why? Away from the Founder, she was all sweetness and light, and he could almost believe she wanted to be friends. Almost.

She stood hands on hips, rocking from one foot to the other, looking like a miniature version of her fierce grandfather, with the same piercing eyes, except hers were lustrous brown, not cool blue. Then she smiled again, and her grandfather's resemblance was gone. Her eyes softened and squinted. She said, "Peter Patchett. They called him Patch. He was lost at sea."

"I remember the story. U-boat."

She shook her head. "Yeah. Strangest thing. Patchett, of all people. I mean, if you were going to pick a hero . . ."

"Your grandfather said he was crippled."

"Yeah, that's him. One of those loose parts every island village seems to have—half beachcomber, half handyman, all worthless. But you can't get along without them. Nobody knows exactly what he was doing out there. They've been telling the story for years. I don't know the details, only that, in the end, he was some kind of hero."

Lots of those around here, Nick thought. "He was the original?"

"You mean Patchett Builders? Yeah, I guess he was. The original. I like that."

"And the mayor?"

"His grandson, Poe."

"Of course." The one who was dodging him. The families again, all the sons and grandsons and cousins and in-laws. "So if he's not buried here, why the stone?"

She shrugged, as if it were a pointless question. "It's not like he's the only one, not on an island of fishermen. People had to have someplace to go."

He pointed to the next graveyard, where a row of headstones ranged along the back fence. All the stones were engraved with the name *ROYAL*. "Your people?"

"Yeah, sure enough. Great-uncles. Great-grandparents."

He noted the names: Malcolm and wife Mary, and their two sons, Charles and Kevin. "All present and accounted for?"

"Accounted for, not present," she said. "Two out of four."

He nodded. More fishermen lost at sea, he presumed.

The other headstones were skewed and weathered, some more than a century old. Most of the names had been scrubbed out by wind and rain. The slabs were narrow and looked chalky and brittle, as if he could break them with his bare hands.

He walked onto the next burying ground. This one had a pole in the middle flying a Union flag. "What's up with that?" he said, aware that she was now walking beside him.

"In the war. The Second War. Some British sailors washed up, and they were buried here."

He took off his Ray-Bans and squinted at the stones. "No names?"

She shook her head. "Unknowns. Burned beyond recognition. All they had were pieces of uniforms, you know. Insignias. They couldn't even tell which ship they served on. It's pretty sad, when you think about it. So far from home. No one to tell their families."

He nodded, and an idea formed in his mind. "Are there any other war graves?"

She looked at him quizzically. The wind ruffled her hair, and she smoothed it with a careless hand—the gesture of a woman who either didn't know she was so attractive or didn't care. "What do you mean?"

He shrugged, as if it didn't matter much. "Sailors, you know—bodies found on the beach from other ships, maybe?"

She paused. "Why? You looking for someone special?"

"Just curious." He hated the lie, however small, but she always had him off-balance, and he still had no idea how far he could trust her. All he wanted was a straight answer to a harmless question. What could she possibly care? At least he could tell his Oma he had tried.

Julia stepped back. "I have to get going. Nobody's minding the inn. Why don't you come along with me? I'll make us some iced tea."

"I think I'll do some more walking, thanks."

Julia seemed suddenly irritated. "Suit yourself."

"Why do you always do that?" he asked.

She crossed her arms. "What? I was trying to be polite."

"No, you weren't. You either don't like me very much or . . . I don't know. Somehow I put you off."

"Whatever you think you know, you don't." And she turned and was already distant before he could answer.

She has a knack for getting away, he thought. And all he wanted was to get his arms around her once. *Stupid,* he thought. *Not with her. It just wouldn't work.* He stood and watched her vanish.

6

He still had a few hours before Fannon would be back from the rig. It felt good to be stretching his legs outdoors, and he settled into an easy stride. He was far down the lane now, and the houses and graves were gone. In their place on either side rose an impenetrable wall of wax myrtle and yaupon holly, mounded into blunt, abstract shapes by the constant wind. He had read in one of the guidebooks at the inn that yaupon leaves contained caffeine and could be boiled into a healing tea.

The lane narrowed, the thicket closing in. Finally he was trapped in a cul-de-sac.

Then he saw it, a small painted sign almost overgrown with myrtle, the neat black letters faded but still legible: *Merchant Marine Cemetery.* And an arrow pointing directly at the foliage.

He stopped and listened. On the other side of the thicket, he heard rustling—birds, maybe, or marsh rabbits. He turned slowly and let his eyes follow his ears. The opening was just a slash of shadow, so narrow he would have missed it, were he striding past it. The gap was barely wide enough for him to slip into sideways. The thicket formed a sort of baffle, so it was impossible to see into the clearing without navigating an abrupt blind turn.

He emerged into a windless clearing partly shaded by a live oak whose branches splayed out from the trunk like the giant gray fingers of an open hand.

This graveyard had no fence. Two rows of perhaps twenty headstones lined the far edge under a bronze plaque, green with verdigris, attached to a rusty pole. The plaque bore the fouled anchor and eagle of the United States Merchant Marine.

Nick stood in the clearing, feeling like the last man on earth. He could not recall when or where he had been so utterly alone. Time seemed to stop. He could hear the wind, but the wall of bushes was absolutely still. The heat was suddenly stifling. The old vertigo returned, and he steadied himself against one of the headstones. It felt like breathing in a vacuum. Sweat trickled into his eyes, and he swiped them free of salt.

The grave markers were lined neatly—straight, plumb, and military-looking.

He bent to read the names. He fell to his knees and traced the shallow etched letters with his fingertips. They were ordinary names—Robinson and Barker, Klein and Tilitch. Names of rough and ready men who manned the Liberty ships and oil tankers and tramp steamers that had dared the U-boat lanes almost half a century ago and had come to rest on this spit of sand.

Many of the markers bore no names—simply the single word *Unknown*. He felt an unutterable sadness.

He recalled what Julia had said about the British sailors, and it felt true in his gut. These were men who had never come home, men whose stories had never been told, who were consigned to oblivion. They might have been ordinary men, or cowards, or heroes, or likely some combination of all three, but their last deeds would never be known. They would inspire nobody's particular admiration or grief.

They were just lost men—lost to a war, lost to their families and the communities they had left. They were the ultimate homeless.

For this kind of moment, he wished he had his Oma's uncomplicated religious faith, the comfort of a benevolent imaginary God holding the souls of these lost men in His loving hand, rewarding them with eternal peace for all they had suffered. But he had surrendered that easy solace when his parents died.

Still on his knees, he approached the last headstone. A vine had crawled up its face and fastened itself in the fissures, obscuring the letters. He gripped it and pulled, but it was tough as wire. Using both hands, he finally yanked it free and cleared the inscription:

> SEPTEMBER 15TH, 1942
> *Goliath*, Galveston, Texas
> Sunk by U-Boat
> Unknown
> Unknown
> Unknown

He stared hard at the last name on the stone: *Nicholas Wolf.*

It felt like falling through a hole in time. He leaned forward, touched the warm hardness of the stone, carved his index finger along the cut grooves of his own name. The name of his lost grandfather.

Somehow his Oma's story of his grandfather had always seemed just that—a story. A tall tale of a mythical figure who had walked out of her life long before he was born. Like the Founder had said with such certainty, *Stories never happened.*

But here were actual graves, the graves of men who were part of that story.

Nick pressed his palms to the stone bearing his grandfather's name—*his* name—leaned his forehead against the slab, felt the heat of it as a fever. Couldn't stop the tears.

7

GOLIATH. The single word in the first note.

Not a person at all but a ship—probably a tanker, if it came out of Galveston.

An oil tanker.

Of course it would be that. Life had a way of slapping you with little ironies from time to time. Oil had brought him to the island, and oil had apparently been connected to how his grandfather's life had ended here.

He stood slowly, stepped backward, felt his balance falter. He planted his feet and took a breath, stared at the name. His Opa's name—his name now. His stomach felt queer, and there was a rushing in his ears.

Of all the things he had expected, he had never anticipated this, an actual gravesite.

What should he tell his Oma?

Nothing, not until he made some inquiries. She would want to know more than just the grave. There must be a village archive of some kind—he could flesh out the details, figure out why his grandfather was buried here, why the War Department hadn't known his remains had been found and buried in 1942, how he had gotten from Germany onto a tanker out of Texas. If indeed he had ever made it to Germany.

He said out loud, "How in the world did you get here, Opa?" and felt emotion strangling his throat so that he turned away, looked skyward for escape.

Overhead the sky was turning to gray haze, deepening into purple with a fast-moving plume of cumulonimbus to the northwest. The first fat drops of rain splashed onto his bare arms, and before he could thread his way back through the alley of myrtle and yaupon he was soaked.

He sloshed through deep, sandy puddles and enjoyed the fresh, shivering chill of rain. The cloudburst transformed the landscape from a still and sultry tableau of humped thickets and square houses to a world in wild motion. Branches waved, spindrift whirled across the lane in front of him, the rain beat a silver froth on the ground, and the sky itself boiled with dark matter laced by threads of lightning. A crack of thunder reverberated off a tin roof, and the whole sky was suddenly shot through with blue electricity. A weird rainy twilight descended.

In the gloom, the little family graveyards at the side of the lane brooded, their cocked tombstones glazed with rain that polished the stones, smoothing the etched lines of the names, one grain at a time washing out of the letters.

Stabbed cockeyed into the sandy yard of a house across from the graves, a two-sided cardboard sign declared, *NO DRILL, NO SPILL!* The weather had faded the letters, and now the cardboard was peeling back from the wooden stake in the rain. There was writing on the back. Nick crossed the lane and peeled it loose and read the reverse side: *FOR SALE by Royal Real Estate.* He pulled the sign loose and folded it, then shoved the sodden cardboard in his belt. Nobody would see him in this downpour.

Suddenly from behind came the roar of an engine. He half-turned, catching just a glimpse of a dark blue pickup speeding toward him. Reflexively, he pitched sideways off the road and landed face down in a shower of mud and water. He felt the truck careen past in a rush of wind and noise, so close he thought for a second it had run over him. He heard it roaring away as he lifted his head.

Ahead of him in the curtain of rain stood the dark outline of a figure wearing a mariner's black oilskins. A ghost of a man.

Nick pushed himself to his hands and knees, waved toward the figure, but it was already gone.

8

"You found what?" Julia Royal said.

They sat together on the back deck of Lifeboat Station #17 drinking strong iced tea and watching the rain. If it was storming this hard offshore, Fannon would have a rough ride in on the *Rascal.* He might just wait it out on the rig. He would call Nick when he got in. Fannon would want to know about the sign, and meanwhile Nick would tell nobody else, not even Julia. Did she know? Maybe it wasn't such a surprise—why wouldn't the Royals want to stop NorthAm if they thought tourism would suffer? Tourism meant rentals, and they had plenty of those to fill.

Nick stared beyond the boathouse toward the breakers, watching the storm sweep up the coast. Already the rain had turned intermittent, and the wind gusted and died between downpours. He said quietly, "My grandfather's grave." He didn't tell her about the pickup truck, or the ghost of a man in a black sou'wester.

"Your grandfather?" She did not look at his face. "So you were looking for someone after all." Her voice was quiet and steady, but he heard an undertone of accusation.

"So what if I was? It was an old family story, just a long shot. Why do you care?"

"Why did you lie about it?"

"I'm sorry about that. I don't know why, not exactly." He was lying again, in a way—he had trusted her, and then he had stopped trusting her, all in a moment. That seemed to happen over and over, and it was maddening.

"Are you glad? Is that what you came for?"

He thought he could hear what she really meant: *Now will you please go away?* "I came because my team came. Because the company is here, and it's my job. It's what I do. I had no idea."

"Well, now you know."

"Know what? I don't know any more than when I started."

"Does it make any difference, knowing?"

He told her, in brief, the story his Oma had always told him. Why not? It had no bearing on oil, on the job. "It was always just a story. A really awful story. I had no idea there would be an actual grave." She listened without any apparent reaction. "You don't look surprised."

She laid a hand on his, and a snap of static made them both startle. "You see," she said, "that's what it's like around here. All the stories are electric. They zap you. Like the storms. They're always bigger, windier, more sudden, completely unbelievable. When they're gone, you can't believe they ever happened. Yet they're real, all the same. So, no, I'm not surprised."

"Well, I sure am."

"What, that a mechanic found his way onto a ship?"

A thought occurred to him. "So you already knew my name. His name. My name. When I showed up."

She shook her head unconvincingly. "Don't flatter yourself. I haven't been out there since I was a kid. School field trip. How in heaven's name would I remember?"

"Yeah, I see what you mean." He felt small for accusing her. "Forget I said anything."

"Just thank God you have closure."

He shook his head slowly. "It doesn't close anything. It was the wrong side."

"Side?"

"He was supposed to be fighting for Germany."

"*Supposed* to be? What does that even mean?" She shrugged. "You mean to tell me you've never changed your mind?"

He laughed wryly. "I can't imagine changing my mind about something like that. I mean, come on."

"People change sides," she said. "Anyhow, like I said, the stories around here are strange but true."

Strange but true, that about sums it up, he thought. "Before I left, I told my Oma I didn't have time to try to untangle her story. I said there was nothing to find here."

She stirred her iced tea with a long spoon, the lemon wedge swirling in the dark liquid. "Well, I guess you're right after all. How could you possibly have known?" When he didn't answer, she said, "You going to tell her about this?"

He finished his tea and clinked the ice in his glass. The excitement he felt was tempered by an awful dread, and he knew all at once what it was: the fear of finding out more. He said, "How can I not?"

But what would his Oma's knowing change? She would want to come out here, that much he was certain of. She would want to see for herself, to touch the gravestone, to be in the place that contained her husband. He was not sure she could stand the journey, or what lay at the end of it: the final death of hope.

She sighed. "I should have served you yaupon bark."

"Yeah," he said. "I understand the tea will really jack you up."

She touched his face with her cool hand. "Not the tea—that's made from leaves. The bark."

"What does the bark do?"

She covered his eyes with her hands. "It cures you of seeing ghosts."

9

When Nick emerged from his room onto the balcony early after a sleepless night, Julia was already down below, a cup of coffee in her hands, leaning over the railing and staring intently past the boathouse.

Out on the beach, an old Willys Jeep was parked facing the ocean, and attached to its front bumper was a long, low trailer carrying a kind of boat Nick had never seen before. It rested on the trailer with its bow pointing toward the ocean. The trailer itself was a strange contraption with a home-built look: long rails and no cross-piece at the tail, under the bow. He figured this would allow the boat to motor directly into the surf without the chance of bending the prop on the trailer. Ingenious.

Julia turned her head, looked up, and shouted, "You're in luck! He's going to splash the lifeboat. Come on down."

He clambered down the stairs and stepped past her onto the cool sand. She followed. The Founder and half a dozen men were standing around the long white boat, using their hands to make arguments about how best to launch it.

Nick approached the hull, pressed his hand against the smooth painted wood. "Must be, what, twenty-five feet long?"

The Founder said without turning around, "Twenty-six. And a good Detroit diesel to push her along."

Nick couldn't help admiring her graceful lines, the power in her upswept bow. Even chocked on a trailer, she was a beautiful vessel, a machine for moving forward through rough water and breaking waves.

Completely at rest, the boat seemed already in motion. "She looks heavy," Nick remarked, standing on the trailer rails now and holding on to the gunwales while he peered inside the boat.

"Oh, she'll go two and a half tons, I guess," the Founder said. His tone was measured, but he couldn't disguise the pride in his voice.

Nick stepped down and stood with his back to the boat. The other men had gathered behind the Founder and were now facing Nick like a little mob, and all at once he wondered if he had violated some kind of maritime etiquette, some unspoken rule that only an islander would know. He might as well have had *Off* tattooed on his forehead. "Didn't mean to barge in," he said. "It's just, I'm staying at the inn, and I couldn't resist such a beautiful—"

"She's built on the lines of the old Monomoy surfboats," the Founder interrupted. "They called them 'pulling boats' in the old days. Men like my father oared them right through the breaking surf toward a wreck. I been rebuilding this one for two years."

Nick tried to imagine how much strength, of how many strong men, would be required to make headway against the sea in such a heavy boat. "What are you going to do with it?"

Liam Royal glared at him. "Only one thing to do with her—what she's made for."

Nick didn't say it out loud because it was too preposterous: *Rescue? Who in the world?*

One of the mob, a wiry, alert man with a crooked face and a red crew cut, squinted and said, "You're him, ain't it?" He reached out a bony hand. "Poe Patchett."

Nick introduced himself while taking the man's hand in its own, feeling the missing thumb and the old broken bones like a bag of marbles against his palm.

Poe Patchett said, "Niver yarn while you're using a band saw," and grinned.

"Nice to meet you, Mister Mayor. You're a hard man to track down."

Poe Patchett grinned. "Oh, I get out and about, I guess." He held on to Nick's hand.

Nick could hardly understand the man's speech. "I've heard all about your grandfather, the famous one. The hero."

Patchett laughed big and let go Nick's hand. "Granddaddy, yeah. And my daddy's famous for being old. You should come by the office sometime and talk. Just make an appointment."

"Yeah," Nick said, "I'll make it a point to do that."

The Founder introduced the others, including Little Jimmy and Hank Littlejohn, both around forty with red crew cuts. Little Jimmy, of course, stood well over six feet and carried a beer belly the size of a keg. Hank was thick but not fat. The others worked for the Royal company one way or another and had come to lend a hand.

Julia was suddenly next to him. "You can pitch in if you want," she said. "It's going to take all of us." For once, she was not keeping him at bay from her grandfather.

To his surprise, Julia stepped up onto the trailer and began unlacing the rope tie-downs. She directed the men to their places on either side of the boat: "Hank, starboard aft line, Little Jimmy, port side aft. The rest of you, line up on both sides and keep her steady once she hits the water. We don't want her slewing around."

Hank and Little Jimmy hoisted themselves into the boat with remarkable nimbleness despite their size.

To Nick, Julia said, "In the old days, a couple of Coasties who knew their stuff could launch this thing, Still could, I guess, but this is the first time we've tried it, and we don't want the prop to get banged around too much."

Nick said, "Where do you want me?"

"Hold the bow painter till the engine turns over, and then get that rope into the boat. You don't mind getting a little wet?"

"Not at all."

"Listen to me." She led him into the surf till he was waist deep a dozen feet to one side of the boat and trailer, put her hands on his shoulders, held him with surprising strength. "Just keep it steady against the waves that are angling in. Don't pretend you know what you're doing if you don't."

"Yes, ma'am."

"Coil the rope as best you can, and when you fling it, fling it overhand, like this." She showed him. "We don't want a line dragging in the water where it can wrap around the prop."

"Got it." He felt scolded.

"Good." She canted her head and smiled at him wickedly.

Then she climbed into the Jeep and started the engine. She waited till the Founder clambered aboard the boat and gave her a thumbs-up. Then she jammed the vehicle into low gear, and the Jeep slowly pushed the trailer toward the water in a perfectly straight line. As the boat entered the water and came closer, Nick felt the line in his hand slacken.

Now the bow of the boat was slammed by a wave. Then it was in, sliding free of the trailer, and Julia was slowly dragging the trailer out from under it. The diesel started with a rattling roar and then surged into full throttle.

Nick felt the line suddenly tauten, pulling him hard through the water—the boat was under its own power now—and he tried to make a loose coil and fling the line aboard. But in his nervousness, he had wrapped it around his hand, and now it dragged him off his feet and tightened, and he was swimming.

He was too startled even to cry out.

Two of the men had his hand now and were freeing the rope, and one of them flung it in a clean arc to land inside the gunwales as the boat pushed off and rammed through the waves. Then, in one quick bounce, it was over the breakers and into the long rollers, moving away fast, the Founder howling with delight at the wheel and the Littlejohn brothers anchored to grab rails in the stern.

Nick got his feet under him at last and stumbled back through the rough breaking water to the surf line. A wave slapped him cold in the face. Not far off, he heard Julia's laughter, full and contagious, and before long the other men were laughing, too. And so was he, drenched and holding his rope-burned hand in the foaming sea.

CHAPTER SEVEN

1942–45

1

Chance Royal was as good a handler of small boats as any boatswain in the navy.

His Higgins boat was lowered from the deck of the auxiliary ship, and he throttled up the two-hundred-twenty-five-horse diesel. Dawn was breaking gray and drizzly over the bluffs of Normandy, and the channel was choppy and swollen with crosscurrents from old storms. He wore a blue steel helmet and a gray flak vest and already was soaked from the driving sea spray.

He had skippered a Higgins boat during the eight days of invasion rehearsals off Slapton Sands in April. By some accident of terrible luck and timing, German E-boats had slipped in among the flotilla and sunk two troop transports, killing nearly a thousand men. Chance had dodged the enemy boats and rescued scores of sailors and infantry amid the melee.

Today was payback day—for those men, for his brother Kevin, for all of it. He understood it was his job to deliver killers onto the beach—as many as he could, as fast as he dared, for as long as it took.

Chance knew what he was doing, all right, but that didn't calm the flutter in his stomach.

His legs felt rubbery, and he took a couple of deep breaths to steady himself to the task ahead. He was about to do what he had bragged he would do that night on the beach back home with his brother and his buddies—a long time ago and a long way from here. He was going to assault Fortress Europe. It wasn't just a catchphrase now but a looming fact, water and rock and steel and a cataclysm of fire to be endured. It was both unreal and the realest thing that had ever happened to him.

Nothing felt accidental about this moment. He was born to do this. He had a skill, and now that skill was going to be tested and used, and when he emerged on the other side of this day he would at last be at peace. He had to believe that. It was a thing to steady him in his purpose.

He knew the drill: Maneuver the flat-bottomed landing craft alongside the transport ship, matching its speed. Load the troops from cargo nets slung over the side of the transport. This was the maddeningly slow part, for the soldiers were not sailors. They mostly hated being on a boat at all, and the only thing they hated worse was getting off a big steel boat onto a little wooden one bobbing around, defenseless under the dive bombers. They were clumsy and overloaded. The commanders made them carry too much gear: rifles, ammo, rucksacks, hand grenades, trenching tools, mines, extra machine-gun barrels, mortar baseplates and tubes, tools and rations and radios.

Then, when they were all aboard, he would take up his position in a rotary file of boats spinning in a tight circle offshore while the rest of the boats loaded.

That was the part that called for patience and nerve, holding formation at a fixed speed while fighters made low strafing runs and Stuka dive bombers screamed down, aiming for a kill. He had learned that the Stukas were terrifying but not very accurate. But in war, everybody died by accident. The violence was random, and he knew better than to think he had any control over his fate.

At last, on signal, he would head for the beach with all the speed he could crank out of the diesel engine. The tricky part would be navigating through the debris, tank traps, shallows, wrecked boats, and other obstacles without slowing down, to deliver the men as close to the beach as possible. Each succeeding wave would leave a litter of flotsam and submerged traps for the incoming boats. A boat could find itself hung up, stranded far from the beach, a sitting duck for the pre-sighted guns on shore.

If he lowered the ramp in deep water, the heavily laden troops would simply step off and drown. Their burdens were strapped on, belted in, and there was no way to shrug them off fast enough.

The boat was just a plywood barge with vertical sides and a ramp at the bow, thirty-six feet long, holding exactly that many troops. Under full power, it could make nine knots, a little slower than a fit young man could run. Chance commanded a crew of two young Coast Guardsmen who manned the .30 caliber machine guns.

He stood in the rear and drove, much like he used to drive an outboard motor boat on Pamlico Sound back home, though the keel-less landing craft rolled like a log in heavy swells. His mouth was dry, and his head burned from lack of sleep, as if he had been awake for days. There was an unreality to it all that stunned him into a dreamlike trance.

He must perform perfectly. Up till now, he always had. But today would count the most. He must use all of himself today.

He was not afraid, exactly. He was just completely immersed in the moment, could not imagine that any future would follow the next few minutes. He was calm and focused and cold in his stomach. His hands were busy, his legs braced against the motion of the boat.

As long as he had something to do, he was all right.

As the troops clambered aboard and the planes stitched the water with their parallel machine guns, he ignored the din. *Do the next thing,* he told himself.

That was the best part about this work: There was always one more thing needed doing. He had no time to daydream, think, worry, or reflect. *Just do,* he told himself. *All will be forgiven.*

He felt sorry for the poor bastards who had to stand there, packed together in the well of the boat, heaving up their breakfasts, bowels clenched against the concussions, ducking with each explosion, closing their eyes against the geysers that sprayed over the open boat. They stared ahead at the high landing ramp, blind to what lay ahead. And everything would get worse once they made it ashore.

He ferried in the first wave of Fourth Infantry through a froth of exploding ordnance. The noise was unworldly, the racing engine drowned out by the rush of shells overhead and the detonations all around. A boat from his flotilla took a direct hit and simply disintegrated. Another, raked by heavy machine-gun fire, slewed around, the headless driver slumped over the con, churning in circles until a shell tore it in half.

But Chance made it in, lowered the ramp, watched the men dodge out lead-footed into thigh-deep water, saw some of them go down and the rest scatter onto the beach. When the last boot cleared the ramp, he was already backing out, the ramp winding closed against the *ping*s of bullets and the louder *whang*s of shrapnel.

He got off the beach in good order and slammed through steep, chaotic seas back to the fleet.

Chance returned to the beach three more times, each time carrying off wounded. This was just dirty work, and he understood work. He settled into it. *Do the next thing*, he told himself, over and over.

He was good at this, made for this, was exactly where he belonged at this moment in history. He did not think of it that way, in words. He was just so completely present in the moment that this day, this hour, this minute, were all that had ever existed. All that ever would exist. He was alertly conscious, hyper-alert even, yet felt in the middle of a vivid dream.

Hit the beach, lower the ramp, take on wounded, raise the ramp, back off, turn, throttle up steady but fast.

Load up and do it again.

The troopships seemed to hold an infinite supply of fresh young men. He could do this for days and never land them all.

2

Liam Royal was drinking a highball at the Outrigger Canoe Club in Waikiki Beach, Honolulu, Hawaii, when the news came over the radio: The Allies had invaded France. Everyone had expected it, yet no one actually believed it would happen. It had been forecast for so long, then postponed yet again, for many months. The radio voice might as well have announced the Second Coming.

The room filled with silent awe.

Details were few. The announcer reeled off some vague numbers—how many hundreds of ships made up the armada, how many tens of thousands of men they carried, how many miles of beach they assaulted, how many troops and tanks and guns were waiting for them. Liam didn't trust the numbers. He knew the high command would exaggerate some, downplay others. You didn't want to give away the truth to the enemy, and maybe your own people didn't really want it either. They wanted good news. They wanted reassurance that their sacrifices were not in vain. They wanted victory.

Liam sat still and listened. Above the bar hung an outrigger canoe. On either side of him stood young lieutenants just like him, one leg poised on the bar rail, mouths hanging open. Occasional captains and commanders sat at tables near the stage, all of them now frozen in mid-sentence, drinks lifted, heads cocked to listen.

General Eisenhower was calling the Normandy landings a great success, and the news reader was stressing that "casualties were surprisingly light." No numbers yet, just that reassuring word: *light.*

Liam turned his glass and pondered the term. What did that mean? Light by whose accounting? Not light for the men cut down on the beach, drowning in the cold surf, blasted to pieces by the big guns. He hated words that didn't tell the truth. To the soldiers on the beach, it was all or nothing. They either made it or they didn't.

Where was Chance? Driving a boat, that much he knew. A ferryboat driver. *That isn't fair,* he chided himself. The landing craft were in the shit right from the start. Of course they were. And Chance with them.

With any luck, he's in it, Liam thought. *Where I should be.*

Instead he had spent the past sixteen months teaching navigation, how to get from here to there using a sextant, the sun, and a little arithmetic. It was not what he had signed on for, just what he was good at. Him, with his big outdoor body and practical hands, a teacher. His father had taught him celestial navigation as a boy, and by now it was second nature. The math never bothered him—it was only simple trigonometry. The rest was just practice. He never should have admitted he knew how to use a sextant.

He should be out there. The humiliation stuck in his throat.

And now Chance was in it, really in it. Chance who couldn't add two and two, who couldn't find Orion's belt in the night sky unless it had a pair of tits hanging off it. Chance was doing his part. And Liam was sitting in a bar on the other side of the world.

The radio voice described a great flotilla of warships anchored off the beach at Normandy, barrage balloons floating above destroyers and troopships and LSTs. Tanks and Jeeps trundling ashore through the surf, the Germans retreating inland ahead of the steel onslaught. He could see it unfolding in his mind's eye as if he were watching it from the bridge of a ship—the great cascade of history breaking onshore, the defining moment of a whole century.

And here he was in a tropical paradise drinking hard and wishing he were part of it. It wasn't fair. The whole enlistment business had been his idea. Somehow they naïvely had thought they could all stay together.

They had joined up at Norfolk as planned, all but Par Patchett. They were determined to serve together, to watch each other's backs and one day bring each other home safely. So the recruiter promised.

But once they signed, they had little choice about their assignments. Men were sent where they were needed, to fill the roles vacated by the dead and wounded. The navy needed officers, and Liam tested into OCS. The navy needed small-boat drivers, and Chance volunteered for PT boat duty, but the navy needed to land soldiers on beaches, across rivers, and put him on a landing craft. Brick Littlejohn found himself running the ship's store on the USS *North Carolina,* the first battleship to arrive in Pearl Harbor since the attack, and Tim Dant wound up a corpsman with the marines.

Liam ordered another drink and listened to the overwrought voice on the radio. The more he drank, the harder it was to resist the urge to smash the damned thing.

3

The current pulled all the boats more than a mile south of their designated landing zones on Utah Beach, but the troops rallied around some general and made a fight. One of the wounded he took off the beach shouted that it was Teddy Roosevelt Jr.

Chance Royal gunned his Higgins boat off the beach and into the churn of gray seas, the well full of injured men groaning in shock, a wounded medic working among them.

On his fifth run, he carried a weapons platoon, mortar men and machine gunners. He felt the bottom grind onto the sand and let go the ramp. The soldiers in front surged forward and then fell back, chopped into pieces by heavy machine-gun fire. Only a handful of the thirty-six troops made it out alive. His two crewmen were weeping as they fired continuously toward the rock face that loomed over the beachhead.

Chance was soaking wet, and his hands were slippery on the controls.

He managed to back the boat off the beach and get it into deep water, headed away from the firing. It took a long time for him to understand that the wetness he felt under his flak vest was his own blood. The dream took him out to sea and then into blackness. He woke up briefly on the *Naushon*—a ferry converted to serve as a hospital ship—as if still in a dream of fire and fury. For a little while, he drifted back to the beach where he had last been a boy, innocent of blood, watching the breakers comb in under cloudy starlight, his head dizzy from the white lightning from Brick Littlejohn's jar.

When he died a little after sunset on June 6, 1944, D-Day, no one noticed for more than an hour.

4

Liam was leading a late-morning class of cadets through the sight reduction tables in a Quonset hut near Pearl Harbor. He was holding up a sextant and explaining how to bring down the sun to get an angle at a precisely timed instant. How you could do that several times, hours apart, and get a running fix, meaning you could plot a reliable course and find your destination.

He was saying, "You navigate by pretending you already know where you are and proving yourself wrong."

Then a pimply faced ensign stood at the open door and held out a telegram. Still gripping his sextant, Liam took the telegram and read it while the ensign stood at attention, as if waiting for a reply.

But there was no reply to this news: Chance, his little brother, was dead.

Liam flinched, as if he had been sucker-punched.

Details were vague. Killed in action on D-Day. More than a week ago. His body would be interred in the military cemetery where he died. *Casualties were surprisingly light,* he thought, and felt the rage back up in his throat.

He felt suddenly old, too old to be in the same room with a bunch of kids. In truth, they were mostly his own age, but their mild looks and smooth, guileless faces seemed to him to belong to another generation. He despised them for what they didn't know, for what they had not yet experienced.

He brushed past the ensign, leaving his cover—the hat that held the insignia of his rank—on the desk. He felt the staring eyes of the cadets on his back, but he didn't care. He clutched the telegram in his right hand and the sextant in his left, and when he exited into strong sunlight he didn't bother to salute the pair of captains who passed him on the parade ground. Liam was in such a black study, they simply stared as he stalked past, a big, angry, bare-headed lieutenant in a hurry.

The telegram came from Patchett. Now Liam pushed through the doors of the Navy USO Club and went to a bank of telephones at the back. A cheerful young operator in a yellow floral dress sat behind a semicircular console. He took a breath. Then, without a word, he scrawled a phone number on the back of the telegram and handed it to her. He laid the black sextant on the counter. He was done pretending he knew where he was.

"North Carolina?" she said. "What time is it there? Same as New York?"

"I don't care," he said quietly, and recognized the alarm in her bright green eyes.

It took her more than an hour to make a connection to the telephone at Littlejohn's store at Kinnakeet. A boy was sent to find Patchett, which took another hour. The operator placed the call again, and directed Liam to the only unoccupied booth. He entered and shut the glass door.

"Tell me everything," Liam said to Patchett across the Pacific distance.

Patchett's voice came through scratchy. "Nothing much to tell," he said. "All we know is in the Western Union."

Liam tried to picture him, lanky and unkempt, perched on the wooden stool at the back of the store where the phone was connected. On Hatteras Island, evening would be settling in. The breeze would be turning out to sea from the overheated sand, and it would be a good time to go for flounder in the sound. "That's it?"

"That's it. I'm looking out for things here. I always look out for you boys. Don't you worry." His voice nearly broke, or maybe it was the static on the line.

But Liam's only worry had been Chance, and now Chance was gone, just like Kevin. There was nobody left to look after. The boys were all gone to the war. "My dad and mom? How are they doing?"

"You want I go fetch 'em?"

"No, don't do that." He and his father weren't talkers. They would just stay on the line listening to silence. His mother would be stoic outside and all ruined by the news inside. What could he possibly say to her? That joining up was his idea? The guilt was inside him now, and shame. His little brother had trusted him and was gone. "I'll send a letter," Liam said. "Goodbye, Patchy."

He gently hung the phone on its cradle and slipped out, caught a cab to Honolulu, and left all gentleness behind.

He started at the tiki bar on Ala Moana and worked his way down the line, slamming beers and then whiskeys and not feeling drunk at all. He toasted Chance at every bar. He started a brawl with some marines at the Punchbowl Club and was escorted to the door by a brace of burly shore patrolmen who knew him from Pearl and put him in a cab for Waikiki, where he wound up back at the Outrigger Canoe Club drinking with a bunch of reserve officers from Naval Intelligence who all looked as carefree and debonair as movie stars.

One of them, who looked like Douglas Fairbanks Jr., matinee-handsome with a pencil-line mustache, somehow got hold of the telegram from his pocket and read it to the others. "Your money's no good in here tonight, old sport," the man said with great solemnity, and ordered round after round of top-shelf scotch.

Liam woke the next morning in a light drizzle on the lawn under a palm tree, a Filipino gardener squatting over him, gently nudging him by the shoulder. "Officer not dead?" the gardener said happily.

"No," Liam slurred, feeling heat behind his eyes, his head a balloon of pain. "Officer just fucking dandy."

He got up, stiff and sore, and felt for his wallet, wondered if he had enough cab fare to get back to the base, and what he would tell his commanding officer.

Holding a wake for my little brother. Now send me to the goddamn war.

5

Tim Dant got into the war fast and in a way he did not expect. Because in high school Tim had worked part-time for a veterinarian—a cousin—giving rabies shots and patching up injured mules, the recruiter coded his application with a *C* before he passed it along. After basic training, Tim was ordered to corpsman training in Hampton Roads.

His instructors were women—seasoned navy nurses. They showed him how to apply a tourniquet, splint a broken arm or leg, suture a wound, perform a tracheotomy, set up a field IV using water and sugar.

The nurses—especially Josie, a tall, middle-aged supervisor with bottle-blond hair—liked him. On his second day, Josie took his hands in her strong grip and inspected his palms. She said, "Hard to believe you're a fisherman, with hands like these."

"Depends on the season," he said, and she nodded, as if that explained it all.

She kept hold of his hands. "Did you know hands have their own knowledge? Muscle memory, they call it. It means when the shit is flying—excuse my French—when the shit is flying, and you can't think straight, and everybody is yelling at you to do this and do that, and guys are crying out 'cause they're hit, that's when you turn it all off and trust your hands. You hear me? Trust your hands. These hands." She shook them hard. "Train them right, and they'll know what to do, even when your brain don't."

He had no idea what to say to her, but he believed she was telling the exact truth. He had a feeling that, when the shit started flying, he'd be scared all the time, and he was right.

After a ten-week course, he was shipped off to the advanced Field Medical Service School at Camp Lejeune. By the time he joined the fleet marines, he could treat for shock, dispense morphine, keep a marine alive long enough to make it to a real doctor. Sometimes.

And now he thought of the memories that lived in his hands. Not just the memories of how to twist a tourniquet or plunge a hypodermic needle into a vein, but all the other things they had learned to do on their own, some of them things he was not proud of.

6

The landing at Tarawa turned out to be what the old-timers in the navy called "a first-class clusterfuck."

From Pearl Harbor, the invasion fleet steamed southwest across the rolling Pacific for the better part of a week, and Tim was one of only a handful in his company who wasn't violently seasick.

Their target was the island of Betio, just two miles long and half a mile wide, part of the Tarawa atoll. After a massive aerial bombardment to soften up the concrete defenses, eighteen thousand marines prepared to storm the beach in the new amphibious tractors—amphtracs.

But the aerial bombardment was delayed. The ships held their stations off the beach as long-range Japanese guns rocked them one after another. They just stayed there and took it. Madness. At last, the order came to load the amphtracs, and soon, in the predawn darkness, thousands of marines were scrambling down cargo nets into the landing craft—except the rough seas kept slamming the balky amphtracs into the ships' sides, crushing men in between. Some were hauled aboard screaming or cursing, but others just slipped away as steel slammed into steel,

By the time the last amphtracs were finally loaded, the tide had dropped alarmingly. Amphtracs skidded onto coral reefs hundreds of yards from shore, pounded by enemy guns. They were supposed to be able to power over the reefs, but this was untried. For hours, the fleet bombardment ceased, and the Japanese had open season on the men stranded on the reefs. Every kind of ordnance rained down on them, making so much smoke and fire that it was hard to believe this was all happening on water.

The men fled the amphtracs—now deathtraps—and swam ashore, leaving behind their heavy mortars and machine guns.

Tim Dant's amphtrac took a direct hit in the bow and spun out, broaching on a swell and coming down hard on a coral head, listing heavily toward the beach, so that machine-gun fire raked the interior. The amphtrac's crew and half of the twenty marines it carried were killed instantly. The others, burdened with packs and weapons, clumsily climbed up the high side. Some were cut down. Others scrambled over the bodies and plopped down into the deep water on the other side.

There was no time to tend any wounded, not while bullets were ricocheting inside the amphtrac. Tim flipped into the water, temporarily safe in the lee of the stranded vehicle. Around him, men were struggling to shrug off their heavy rucksacks. Plenty were drowning.

His corpsman's bag slung by its strap over his neck, Tim struck out for the beach.

The swim seemed to take hours. The scene was surreal: fire and water and smoke, the din of explosions and big diesel engines roaring past, men shouting and crying out, men run over by the churning amphtracs, a huge burst of water that hurt his chest, and then deafness, eardrums blasted.

He staggered ashore, the beach alive, erupting in billows of sand. Bullets zipped across it in ragged lines like raindrops. Dark forms in jungle-green camouflage crabbed across the white sand of the open beach, moving from the bloody water toward the flash of gunfire lighting up the tree line ahead of them.

Sloshing in the surf was the detritus of battle—packs, jagged parts of wrecked landing craft, life jackets, weapons, and bodies. Everywhere bodies.

Somehow, in the first hours, five thousand marines made it ashore. All Tim knew was that men were crowded into every shallow hole, behind every sandbank, many of them yelling and crying out in pain. Fifteen hundred died trying to make it across the beach, and many more were wounded.

The rest were mainly exhausted, lacking heavy weapons, piled on the curving beach in a mob of confused units. There was no safe spot anywhere. Men kept falling all around. The navy guns had recommenced their fire, rocking the tiny island so that the whole world seemed to be erupting. Every blast brought a hail of sand and coral down on their heads. The thick copse of trees ringing the lagoon was already a stand of shattered bones blackened by fire. The island didn't seem big enough to contain so much violence.

Tim went to work with his hands.

He did not think or ponder or reflect. He simply went from one man to the next, doing whatever his hands remembered to do. He was soon out of bandages and morphine.

He approached a fellow corpsman who was kneeling over a legless marine. He put a hand on the corpsman's shoulder and was about to ask if he could spare some gauze. The corpsman looked him in the eye, and then Tim heard a muffled zip, and the corpsman's head came apart in a spray of blood and bone, slapping Tim in the face. His cheek was gashed by a piece of the man's skull. He half-expected to feel a bullet plow into his own face, but nothing happened. The corpsman lay collapsed, headless, over the wounded man. Tim's hands moved him off the marine. His hands then looted the dead corpsman's bag, which was still full, and wrapped tight compresses of gauze around the marine's blood-soaked stumps of legs.

Tim continued his rounds.

Trust your hands, he told himself. There really wasn't anything else to do.

Beyond the beach loomed sand heaps and pillboxes and bunkers made of palm logs. Tim followed the flow of troops off the beach. At the edge of his vision, on a small rise, he saw flames outline the forms of four men in a livid tableau, and all at once, in a fury of black smoke and erupting sand, the four disappeared.

The beach was littered with bodies, none of them Japanese.

At darkness, Tim experienced a momentary displacement. The failing light reminded him of his own island, how the darkness fell hard, but how in the short interim between daylight and true dark the sky took on a purple cast, the clouds solid as steel, the wind settling, the ocean lying down.

The blackness on Tarawa was absolute.

From time to time, the muzzle flashes of artillery and machine guns erupted, leaving him night-blind. Mercifully his hearing was still mostly gone. In the rushing silence of his head, he felt less terrified, as if whatever was happening outside his body were less than real.

As the firing died down and the men waited for a counterattack, the cries of the wounded started. Cut down earlier, they had lain in the blistering sun for hours. Now, in the terrifying darkness, they cried out for water, for their mothers, for the corpsmen.

For Tim.

All through the night, he belly-crawled toward the muffled sound of American voices—hoping they were really American and not a fatal trick. Some of the men were too far gone to help. He laid hands on their bodies and carefully felt along their limbs, their trunks, their faces, discovering the damaged parts. Thankfully, in the darkness, he could not see their faces.

He trusted his hands.

Feel for the pulse in the neck.

Touch the face to register the temperature of the skin, whether warm and dry or cool and clammy, to assess shock.

Squeeze the hand and find out if it can squeeze back.

Carefully touch all the limbs and digits to learn which ones are missing.

Stick in the morphine dart with the telltale red fletch, so the doctor will not overdose him later.

Hold the compress firmly on the bleeding wound and wrap.

Wind the tourniquet around the stump of the severed limb and twist. If the patient is conscious, recruit him to hold it and release it every fifteen minutes. If not, call his buddy—if he has a buddy.

Seven times, Tim dragged wounded men through the blackness to the palm-log bunker, where other marines could help get them off the beach. Four of them survived the day.

For this action, he would be awarded the Navy Cross. But all he thought by the end was, *I have not saved enough.*

He himself was slightly wounded by shrapnel and a grazing bullet, but in the adrenaline rush of combat he never even noticed. The battle lasted seventy-six hours and left behind more than two thousand wounded men.

When it was finally over, Tim Dant's corpsman's bag was beyond empty.

7

Brick Littlejohn couldn't believe his luck.

For reasons only a military bureaucracy could explain, he was told to report for boot camp not at nearby Norfolk but all the way across the continent in San Diego. The navy even provided the rail pass.

Brick traveled in style, a Pullman berth all to himself, free meals at every stop, the country reeling by outside his window like a movie about America: Pennsylvania coal mines; the giant, glittering sprawl of Chicago, all those lights; the endless panoramic wheat fields of the prairie states; then the rugged, otherworldly desert and the last breathtaking mountains, the train clinging to the right of way blasted out of rock, the world disappearing in a haze below.

He'd always wanted to see California, to check out all those movie stars. He still had a dog-eared copy of *Life* magazine from the past August, which featured a full page of Rita Hayworth lounging in a sheer black negligee. Maybe he could look up Clark Gable or Humphrey Bogart and buy him a drink.

He thought, *The farther from home, the better.*

He was told boot camp would last six weeks, with a two-week leave at the end. He'd have all the time in the world to sport around Hollywood and see what was what and who was who.

Meantime, each day was ten hours of hard labor—marching, running, drilling, gunnery, and classroom lectures. He didn't much like any of it, but there was some comfort in being told exactly what to do, having your hours scheduled for you, and always having your pals around. And each night when he hit the rack, he fell asleep at once and dreamed away his fatigue as his body strengthened. Brick got along with everybody. He kept his mouth mostly shut and grinned a lot. He counted down the days until he could head for Hollywood.

Then, at exactly 2:00 A.M. on a drizzly morning twenty-seven days into basic, the barracks exploded into light, and there stood the chief flanked by two sailors wearing sidearms. "Congratulations!" the chief shouted. "You are no longer seaman recruits. You are now seaman apprentices. Now grab your sea bags!" he ordered, and followed with a string of colorful profanity.

They carried the heavy canvas duffels outside and loaded them into six-by trucks, then piled themselves into other trucks, wedged onto parallel benches on either side of the bed, covered by a canvas roof. An armed guard with a .45 pistol on his belt anchored the last spot on each bench, nearest the tailgate. They drove all night up the coast, the drizzle slackening into fog and then resolving into gauzy sunshine as they passed the fortified guard post at the entrance to the San Pedro wharf.

Then they lined up and waited. The line ended at a long table set up on the wharf. Behind the table sat a dozen or more young lieutenants, each behind a sign announcing, *A-C, D-H,* and so on. "Find your line," the chief told them.

Brick queued up in the *I-L* line and soon was handed an envelope—his orders. From now on, he was assistant storekeeper aboard the USS *North Carolina,* a brand-new battleship.

He was hustled aboard, shown to his billet, assigned a high bunk crammed into a corner under pipes and wire harnesses, and put to work in the warren of steel rooms in the belly of the ship. They sailed the next day. For the first week, he was almost always lost. But he paid attention, he listened, he did as he was told. He was a good sailor.

When they steamed into Pearl Harbor, they were already heroes. The harbor was a junkyard of burned-out buildings and shattered wharves, a mess of sunken ships sheened with bunker oil still leaking from the *Arizona* and some others. The *North Carolina* was the only American battleship in the Pacific. Along the shoreline, thousands cheered their arrival. It was like they had just won a great battle. They were being cheered just for being there, alive and afloat.

Brick stood on deck in formation with the rest of the twenty-three-hundred-man crew, awed by the wreckage around him, thinking, *So this is what war looks like up close.*

But it wasn't really war, not yet. This was just the wreckage of something that had already happened. He shuddered to think of the men who had been under the bombs that made it.

For the duration of his stay at Pearl, the war was flurry and tension and everything moving fast, too many soldiers and sailors and marines packed into too little geography, jostling guns and ammo and equipment, a circus of activity, crowds and vehicles all over the docks at any hour, uniforms of men from half a dozen nations—Brits, Aussies, Kiwis, Canadians, even French and Dutch, every service and rank.

Brick bided his time, did what he was told, bemused by all the confusion, feeling like an imposter in his loose uniform, willing to play the part. The days slipped by without his keeping any track. He followed the routine and found reassurance in the repetitive familiarity of life aboard ship.

Before long, the *North Carolina* was at sea again, cruising in the company of destroyers and aircraft carriers. Brick would stare out over the heaving gray seas and think, *Holy smoke, this is the real thing! I am really here, and this is really the war.* If the Royal boys could see him now. And Patchett, that old skunk. And Tim Dant, the baby of the bunch.

But it was still just cruising on a big steel island. He felt it pitch and roll under him, a sensation that made him queasy. Not seasick, not that bad, but nervous and slightly off-balance, never quite relaxed. He was surprised, since he'd spent his life on small boats, one way or another. This was different, like the world itself was shifting under him, always moving, rolling and yawing. The bigness was the problem. *Something this big shouldn't be moving like this.* It tricked a person into expecting it to be solid and permanent, but it was floating on salt water. All those thousands of tons, buoyed up by water.

How was that possible? *All it would take is one hole,* he told himself. *Just one big hole.*

Alone in his cramped bunk, just when he was beginning to feel steady, the hum of the engines vibrating the steel bulkheads in a reassuring monotone, there'd come a sudden lurch, a slight bump, something to remind him that under him was not solid earth but floating steel plates, and under that green water with no bottom.

8

There was nothing glamorous about the work, but he liked it well enough. Guys would stop by all day long to buy shave cream or writing tablets, cigarettes and candy. The store was a chatty place, and after his shift there was always a poker game somewhere, and so far he was slightly ahead. His best pal was a lanky guy from Jersey everyone called Sketch, because he was always drawing pictures. He could make a caricature in about five minutes and a serious portrait in an hour. He made his pin money selling these to the men to send home to their sweethearts and wives.

He drew Brick and made him look handsome and heroic, his Dixie Cup sailor's cap jaunty over one eye, a sly smile on his lips. A movie-star pose. Didn't even charge him, just wrote on the back, "For my best pal, Brick." A good guy, Sketch.

Everything changed on September 15, 1942. The *North Carolina* was steaming in a task force. The whole crew, even the officers, were jumpy as cats. It was in the air, an ineffable something, the inevitability of action, like they had been stalling for too long, and now they were due. The horn for battle stations sounded a couple times, but they were false alarms.

Then it sounded for real.

Brick wasn't on duty. He'd gone forward to grab an ice-cream sundae at the soda fountain. When guys started scrambling all around him, he wound up with chocolate syrup all over his blouse. But at that moment, he didn't care. He rushed up the companionway to his battle station at the 20 millimeter antiaircraft gun on level two, aft. He was just the loader, not the gunner, but still it was a crucial post.

The word came round that submarines had been spotted. The men watched across the water as the carrier *Wasp* erupted in a sky-high geyser of flame and burned magnificently.

Brick said to the gunner, "God help the poor sonsabitches on the flattop."

The gunner snapped his gum and said, "God ain't out here today, son."

Then an explosion tore into the battleship and knocked Brick to the deck so hard he thought at first his right arm was broken.

Somebody yelled, "Torpedo!" and other men took up the cry.

Though she never lost speed, the ship slewed violently and suddenly was listing hard to port. He scrambled to his feet and rubbed his aching arm and stayed at his station for the next four hours, waiting for the call to abandon ship, while the lookouts scanned the horizon for the telltale wakes of more torpedoes.

Under him, the steel deck felt flimsy and temporary. The big ship moved with a heaviness inside her, the weight of the sea trying to pull her down while she resisted. That's how Brick thought about it. He didn't know if a battleship could suffer a direct hit from a torpedo and stay afloat. In truth, he knew the battleship mostly as a warren of small steel rooms, each separated from the others by steel bulkheads and hatches. Down below, it scarcely seemed like a ship at all. More like a factory.

Except it constantly moved, restless and unquiet. And Brick knew that a warship carried no lifeboats.

At last, they stood down. The captain addressed them over the loudspeaker. The ship had taken a hit, but she wasn't going to sink. They'd be heading back to Pearl for repairs.

Released from his battle station, Brick checked the storeroom and found the steel bulkhead peeled open like a giant can of peas. Cagey, the bosun's mate, was inspecting the damage. Cagey said, "Blew a big damned hole in her, that's for sure. They sealed off the watertight hatches from Second Division."

"That means we won't sink, right?" Brick asked nervously, still not quite believing the ship could stay afloat with all that damage. Just one big hole. Under that, deep water.

"Oh, we'll be all right." Cagey shook his head ruefully. "But those poor bastards down below. Christ, that's another story."

"What you talking about?"

Cagey mopped grease off his face. "We had three guys down there, dirty job. Sounding the fuel tanks. They say another guy was up in the forward shower space, you know, just before. So four guys. We think."

"So they're in sick bay? Hurt bad?"

"Shit, Brick, listen at what I'm saying. Had to dog the watertight doors. You know, seal 'em inside."

The news staggered him. "Jesus. Jesus, that's cold."

Cagey nodded. "Yeah, but what else you gonna do? We leave them doors open, we lose the whole ship. Anyhow, they probably died on impact." He shook his head and stuffed the greasy rag in his back pocket. "We can hope."

Brick retired to his rack and turned Cagey's words over in his head. He could almost hear the rushing water down below, where the men were trapped. The world rocked under him. He couldn't stop thinking about it. *Sealed inside*, he thought, over and over. *Christ, I can only hope they died on impact.* The alternative was simply too awful to contemplate.

9

It was all they talked about in the mess: *Those poor sonsabitches.*

Some guys claimed they could hear pounding and cries for help from inside the sealed-off spaces. Till they didn't hear them anymore. The carpenters shored up the damaged bulkheads with timbers and hammered together four pine coffins. Meanwhile the watertight doors remained sealed until the ship dropped anchor off Tongatabu four days later.

By flooding some of the aft trim tanks and shifting bunker fuel between tanks, the engineers squatted the stern and floated the bow high enough that damage-control parties could survey the hole from the outside. It was massive—eighteen feet high by thirty long. Cagey, the bosun's mate, said to nobody in particular, "You could literally drive a truck through there."

Only the watertight bulkheads had saved the ship. Enough water was pumped out to allow another party to open the watertight door sealing in the bodies and try to retrieve them.

But before long, the men came out, unnerved, panicky, slimy with oil, and sickened by the stench. Things were at an impasse. Nobody else wanted to go in.

After a while, the chief pharmacist's mate volunteered—but only if he could have a good slug of bourbon first. Brick, who wouldn't have dreamed of helping out otherwise, thought this sounded like a daring idea, a story he could tell later, back home. He piped up, "Hey, if I can have a jolt of corn, count me in!" He knew liquor was banned at sea, and the captain couldn't possibly allow it.

But just this one time, against all naval protocol, the captain nodded his approval, and a steward was sent to the officers' mess to fetch a bottle of Four Roses and a shot glass. Each of the volunteers took a healthy slug and passed it on. Brick held the shot glass in his fist, felt the burn at the back of his throat, tasted a sour belch of bile. Then, single file, they entered the chamber.

When Brick stepped across the steel lip of the doorway, second in line, filthy waist-deep water sloshed around his legs. Invisible things bumped against him underwater—some soft, others sharp and solid. The water was colder than he expected—frigid, in fact. Their flashlights swept the blackened bulkheads, the wavy light shivering across them. The overhead was buckled in places like a sheet of tinfoil.

The surface of the water was clotted with debris, and the bodies, when they found them, floated half-submerged. The clothes were tight as inflated balloons, the bodies were so bloated.

The skin felt soapy. It was hard to find a way to grab and hold them, but they did it. Two men to a body, slowly towing and lifting and handing it through the narrow doorway, as gently as they could manage, to a team who waited outside.

When they had brought out the last man, Brick vomited at the hatchway, the bourbon hot in his throat. He felt dizzy and utterly sober. He went as far aft as he could and showered for as long as the chief let him. Then he tucked himself into his rack, pulled a blanket around his shoulders, and cried his eyes out.

Other men cleaned the four bodies and wrapped them in canvas, then laid them in the newly built coffins and nailed shut the lids. No one would be allowed to see the men's faces.

Next day, the ship's company assembled ashore for the burial service.

Brick had not saved anybody, but he had helped do the next best thing. He told himself that, over and over. That had to count for something against his sins. He could hold on to that much.

10

There were other battles after that, more submarine scares. The *North Carolina* sailed for months into and out of combat, and the battle alarm always put Brick's heart into his throat. Some days, it felt like he had been on the ship forever, that the cruise would never end, that the rest of his life would be spent between boredom and terror, always the steel world rocking under him, never solid, just one big hole away from oblivion.

But even so, for Brick, the worst moment of the war was carrying out that last man.

The guy had been in the forward shower, well away from the blast. His body was unmarked by wounds. He must have survived the torpedo impact. For long minutes—a lifetime of minutes—he must have known what was happening, as the cold water rushed in and the chamber went dark, and all around him was steel, no way out.

For months afterward, Brick Littlejohn suffered nightmares. The dream was always the same—waking up naked in the dark, the rush of water filling his ears, steel walls all around, a steel deck below. Then he'd awaken for real, pounding the bulkhead beside his rack with a bruised fist.

He never told anyone about the dreams. He never told anyone that the last man he'd carried out was his best pal, Sketch.

He vowed that if ever he returned home, he would stay ashore, on solid ground, and keep store like his father and his father's father before him. His store would be big and have plenty of windows. It would be full of light and air. Full also of visitors—his pals and even tourists, maybe, dingbatters come for the fishing, all sitting around the pickle barrel and trading news and stories, telling bawdy jokes and filling the room with talk and laughter, a big, airy room full of company and light.

He would never venture into any room that didn't have at least two ways out.

And he would never drink bourbon again. Just the smell of it made him gag.

11

Liam Royal finally got his wish—he was steaming toward the war zone, navigation officer on the *Fletcher*-class destroyer *Carl Stach*, to join the Fifth Fleet as part of Operation Iceberg, the assault on

Okinawa. The fighting had been fierce and unrelenting for more than two months. More than one hundred eighty thousand American soldiers and marines were slugging it out against a hundred and twenty thousand Japanese troops and conscripted Okinawans. The fighting was primitive and savage—bayonet attacks and flamethrower assaults, heavy artillery pulverizing the island acre by acre.

Kamikaze attacks had already sunk twenty ships and heavily damaged scores of others. The action was so constant and horrific that naval officers, even captains, were breaking down under the strain and had to be rotated out for recuperation. The ones who stayed functioned in a permanent daze, a kind of low-grade shock, zombies in uniform, and many would never be the same again.

Thus, in 1945, Liam was plucked out of the classroom and onto the *Stach*. Unlike nearly every other officer he knew, he had lost weight in Hawaii, working late and drinking hard and tirelessly angling for a chance to get into the war. He had called in every favor he could, pestered every staff officer he knew.

For Chance, he thought. But that was a lie. He was not seeking vengeance, only a kind of vindication. He would be ashamed to go home when the fighting was done and admit he had sat out the war in a tropical paradise, safely ensconced in a soft billet, his only danger driving drunk on the twisty, narrow North Shore highway.

In the company of a small task force assembled at Pearl Harbor—three destroyers and a light cruiser escorting several slow transports full of reinforcements, a hospital ship, and a train of supply ships—the *Stach* plowed slowly toward the war.

It arrived on June 22, the day after the fighting ended.

12

The *North Carolina* stood offshore with a carrier task force, protecting the carriers as they launched air strikes against Okinawa and retrieved their planes. Brick Littlejohn manned his 20 millimeter gun station, which fired almost constantly at the kamikazes as they bored in low over the water.

After the second day of constant battle stations, his gunner was so fatigued that Brick changed places and fired round after round. The gun felt like a jackhammer, shuddering him with each recoil till he felt himself jarred loose from his body, simply floating above it in a kind of bemused daze. He watched the kamikazes spin and burst into flames and shatter as they cartwheeled across the gray scalloped waves. The din of all the guns felt like a solid thing, as if the air were suddenly thick and impenetrable, as if the noise itself were an enemy.

The kamikazes fell by the hundreds, the novice pilots flying straight into the maelstrom of fire from the massive fleet. But there were always more. And some of them always got through the curtain of tracers and explosive rounds. It was his job to help keep them from hitting the battleship. There was so much powder aboard to serve the nine massive 16-inch turret guns that a direct hit could send the ship sky-high in an instant.

On the sixth day of battle, gunners on the *North Carolina* knocked down another Zero skimming low over the water toward one of the carriers. But a flanking destroyer was also firing at the same airplane and missed, its 5-inch shell punching into the battleship instead and wiping out a gun crew. Brick didn't witness what was happening, but later he was slightly wounded in the left arm by a shard of shrapnel, and in the sick bay he saw the three mangled bodies lying under bloody sheets.

By the end of April, the *North Carolina* was no longer needed on scene. The Japanese had run out of airplanes and gone underground, fighting with suicidal mania from caves and a warren of concrete bunkers. Only ten thousand would survive the banzai charges and mass suicides, men clutching hand grenades to their bellies or leaping from the high cliffs. American soldiers and marines continued to die in record numbers, and in the bays the hospital ships filled up with more than thirty thousand wounded. The war at last came down to numbers, an accountant's ledger, and the balance sheet made the rounds of scuttlebutt across the fleet—along with wild rumors about a final assault on the Japanese mainland that would cost a million casualties.

But there was no more work for the great battleship, and she steamed back to Pearl for repair and refitting, and Brick Littlejohn left the war for good. When at last he was mustered out in Philadelphia, he changed into civvies in the restroom at the Greyhound terminal and left his sea bag containing his uniforms, his bluejacket manual, and every other vestige of his naval service under a bench. He carried home only the clothes on his back, his discharge papers, and the pencil drawing Sketch had made.

13

Tim Dant survived the nightmare on Okinawa.

And for him, the battle was just that—a waking dream of noise and fire and blood. Time and again at night, the marines were hit with human-wave attacks, and they did not need even to aim—just to hose down the terrain in front and at dawn count the bodies heaped on their perimeter, some of them with swords still in hand. But always some attackers got through, and the marines kept falling. And Tim Dant kept trusting his hands, touching shattered limbs, bandaging bullet wounds, pressing intestines back inside bayoneted bellies.

After the battle, he shared a tent with other medical personnel at the makeshift naval base near the Yonabaru airfield on Nakagusuku Bay at the south end of the island. There was plenty of work at the field hospital—men came limping in for a whole week after the fighting ended. The worst were evacuated, but there were plenty of gunshot and bayonet wounds to dress, plenty of amputations, whole squads sick with diarrhea and a dozen exotic infections.

And worst of all were the shell-shocked, the men suffering what was called "combat fatigue." They wandered in like a legion of the walking dead, hollow-eyed and silent or belligerent and babbling. They had gone into battle and never really come out again. Some of them could not stop crying, while others could not cry, could feel nothing at all. You could poke their arms with needles and they wouldn't even flinch. The docs called them "hollow men." Tim Dant had no medicine in his bag for them. His hands held no muscle memory that could be of any use in exorcising whatever evil thing had gotten inside them—or for putting back whatever had been sucked out of them, leaving them empty shells. All he could do was sedate them, get them hot showers and chow, move them along.

He bided his time. After a while, the wind no longer carried the stench of a quarter-million bodies—half of them civilians driven to suicide at bayonet point by the Japanese—rotting in the fields, in the surf line, in every cave and grotto. After a while, it seemed normal that the surviving islanders—their villages obliterated by the holocaust of seaborne guns, artillery, and aerial bombardment—should inhabit the stone sepulchers of their dead ancestors, cooking their meager meals on the stone pediments, as if barbecuing on suburban porches.

After a while, it was almost like peace.

Tim Dant sat in his sun-rotted tent and chain-smoked Chesterfields, a new habit, and waited to invade the home islands of Japan. It was the inevitable final act, the curtain on the war. Sometimes he would rouse himself before dawn to watch the B-24 and B-29 bombers lift off from airfields around the island, bound for targets of ships, planes, and steel. Those very words were printed on their targeting maps for Honshu, Nagoya, Yokohama, Yawata, Nagasaki, Tokyo. To remind the pilots and bombardiers, as if they needed reminding.

Tim Dant tried to imagine living in a city of paper and wood while the firebombs rained down. Sometimes he would walk the beach, vaguely aware of the commotion of small craft plying their way back and forth between ships and shore, thinking, *I should see fishing boats out there.* But the fishermen were all dead or gone, their boats wrecked. For all he knew, the fish were gone, too, stunned by the concussive violence that had overwhelmed both land and water.

It was an empty sea except for warships. The restless rhythm of the breakers reminded Tim of that last night on the beach at Hatteras Island, before they all enlisted.

After all this, after Tarawa and Okinawa, why was that night still so clear?

The cataclysms he had survived, the death and suffering he had witnessed, the wounds he had touched with his own two hands, should have driven it from his memory, tamped it down into a vague and muffled distance. Yet he could close his eyes at this moment and smell the salt on the night breeze, hear the thrashing breakers, taste the hot white liquor burning his throat. Hear their young bragging voices, feel the weight of the rifle in his hands. Remember all of it.

He thought of everything he would carry home with him, the dead weight of it.

14

Liam Royal understood the war was coming to its climax. The Nazis had already surrendered. Okinawa had fallen. Nothing remained between the deadly magisterial might of the Allied armies and navies and Japan itself.

He was billeted ashore at the naval base at Yonabaru. His destroyer had been dispatched on submarine patrol, but he had been left behind to conduct field navigation classes for naval aviators and Army Air Corps navigators. Many were young replacements flying their first missions who had sped through accelerated training courses to get them into the war. Bombers were getting lost, ditching in the sea a hundred miles off course. His job was to make sure the men knew how to get their planes and crews where they were going—and get them home again.

This time, Liam approached the duty with equanimity. His condition for accepting the temporary assignment was a guarantee that he would sail with the fleet for the invasion of Japan.

On August 6, Liam was sitting on the beach, sipping from a bootleg bottle of Johnnie Walker Red he had bought from an enterprising master chief, when he spied a familiar figure ambling up the beach, barefoot, just beyond the surf line. *Impossible,* he thought. *Here, of all places. After all this time.*

He must be mistaken. He watched the skinny kid draw near, shirtless and tanned, straw-blond crew cut shining in the sun. There was no mistaking him now. Liam stood, waved.

The kid stopped, put a hand to his forehead to shield his eyes, cocked his head in recognition, walked slowly across the sugary white sand.

"Timmy," Liam Royal said, and held out a big hand.

Tim Dant grabbed the hand with both of his and held on, squeezing hard, his eyes brimming.

"Cut it out," Liam said, himself tearing up. He pulled Tim Dant close and crushed him in a bear hug.

"Goddammit," Tim Dant said. "Goddammit. You here. Of all the fucked-up places on earth."

"*Me* here? What the hell! *You* here." Liam laughed and felt a strange elation he had not felt in years.

Liam sat on the sand, and Tim Dant collapsed beside him. For a few moments, they had no words.

"Heard about Chance," Tim Dant said at last, almost in a whisper. "I'm so sorry."

Liam looked out to sea. "Don't speak on it," he said huskily. "There's nothing to say."

Tim Dant nodded. "All right." He knew there were other things they wouldn't speak of as well. Most of what mattered between them would go unspoken. That was all right. They had never talked much with words anyway.

"Tell me where you've been all this time."

It was the usual ritual, the months and years, the highlights of service, an anecdote here and there to punctuate the telling, the illusion that all that time could be accounted for in some reasonable way, that the arc of their wartime lives somehow made sense, earned them something they could take back home with them. That their lives could continue back home with both of them as they were now, not as the reckless boys they had been, that it could be both continuous and new, a hard, sharp line between then and now. And so they traded their stories, but neither one could really tell the truth of what he had seen and done, only relate place names and dates and broad strokes of events. Probably it was better that way.

When Liam finished his tale, Tim Dant jerked his head toward the bottle. "You sharing that, then?"

Liam handed over the bottle, and Tim Dant took a long swig. He wiped his lips and belched and said, "I guess we may as well celebrate."

"Yeah," Liam said, taking back the bottle. "Here's to all the boys."

They shared the bottle back and forth and drank freely. They drank to Chance and Littlejohn and even Patchett. They drank to each other, solemnly. For a little while, the world went gauzy and soft at the edges, blurry with good fellowship and more peace than either of them had known in a long while.

At length, Tim Dant said, "So I guess we're all going home now."

Liam shook his head. "Not me, Timmy. I'm going with the invasion fleet."

Tim Dant gave him a quizzical look. "Invasion fleet?"

"The last battle," he said. "The Nippon homeland."

Tim rubbed his crew cut and then put a hand on Liam's arm. "Haven't you heard? The invasion's off."

"What are you talking about?"

"Jeez, don't you get any news at all? The secret weapon. The atomic bomb. They dropped it this morning. Scuttlebutt's all over the island."

"On Tokyo?"

Tim Dant shook his head. "Tokyo's already flattened. This time, they disappeared Hiroshima."

"*Disappeared?* What the hell kind of word is that? With just one bomb?"

"I got it from a crew chief. One big, fat bomb. One city wiped clean off the map. They're going to do that to the whole place, unless the Japs surrender."

Liam stared out to sea and let the fact sink in: There wasn't any war left for him. He would go back home as he had left it.

Tim Dant squeezed Liam's shoulder. "So you see, you poor son of a bitch—there's nothing left to invade."

15

Liam Royal and Tim Dant languished on Okinawa for two more

months. The *Carl Stach* had gone back to Pearl, stranding Liam. September came and went without any further drama.

In early October, the storm warnings came. Each day began with an announcement on the base public-address system tracking a big disturbance off the Caroline Islands to the southeast. The storm was expected to track northeast toward Formosa. But it took an unexpected hard turn northward.

Liam and Tim were miles north of their base, seated on split-log benches behind the railroad embankment watching Fred MacMurray and Barbara Stanwyck in *Double Indemnity*. The film had nearly run its course, MacMurray as insurance investigator Walter Neff recording the last facts of his confession of murder onto the Dictaphone, when the projector suddenly switched off. A voice came over the loudspeaker warning that a tropical storm was bearing down. "Seek shelter and batten down," the voice said. "I repeat, seek shelter immediately and batten down."

Before the loudspeaker quit, a gust of wind shuddered through the audience, blowing away hats and splitting apart the movie screen. The men scattered as the wind picked up, and before long the first rainy blasts drenched the compound.

Liam and Tim were caught too far from their quarters—there was no question of making it back in time to beat the storm. The horizontal rain was already pelting them like buckshot. So they simply followed a crowd of marines into a Quonset hut—not a barracks but a commissary office. Almost at once, a poker game commenced, and just as quickly men began raiding the stores for cigarettes and canned peaches and whatever else they could lay their hands on. Other men sprawled on the floor and chairs, making themselves comfortable, settling in for the long haul.

One of the marines groused, "All them fancy weather stations, you'd think they'd give a guy a little more warning."

A sailor said, "Just thank your stars it ain't fuckin' kamikazes."

Liam looked around. It was the first time since entering the service that he had ever seen officers and enlisted men sharing the same space in such an informal manner. The wind flung itself at the arched corrugated-metal walls, and Liam watched them pulse in and out, as if breathing with the storm.

All night long, they could hear the storm building outside. From time to time, large objects banged against the walls, so that the Quonset hut reverberated like a giant drum. Nobody slept. The rain hammered continuously.

Toward dawn, a large piece of something solid blasted through the back window, and the sudden rain and wind brought the fury of the storm inside, swirling papers and drenching the men, who sprang up cursing. A gang of them disassembled some plywood shelving and hammered it over the broken window.

"Jesus," Liam said, "look at that!" The object that had crashed through the window had numerals painted on it. It was a jagged piece of the tail assembly of a spotter plane.

The wind continued to rise, and the din became overwhelming. Tim Dant covered his ears—it was too much like Tarawa, like Okinawa during the battle, a relentless chaos of noise. It sounded as if the whole world was in violent motion, tearing itself apart. The wind had risen from a howling rush to a blood-curdling shriek, keening like the cries of the slaughtered dead.

The shrill wind filled Tim Dant's head, made him feel crazy.

Liam had endured many storms, but this was one for the ages. Outside he heard the ground-shaking thuds of large objects being blown around, sounds as sudden and unnerving as an artillery barrage. He heard voices shouting in alarm, someone screaming in terror. He heard sharp reports like gunshots, the splintering of wood, and the tearing of metal. Judging by the shrill wailing sound, the wind was approaching a hundred miles per hour.

And at last, it happened. The wind lifted the hut and tore it in half. All at once, men were lashed by stinging rain, pelted by airborne missiles. A square of sheet metal spun out of the darkness and cut an Army Air Corps sergeant's throat. A private went down unconscious under a flying chair.

Liam and Tim hit the deck. They crawled through sticky mud and blundered into an air-raid hole, now full of water. They slid down the sides and huddled in the wet morass, listening to the typhoon rage over their heads. It felt like lying between the rails under an eternal freight train, all roar and racket, the ground shuddering and slopping under them. They burrowed into the mud, their bodies tucked protectively into each other's, hands covering their faces. They remained hunkered in that mud hole all night and all through the next day as the storm squatted over the island.

At dusk, Liam woke to a strange calm, hardly believing he had slept amid such violent upheaval. The storm had moved north, up the island. Tim Dant sat facing him, eyes wide open and staring. Liam laid a heavy hand on his shoulder. They were both covered in muddy slime, their faces blackened with it. "You and me," he said hoarsely. "You and me."

They helped each other scramble out of the hole. Other men were moving around in dead silence, ghostly figures in slow motion. Their actions seemed random and aimless to Tim, movement for its own sake. No one seemed to be doing anything useful.

Tim Dant spied something and began walking toward it, stepping over and around the debris scattered by the storm: splintered boards, overturned Jeeps, battered jerry cans, great balled-up clumps of wet canvas. He bent and lifted something off the ground and held it for Liam to see: a cardboard carton of eggs. Carefully, as if he were dressing a wound, he opened the lid. All twelve eggs were intact. He grinned stupidly. Liam cursed.

The typhoon had accomplished in hours what the Japanese could not in three months. The camp was utterly destroyed. Out on the airfield, B-24 bombers lay overturned, their great nose wheels pointed to the sky. The smaller observation planes, PBYs, were in a pile at the far end of the runway, as if pushed there by a giant plow. And it was the same all over the island. Hardly a building remained standing.

The island had been blown clean of tents. Men had died. Villagers in the countryside had been swept away. A dozen ships had been overwhelmed by thirty-five-foot waves and lost at sea. Hundreds more had been driven aground, and a hundred landing craft were lost.

Liam took the carton of eggs from Tim. *The cruelest piece of wreckage,* he thought, *to survive unscathed.* He smashed the eggs on the ground.

CHAPTER EIGHT

HATTERAS ISLAND, 1991

1

Caroline Dant explained it to Nick, the phrase he had heard Liam use. "*Dark of the island,* hon," she said while she gathered his signature on the invoice for fixing the car. "That's what the old-timers call a scawmy moonless night, no stars. That's the time the mooncussers and wreckers used to come out. Raise a false light on the beach to lure in the unwary captain feeling his way along the shoreline in the dark."

Mooncussers and wreckers, he thought. Maybe one of them was the son of a bitch who had sabotaged the Land Rover.

She motioned with her fingers. "He come to grief, steering by that false light, and lo and behold, when his vessel was hard on the bottom, the wreckers would row out to loot the cargo."

"What a charming custom." They both laughed.

"Well, it kept a lot of families fed through the stormy winter. Although once there was a load of top hats—top hats!—come ashore, and lo and behold, every ignorant waterman from here to Corolla was sportin' around in a topper. I got a picture sommers. Revenuers come around, all them old prousers played dumb, like nobody gonna notice a hundred top hats walking around loose."

"That must have been a sight." He found himself enjoying a rare sense of being included. It was only small talk, but Caroline Dant struck him as someone strangely familiar, as if he'd known her for years. The older sister he could confide in, even if she salted her talk with unfamiliar words, words that seemed to belong to her private memories. The high-school teacher who looked out for him. She radiated a disarming openness, a nature that was trusting but that also had been bruised a time or two. She always welcomed him with a smile, but in a flash that smile could be wiped clean, replaced by a hurt look, lips pursed, the corners of her mouth turned down.

She cocked her head and observed him with a squinted eye. "I don't mean to get into your business," she said, and instantly he understood that was exactly what she was about to do. And oddly, for once, he didn't mind.

"Go on," he said.

"You want a coffee?"

"Day like this? Rather have a cold beer."

"Makes two of us. Come on, hon. I'll show you a picture."

2

Caroline Dant's house stood behind the garage on a sandy knoll, the front and sides hemmed in by thickets of wax myrtle and yaupon. It was not one of the new palaces raised on pilings but old and cottagey, the cedar shingles silvered by weather. Inside, the floors were sway-backed and worn soft from bare feet and decades of brooming, and the walls were white beadboard hung with old photos of men in boats.

"Looka there," she said.

He studied the old sepia print of a dozen watermen, all wearing top hats. Someone had penned a date across the bottom—April 18, 1912, just three days after the *Titanic* went down. "Quite a picture," Nick said. Ridiculous, sure, but also funereal. All those dark hats and grim, fixed, staring faces—like a gathering of mourners.

"That's not the one I meant," she said, and led him to the kitchen, where hung a black-and-white photo of four boys, all bare-chested, slim, and loose, arms slung carelessly across each other's shoulders, grinning for the camera.

He looked closer. Across each boy's chest was a name scrawled in cursive. And the year was noted: 1942.

"The two brutes on the left are the Royal boys, Liam and Chance. Chance is the black-haired one—the handsome devil."

He started. "Wait, Chance is a person? The name of an actual person?"

"Sure," she said. "Chance Royal. His real name was Charles, but nobody ever called him that. They say he was his mother's last chance. A rakish name for a hell-rake boy."

So *Chance* was a person, like *Goliath* was a ship. All the names somehow were part of the same story.

"Next to him is Brick Littlejohn—you know Littlejohn's stores?"

"Sure," he said. "They're everywhere." Two members of the family had helped launch the lifeboat.

"And this skinny fellow on the end with the blond crew cut and the big grin—that's my daddy. He grew up down in the village and built this house when he married my mom. His name was Tim. It's the only photo I have of him."

"I take it he's passed—I'm so sorry."

"Gone off his boat," she said. "Drowned at sea." She suddenly teared up. "Oh, my," she said. "I never expect to cry, and I always do."

"There," he said, and laid a hand gently on her shoulder.

"I promised you a cold beer," she said, and smiled and turned from him.

They sat in her kitchen, broad and full of light, at an old Formica dinette table with a mottled orange top. It was the most comfortable place he had been in years.

"I've lived in this house my whole life," she said absently. "Sometimes that seems strange, never to have gone out and seen the world. And other times, it feels just right."

Nick thought of his Oma, refusing all those years to leave the little apartment over the candy store, until the city forced her out.

Through the kitchen window, he watched a pair of white trawlers working the sound, their nets gathered like wings under the spread booms, the water shimmery with sun and heat. Delegations of raucous gulls trailed each boat, swooping erratically, diving into the wakes and fluttering back up into the air.

Caroline Dant said, "I was supposed to be a fisherman, like my father. Supposed to be a boy, for that matter." She laughed. "They were so sure I was going to be a son that they had the name already picked out—Peter, after the man who saved my dad in the First War, when he was just a kid. Peter Patchett." She laughed again. "That no-good scalawag. Of all people."

"But you weren't a boy."

"No, I surely wasn't. I wasn't a Peter and weren't niver going to be. Niver cared for fishing neither. But I do love boats, God help me. You'd think I wouldn't, you know."

"It's lucky you've got the marina."

"Oh, they're all Gulf Stream boats now, or else those cabin cruisers that look like a cross between a cathouse and a rocket ship. I like the old boats, the wooden shad boats like my daddy had. Built over on Roanoke Island by old George Washington Creef—'Uncle Wash,' they called him. Had a great white beard, and boy did that man know how to build a boat! Sharp, high prow to take the seas, shallow, but don't roll much."

Another one of the heroes and giants, Nick thought.

Caroline Dant lifted a photograph off its hook and showed him—a sleek boat with a sprit mains'l and a flying jib, heeled over in a stiff breeze with a grinning man at the tiller—her father. Nick recognized it. Its exact wooden model stood on a shelf at Lifeboat Station #17.

"They say Uncle Wash used to keel two boats at a time out of the same juniper log and build them as twins, just two every season. When his wife took sick, he built two juniper coffins. Buried her in one and set the other one on the rafters of his boat shed. There it waited for twenty-four years until the old man passed. They carried him to his grave in it. I always think of it as his last boat. Anyhow, that was way back during the First War, long before my time. It's just a story to me. But that boat my daddy ran. Not many of those around anymore, unless you know where to look."

"I guess the place has changed a lot from the old days."

She carefully rehung the photo. "Yeah, you can say that again. The tourists, well, they're a mixed blessing. They sure crowd things up, you know? But we need their business, I guess. Otherwise we're just a backwater, just one more little place that don't matter. But I do love the legacy of this mean little place, a whole community built on fishing and lifesaving. Isn't that something? Feeding people and rescuing them. In the old days, at least. All the Royals, the Lords—that used to be their business. Rescue."

"Never thought about it that way."

"It was part of their marrow, those old-timers. It was in the . . ." She searched for a word and cramped her hand into a fist. "It was in the *bones* of the island, you know? We were always looking to the sea. And the lifesavers, they were the tallest men around. That was how you reckoned a man's value. How many times did he go out? What did he do when the wind blew hard and the seas got up and sensible people stayed indoors?"

She poured an amber beer into a frosted schooner and handed it across to him. The beer was sweet and wheaty, with just the aftertaste of bitterness he craved.

"Mud in yer eye," she said," and they clinked glasses. "Don't mind me—don't get much company, and I get to rambling on." She laughed self-consciously.

"I don't mind," he said. "I love the talk." He sipped his beer and licked foam off his upper lip. "And I'm glad I've got at least one friend here. Somebody who doesn't see me as the enemy."

"Bless your heart," she said, her eyes sparkling. "You're a charmer. I know why the company sent you here." She wagged her finger playfully.

"Well, there's at least one person who doesn't find me so charming."

"She's a troubled girl," Caroline said. "I'm not speaking ill, you understand. She's got a lot to carry, is all."

He smiled and then shook his head. "Maybe she's not the only one.

All those protest signs. I'd love to talk to the leader, find out what we can do to reassure them. But every time I ask, well, nobody seems to know about any organization. No meetings, no demands, nothing. Just a lot of damned signs."

"And?"

"All courtesy of Royal Real Estate."

She nodded. "You act surprised. You spoke to her on it?"

"Not yet."

She shook out a pack of Marlboros. "You mind?" He shook his head, and she lit up and inhaled luxuriantly. The smoke trailed out the open screened window. "Hon, from where I sit, the signs is the least of your worries."

"Yeah, the brakes."

"Yeah, and the boat, too—heard about that. Somebody sure is trying to put out your light."

He shook his head and grinned, though it wasn't funny. "No secrets around here."

"Not on an island, hon. We read the paper every morning just to see if what we heard last night is true."

"Thanks for, you know, being straight with me. And nice."

"Aw, honey, you already got a nicer girl than me to talk to."

"If you say so." So far, Julia Royal had been mostly a puzzle and a vexation.

"She's a good girl. Like I say, she's carrying a lot, but she's good in her heart." She leaned in confidentially, though nobody was around to hear. "But that old Liam, he's a pure devil. Whatever's in his heart is mean and mad. If he even has a heart. You watch out for him."

Her passion surprised him. "Okay, but so far he's just been telling stories." Nick glanced behind her at the photograph on the wall. "They were all pals back in the day?"

"Tight as any brothers," Caroline Dant said. "That's what I've always heard, anyway. I never met my daddy."

He started. "Oh, I didn't realize. You said . . . I mean, he survived the war?"

"That's a matter of opinion around here," she said softly. "Mama was pregnant when he died. Like I told you, lost at sea. More accurate, out on the sound. Pound-netting. They towed in his boat, but he wasn't aboard."

Nick thought of Peter Patchett's false grave. How many graves on the island were just as empty? "They never found out what happened?"

"Fishermen go missing, that's all anybody ever said."

"Must have been devastating for your mother, pregnant and all."

"Mama lived till I was in high school. Then she just laid down and quit. They said it was pneumonia, but I think she just gave up." She was quiet for a moment, staring out the window, a thin filament of smoke curling off her cigarette. "All they left me was something I couldn't even use," she said vaguely.

Nick waited, but she didn't say more. Maybe she was done talking for today. So he just nodded and drained his glass. He always did know when it was time to leave.

But as he started for the door, the phone rang. Caroline Dant lifted the receiver and spoke briefly, then handed it to Nick. "Your boss has some news."

On the other end of the crackly line, Fannon's voice sounded faraway but infused with urgency. "First core samples are up," he said.

"Already? That was fast."

"I told you, everything's fast-tracked. We need you back here pronto."

"That good, eh?"

Fannon laughed. "Bloody marvelous," he said. "Time to get your arse in gear." And hung up abruptly.

Caroline Dant gave him a quizzical look, but Nick knew better than to talk company business. It was his job to listen. If Fannon was right, he'd have plenty to talk about later. He felt a little flutter in his stomach.

3

After Nick Wolf left, Caroline Dant reached into the top kitchen cupboard and brought down a corpsman's medical pack, olive-drab canvas with a faded red cross stenciled across the flap. The canvas was salt-stiff and discolored with dark stains. Her father had carried it on Tarawa and Okinawa and other bloody places, survived all that, then came home to a lonely death at sea. Everyone said it was an accident, but her mother always said he had just slipped overboard, the weight of it all too heavy to bear.

She hefted the weathered bag by its strap. The weight was still inside. Carefully she unfastened the strap and peeled back the flap. She looked at the contents for the thousandth time and shook her head. This was stupid, she knew. It always made her cry, and she dabbed her eyes with the heels of her hands. It was all neatly bundled, crisp and new-looking.

All that damned money.

4

When Nick stepped aboard the *Lady NorthAm*, Fannon was talking fast into a telephone. He waved Nick to a desk, where Fannon had already set up his keyboard. Piled next to it were reports, pages of numbers and technical jargon from the drilling engineers that Nick would have to translate into readable English for press releases, company announcements, and the update for corporate. He would have to work fast and get it right.

Fannon hung up and slung himself into a chair beside Nick, clapping his hands. "Right, well, get down to it. The numbers are fucking gorgeous, and corporate will want them ASAP with some language they can take to the board. This is priority."

"Got it. Anything else I need to know?"

Fannon slapped him on the back. "Investors, my boy. This will really gin up interest. The majors haven't found shite lately, so they'll be circling us like wolves."

"It's our lease—what can they do?"

Fannon grinned. "To begin with, they can ante up. We own four adjacent leases. Nobody else saw any prospects out there. Nobody thought we could swing the federal approval. Now they can pony up or kiss our arses."

"Can you show me the core samples?"

"Still out on the rig, mate. And what are you now, a fucking geologist?"

"Come on, you know my rule. I always see them." *Even if I don't always know what I'm seeing,* he almost said.

"Yeah, we'll get you out there soon enough, before we chopper them back to corporate."

Nick knew where they went from there: the secure warehouse in La Grange, where thousands of core samples were inventoried and stored, a vault of geological intelligence in the global oil war.

"Get crackin', eh?"

So it begins, Nick thought. *It won't be just one transitory well. It will be hundreds. It will be Gulfport. Julia will never . . .* He put her out of his mind. It was time to focus, to work. Later he could ponder *Goliath,* his Opa, Chance Royal the hell-rake.

He worked for five hours straight. His report to corporate was a thing of beauty—understated, yet smacking unmistakably of triumph. NorthAm had gambled, and now it was about to pay off. He tracked the core samples and translated the engineers' and geologists' reports into a delicious investment opportunity. He had to extrapolate based on the preliminary data, but the preliminary data was compelling—and, for once, unambiguous.

He got rid of all the extraneous numbers and highlighted just one, the amount of oil now estimated in what they were calling the Cape Point Reserve: twenty-eight billion barrels.

Three billion more than the North Slope of Alaska, the largest oil field in the United States.

Buried treasure, Nick thought. *The all-time jackpot.*

5

For yet another night, Julia lay awake, restless and exhausted, yet unable to sleep. She tried singing songs in her head to quiet the clamor, but that just reminded her of Nick sitting on the porch looking dopey and cute, strumming that beat-up guitar like some vagabond from another century.

Every time she talked to him, he stirred up an anger in her that she could not explain. She heard mean words come out of her mouth, a cutting tone, impatience because he was so naïve. He had traveled the whole world, yet he seemed to take everything at face value. And he expected the whole world to take him at face value.

He had that simple sureness about him—not cockiness but maybe its opposite, a settled confidence in what he could do. He laughed easily, didn't complain much, did his work with conscientious pride. And that's exactly what made him so dangerous, she understood. He was disarming, like a big dog, eager to please. Caroline Dant had practically adopted him. And he had puppy-dog eyes that could go all mushy with affection, eyes that also instantly reflected disappointment and hurt in a way that made her feel guilty, like she had just kicked him.

Whenever he looked at Julia, she felt like a big spotlight had been turned on her, highlighting every bit of her, every flaw, every secret. It made her blush and say stupid things. And that made her self-conscious, sometimes angry, so she said mean things.

It would be so much easier if he were some sleazy, despicable character. By all rights, he should have been—after all, he worked for an oil company. She had expected a slick corporate type, a guy who acted like he was handsomer than he was, the kind of guy with gelled hair and monogrammed shirts who took off his wedding ring when he went to the bar and tried to pick her up with a corny line. That guy she could have cut down to size.

But Nick was this big aw-shucks kid in a man's body, still dazzled by the world, caroming through it on his big adventure. The only slick thing about him was his Ray-Bans, and apparently they were a birthday gift from his pal Fannon. Sure, Nick was a shill for the company, its head cheerleader. But he believed all the crap he said. He was ridiculously sincere. You'd think he'd have a hard shell, but she had discovered exactly how to hurt his feelings. Instinctively she had found his weak spot and jabbed it.

He had no business coming here. Had he really not known about his grandfather's grave? How could he not? And yet she believed him.

She wanted him gone, and she wanted him to stay forever, to be her deepest confidant. She could tell him everything, explain it all. Surely he, of all people, would understand.

It wasn't fair that she had finally met a man who could stir her so deeply, and it had to be *this* man.

6

Nick's Oma used to tell him stories about his grandfather, and each story had a title and a plot, for she had rehearsed them many times. It was her way of keeping her husband alive all those years, by creating a living memoir. The fiction was that their life together was still going on, that he would come home to her, that he was not dead but just a wandering soul lost out in the world, and somehow her stories would call him back.

Each night before she went to bed, his Oma turned on the table lamp beside the kitchen window, in case her absent husband needed to find his way home in the dark.

Nick pondered this late into the night, too keyed-up to turn in. He sipped a beer and stared out over the dark ocean, the stiff breeze and the breaking surf down on the beach infusing the darkness with a rush of pleasant sound. He settled deeper into an Adirondack chair on the balcony.

At the moment, Chicago was a place he couldn't even imagine. Julia wasn't there.

His Oma's stories always reminded him of what it meant to love, really to love—a feeling he had witnessed but never really felt before. The soaring joy and surrender, the pain that cut deep into the bones, the memories that both propelled you forward with boundless faith and stopped you in your tracks and paralyzed you—as they had kept his Oma in her little apartment over the candy store all those years, waiting for her beloved man to come home.

A dead man, he now knew.

All those years. Was she happy? She had not seemed so, though he would never have called her unhappy. She lived in some other universe entirely, where happiness and unhappiness were simply not relevant. Instead of happiness, she had purpose, and maybe that mattered more. She seemed in a constant state of reminiscence or anticipation, living either in the storied past or the imagined future, when her husband would come back to her—but never in the present.

Whatever else Nick did, he had determined to live his life in the present—in whatever minutes and hours and days he had right now. Never mind years from now, some indefinite future. People got lost long before then.

His Oma should have known. Despite her guileless faith, her blind, unreasonable hope, her beloved was already sleeping in the sand with his unlucky shipmates long before Nick was even born. He lived on only in her stories, told so often and so vividly that now they were Nick's memories, too, as if he had known both his grandparents when they were newlyweds.

"Did I tell you about the harmonica?" she would say. And he must always answer no, always allow her to unravel the tale and then gather it up again.

The harmonica was an old Hohner Tremolo model her husband had brought with him from Germany. He carried it in his pocket in a snap-buttoned leather case and used to pull it out at lunchtime and play for the men at the Pullman factory. He loved Strauss waltzes and wild polkas and even the marching songs he had heard from veterans of the Great War. Oddly, their favorite was "It's a Long Way to Tipperary," maybe because it had absolutely nothing to say about war. It was a comical ballad about an Irish bumpkin in the big city, London. The added wartime verse started, "That's the wrong way to tickle Mary!" and went on in bawdy fashion.

Nicky the machinist would play for drinks at the *Biergarten* after work, and sometimes at weddings and parties.

Nick thought about his grandfather now as he sat on the deck idly picking out a tune on the guitar.

His Opa should have stayed home with his wife, in Chicago. The war had nothing to do with them. He had a vital defense job, he was old to be drafted, and he had already made a good life. Maybe not the life he wanted, but you didn't always get the life you wanted. But maybe every man needed an adventure, a call to action, the urge to go, coursing in the blood. Nick himself had felt it, sitting in his office in the city when what he craved was to be out in the field somewhere, anywhere, the sun hot on his neck.

But that was different. Nick tried to imagine how a man might be infected with a fever to fight against his own country, the place where he had come to manhood and made his living and met his wife.

What could drive him to leave all that to fight for a fanatical ideology that glorified power and death?

How could the man who lay at night in his Oma's arms, the gentle musician who made her laugh and saved her from harm time and again, how could that man turn toward the darkness, work so hard to find the war? What was it he wanted, if not a life and a love, if not decent work and a place to belong?

On the breezy deck far from his Oma, far from the place where his grandfather had started his strange odyssey toward death, Nick made soft music with his hands, felt the same wood his Opa had felt. He cradled the soundbox to his chest and closed his eyes and let the music into his body.

He dozed awhile, dreaming vividly in that space between sleep and wakefulness. A shadow passed in front of him. A screen door slammed on the deck below, and he opened his eyes, disoriented for a moment. Then he remembered where he was, felt the stiffness. He leaned the guitar carefully against the railing, bent forward and rubbed his neck.

It was lying at his feet, another note: *LITTLEJOHN.*

7

LITTLEJOHN. Well, he knew that was a name for sure. He had met the man—Brick Littlejohn, Chance's pal. Caroline Dant had shown him the picture. Liam Royal's pal, too. And Patchett's. But Patchett didn't go to war.

Whatever had happened had been in the war. Somehow. Something. Which meant that one or all of them—the ones still left, at least—were involved. But involved in what? And what did his Opa have to do with that? He was dead and buried under a monument Julia and her grandfather must surely have known about. And therefore had lied about to him. Or maybe not, if all she knew about that graveyard came from a grammar-school field trip.

And what did any of this have to do with him? Was it about the company after all?

Use what you know to find out what you don't know.

What he knew were riddles and scraps of ancient history. He'd go to the place where the scraps might be pieced together. One more place where his calls had gone unreturned. It wasn't much of a plan, but it was the best he had.

8

At nine o'clock sharp, Nick arrived at the *Island Times*, housed in a cottage that resembled a fishing camp more than an office. Crab pots littered the side yard, and bright red and blue floats hung beside the door. The doormat was made of thick woven rope, and the door handle was a salt-crusted cleat from an old dock. He pushed open the heavy door, made of rough hatch boards, and inside found a trim sixtyish-looking black man wearing jeans and a black T-shirt, drinking coffee, feet propped on a stack of old newspapers.

He pushed his spectacles down his nose and regarded Nick. "Well, come in, if you're coming," the man said.

Nick stepped inside and smelled the dusty reek of old paper, newsprint, and darkroom chemicals. "Took a chance," he explained. "Wasn't sure anybody would be here on a Sunday."

"We're a weekly. We come out on Tuesday, which means we have to go to press tomorrow."

Nick nodded. “Makes sense.”

“We got your telephone message.”

“More than one.” Nick smiled.

“We’ve been rather preoccupied with other matters. Anyhow, my granddaughter told me you’d be coming around.” He stood and strode toward Nick in easy, gliding steps. He was a head taller than Nick. His hair was balding on top, graying at the sides. “Rosa? The waitress?”

“Right.”

“I’m Diogenes Lord.”

“Very pleased to meet you. And please accept my condolences.”

“Thank you kindly.” He took Nick’s hand in a firm handshake and did not let go.

What is it with these people and their handshakes? Nick wondered.

Diogenes Lord turned it over with his other hand, felt the individual fingers, squeezed Nick’s palm, and at last dropped the hand. Then he suddenly grabbed Nick’s left hand and did the same. When Diogenes Lord squeezed the knuckle of his index finger a little too hard, Nick winced and let out a rasp of breath.

“A man’s hands tell you most of what you ever need to know about him,” Diogenes Lord said by way of explanation.

Nick rubbed his knuckle. “What do mine tell you?”

“You’re right-handed. You play the guitar, but not often enough—calluses on the fingertips. You work outdoors a lot. You used to throw a baseball pretty good. And you’re falling in love.”

Nick smiled. “My hands tell you about baseball and love?”

“You’re not built for football, so that limp from your bad knee says baseball.”

“That’s a knee, not a hand.”

“Your left hand has some arthritis in the joints, from catching all those hard throws.”

“And love?”

Diogenes Lord grinned. “You white people sure know how to blush. Want some coffee?”

9

"So the boys all went off to war together," Diogenes said. They sat inside a fortress made of stacks of old newspapers.

"But not Patchett."

Diogenes shook his head. "Bad lungs—scarlet fever as a kid. He just stayed home and proliferated. There's all sorts of Patchetts under lots of names all over these islands. Families the girls married into."

"And Chance Royal never made it home."

Diogenes took off his spectacles and rubbed his eyes. "Died a hero on D-Day. I've got it here somewhere—dug it out last week for Rosa. She's doing a master's thesis down at the university—how the war came to the island." He riffled through a sheaf of newspapers piled on a cabinet and snatched one. "Here it is. The story didn't run until June twelfth, the following Monday. I guess it took that long to notify the next of kin."

Nick took the yellowed page and read it out loud: " 'Boatswain's Mate Charles M. Royal of Hatteras village died heroically while landing troops on Omaha Beach.' That's it. Not much."

Diogenes wagged a finger. "I'm surprised there's that much detail. There was a war on."

"So he's not even buried here."

Diogenes nodded slowly. "That's right. According to Rosa, he's in the American cemetery in Normandy. Of course, there's a marker for him here in the family plot."

"Of course. Didn't his brother enlist with him? Was he there at D-Day, too?"

"Liam? No such luck. By then, they were separating brothers anyhow. On account of the Sullivans."

Nick looked at him blankly.

"In 1942, five brothers named Sullivan went down on the same ship. That was the end of brothers serving together. Liam went to the Pacific war. Navy."

So they didn't even serve together, Nick thought. *What the hell happened, then? And where?*

Diogenes said, "But here's the thing. When Liam Royal came home in forty-five, the family's fortunes suddenly took a turn."

"Meaning what?" Nick studied the photo of the handsome boy that had run alongside the notice of Chance's death.

"Money." He rubbed his thumb against his fingers. "That boy came home with loot. Nobody knew where he got it, or how, but it was obvious to anybody who had eyes."

Nick heard the door open and shut and peered over the stacks of newspapers, suddenly feeling like part of a conspiracy.

Diogenes called out, "Hey, pretty girl!"

"Hey, Daddy. That coffee still fresh?"

"Help yourself." To Nick, he said, "My daughter, Sallie, the editor."

"You're not the editor? Then what do you do?"

Diogenes smiled. "Me? I just tell stories."

"Then tell me about the money."

Diogenes leaned in and whispered. "Oh, they were circumspect about it, you know. They weren't buying Cadillacs or diamond rings, not like that. I mean, I was just a kid, but my mama would say, 'Something fishy goin' on with them Royals, Di.' That's what she called me—my mother had all the education, and she was who named me. My daddy drove the mailboat and served as postmaster in those days, never gossiped. He was famous for keeping secrets."

"So what did they buy?"

"One thing, mostly: real estate. Just like now. Lots of island men went off with the Coast Guard, the navy, some to the army. Me, I had three uncles and four cousins never came back. They weren't even supposed to be in combat, being colored, as they called it in those days. But truckdrivers still got blown up on the front lines, and mess stewards went down with the ship, same as the captain. The Royals bought my uncle Bannister's fishing shack on the sound, and he used the money to help his sister, my aunt Delia. She ended up selling out anyway, moved off to find work on the mainland."

"The Royals bought her house."

"For a song, as the man says. Suddenly all kinds of people are selling off their fishing shacks and homes and either moving off or going to work for the Royals. Now you've got to realize those properties weren't worth then what they are now, but all the signs were there—talk of a bridge to the mainland, all those ex-GIs with their shiny new cars looking to take the family on vacation. It was only a matter of time."

"So, somewhere along the way, Liam Royal found treasure."

Diogenes rubbed his big hands together and leaned in, though nobody else was around to hear except his daughter. "It gets even more interesting. All the sudden, Brick Littlejohn has his own store—not his daddy's old saltbox, but a brand-new big place—and then another, and pretty soon he's got a whole franchise. Now my mama told me that before the war, Littlejohn—his old man—was having money troubles. Bad investments or some such. If it weren't for moonshine, he'd have gone bust. My mama often went with my daddy on his mailboat, so she knew every bit of news coming on or going off the island. Like registered letters from banks and such. So where did all this sudden prosperity come from?"

"And Patchett?"

Diogenes laughed outright. "Now, to hear my mama tell it, that man couldn't sell a pork chop to a starving dog. Came from a family that never had nothing, I mean, *big* nothing. A scrounger and a scamp, that one. She'd say, 'No common sense, no business sense, no dollars and cents.' So, all of a sudden, he's building a new house, a painted house, for his family. Tucked it back on the sound side, thought nobody would notice, but my mama saw it every Tuesday when they made that turn around Pogie Point with the mailboat. It just got bigger and bigger. And then, next thing you know, Patchett's building houses for all sorts of people. Suddenly he's a success. As my mama always said, it weren't natural, the way that man succeeded."

Nick had the feeling Diogenes Lord had been waiting a long time to tell this strange story to someone. To an off-islander. Only someone from off would be a satisfying audience. Nick nodded, taking it all in, and when Diogenes reached for his empty coffee cup to refill it he suddenly grabbed Diogenes's right hand, a big, strong hand with long, delicate fingers, softer than he expected. The hand relaxed in his own, and Diogenes smiled while Nick studied it.

"What's my hand telling you, Mister Baseball?"

Nick let the hand slip out of his grasp. "That you work indoors. That you know some pretty good stories."

"My hand told you that?"

"You didn't yank it away."

Diogenes nodded. "And the stories are all true."

"I don't doubt you."

"Well, it wasn't all bad news. Wherever the money came from, it also did plenty of good."

Nick cocked his head. "How so?"

"Just about every charity and church from here to Corolla gets support from the Royal Foundation. How do you think Rosa can afford graduate school?"

"Scholarship?"

"The Malcolm and Mary Royal Fellowship. There's a dozen more like it."

"This story gets better and better."

Diogenes considered for a long moment, let out a breath, nodded, and held up a finger. "Let me tell you one more. I mean, if you've got the time."

"So tell me another story," Nick said

Diogenes opened the desk and pulled out a brittle yellow envelope, still sealed. "I don't know why my daddy came to have this." He paused, frowning. "I guess he was the only one the poor boy trusted. Tim Dant, I mean. Caroline's father. It was stashed away in a box with my father's papers. I went through it after he died."

Nick thought of the funeral procession that had held him up when he first came to the island. "I heard your father was somebody special."

"Isaac Abraham Lord. Eldest son of Chief Lord. Mailboat driver, postmaster, and preacher. He had the gift. People would tell him everything in their hearts. Strangers, people he didn't even know, would come to him and spill their guts. Even before he got the call. Folks just knew he would keep his counsel, I guess. That's a rare thing, you know."

"Yes, I imagine it is."

"Got religion in the war and preached the gospel for forty-six years. Not the fire-and-brimstone gospel, but the gospel of healing and forgiveness." He faltered, seemingly embarrassed to get so carried away. "Like I said, I was going through his stuff."

"And helping Rosa with her project."

"Yes. And helping Rosa. Actually she was helping me. She was the one found it." He held up the yellowed envelope. "There was a mention in the will."

"What? In the will?"

"And I quote, 'Give it to the messenger from off. You will know his name, for he has dwelt among you.' "

"My God. What's that supposed to mean?" Nick thought, *Maybe the old guy suffered from dementia.*

"People tell you what's in their hearts, don't they, Mister Wolf?"

He said quietly, "Sometimes it's just about listening, that's all. Most people don't."

"Yes," Diogenes said. "Listening." And fastened his unblinking eyes on Nick.

"Wait a second. You don't believe I am *him*, do you? The one your father meant?"

"You're from off."

"Lots of people are from off. Most people, in fact."

Diogenes nodded slowly. "Rosa said you're him. Me, I wasn't so sure. So I waited. I wanted to see you for myself. She said to give it to you. She told me her reasons, and now I'm inclined to trust her judgment."

He handed the envelope to Nick, who held it gingerly between thumb and forefinger, staring, then started to open it.

Diogenes gently touched his hand. "Not here. Take it to her yourself. Tomorrow. I'll let her know you're coming. It's up to her whether you read it."

"Fair enough. But how am I the messenger? How have I dwelt among you?"

"Because of who's in the graveyard."

"I don't understand."

Diogenes tapped the envelope in Nick's hand. "See who it's addressed to?"

"Yes."

"You know the name already. I can see it in your eyes."

"So what?"

"There's nobody by that name in that family."

Nick touched the name on the envelope. "Of course there is," he said. "But not the way you think."

10

The big boardinghouse was empty. It was Sunday night, and all the guests had fled home to Pennsylvania and Ohio and elsewhere. The day had been overcast and dreary, spitting rain on and off and finishing in a blow that rattled the windows and kicked up the sea and then settled down again, so that by eight o'clock the sun was mostly down and the place felt abandoned to shadows.

Nick sat on the lookout deck with his guitar, fingering soft blues. He wasn't playing any song in particular, just letting his fingers find the notes they wanted. He had taken lessons briefly in high school from a jazzman who used to say, "Don't work it so hard. The music is already in the guitar. All you have to do is let your fingers find it and let it loose." He played that way now, hardly conscious of the act, letting the guitar play to him.

From time to time, he paused and sipped from a bottle of beer on a small table. But mainly he just watched the sea, felt a lethargy of exhaustion mingled with confusion. Now, among all other things, he was some kind of anointed messenger. From whom?

What the hell was in that letter? He burned to know, but he understood his promise to Diogenes. *First thing tomorrow*, he thought. *Very first thing.*

He was eager to give it to her, but it also gave him pause. Maybe it would change everything. Bringing the news—especially bad news, if that's what the letter contained—could mark him forever. The soccer buddy he'd been staying with when he got the news about his parents was a case in point. He never hung out with that kid again. He saw the mom at the funeral and deliberately avoided her. In his mind, she was the one who was forever the bearer of tragic news. He simply could never face her again.

As the bearer of an unopened letter, he was the agent of knowledge. That knowledge could change everything, maybe cost him the only friend he had made on the island.

All this was a new responsibility, and he felt the weight of it almost physically. It was lucky he had the guitar tonight, something to hold on to, quite literally, while he passed the hours.

Usually the job was enough to focus him. He always had enough to do, reports to write, facts to gather. He had finally pinned down Poe Patchett, the mayor, who wanted no part of oil. He had expected that. This was a tourist place, and the beach was the golden goose. Sure, there might be oil dollars down the road, sales taxes and jobs, subsidies, what have you. But any threat to the beach was an existential threat, and the only way to counter it was to make damned sure the drilling was handled responsibly.

Because Cal Root was bothered by the crease in the rig's jackleg, Nick worried, too. Enough that he had sent a heads-up to corporate appended to one of his routine reports. Cal Root and Bucky Malagordo were pros, veterans of a working lifetime of difficult jobs. Nick wanted this to be a clean operation, squeaky clean. He owed that much to Julia, to Caroline, to the island.

Funny that he felt such a nagging sense of loyalty to the place, to the people. He'd always been conscientious, but this felt different. This was them getting under his skin. This was the island tugging at him to stay.

The Nature Conservancy woman had turned out to be pleasant enough. Sometimes Nick had to endure shouting, insults, even ranting anger. But this young woman wasn't the ranting type. She had trained as a lawyer and also had a master's in environmental science. He finally corralled her at her trailer office, and they sat in hard chairs and talked over the air conditioner, which flooded the small space with a supercool draft that gave him goosebumps.

She sat across from him, a slip of a woman, tan and muscular, wearing khaki shorts and a green Nature Conservancy T-shirt, her sun-bleached brown hair pulled back into a neat ponytail. He liked her at once—recognized her, in fact, from seeing her at Lord's Manor a couple of times. In another circumstance, they might have been friends—she was a rabid Cubs fan from Wrigley-town and had a biting sense of humor—but in this context he was the enemy. She made that clear up front. No middle ground. "Everybody knows there's no oil out there," she told him flatly, as if it were settled fact.

"Then there's nothing to worry about, is there?" he said.

She smiled slyly and wagged a finger at him. "Oh, there's always something to worry about when Big Oil shows up."

"Come on," he said. "We're not Big Oil. We're a small independent outfit just trying to make a go of it."

"Everything you say is probably true," she said. "I like you. I do. Personally. But there's no room for 'personally.' The environment here—the beach, the maritime forest, the back marsh—that's the whole ball game. All it takes is one mistake. No second chance. It's fragile. A whole complex system, every part vulnerable. You screw that up, it's game over. You know?"

"Which is why we won't," he assured her. "All I'm saying, give us a chance, okay? Let us prove ourselves to you."

"You mean, like, trust but verify?"

"Something like that."

She stood to signal that the meeting was over. "Think I'll verify first."

She had still been smiling, arms folded across her chest, when he left. All in all, he figured the meeting had gone pretty well.

He had finally managed to talk to business owners and council members up and down the island, interviewed the head ranger at Cape Point, and even walked the campground, chatting up the campers. He had read the island newspaper front to back, paid attention to the tenor of things. Nobody was happy to see him. Nobody offered any encouragement. Nobody even seemed curious about whether or not there was in fact oil off the coast.

All of them told him some version of the same line: "Everybody knows there's no oil out there."

But there was oil—that was the thing.

Fannon was updating him daily. The core samples were coming up loaded with shale at ridiculously shallow depths. NorthAm engineers were now cautiously suggesting that this might be the mother lode of all time. You never could be sure, of course—the proof was still in the drilling. But all of a sudden, NorthAm stock was trading high. The company was grabbing air. All of a sudden, there were rumors that two of the majors were about to bid to buy it outright. Investors were banging at the door. They liked the story Nick was telling. When it was all sorted out, he was in line for a hell of a bonus.

So the Founder was wrong. Sometimes there really was buried treasure. And he, of all people, ought to know.

Nick had worked all day on reports for the home office, had written a couple of short human-interest stories about the beauty of the Outer Banks, stressing how invisible the rig was and would remain. He advised corporate to initiate a significant grant for the Nature Conservancy to expand its holdings of wild habitat on the island. Let her verify *that.*

Meanwhile he was putting off the time when he would have to write the rest of it: how it was all about to change. The change would not be for the better, not for the islanders. And it would be irrevocable. It was always so.

The corporate types would dismiss his concern with some glib board-room saying like, "You can't put the toothpaste back in the tube." But this was a way of life they were messing with, not toothpaste.

From the high deck of Lifeboat Station #17, Nick watched the ocean, tried to imagine the orange rig beyond the horizon, pictured Cal Root and Bucky Malagordo grinning under their hard hats with each new core sample, waiting for their big strike. They'd been in the business long enough to see it all, boom and bust, but—if Fannon was right—never anything like this. Not even close.

Then Nick thought again about that creased jackleg. The wind picked up, and now he imagined the rig taking the brunt of a storm, a hurricane, the waves piling up against its metal legs, pounding the joints, the wind screaming through the drilling tower, Bucky Malagordo with his hands full trying to keep the rig intact, Cal Root cursing the company for being so skinflint and putting his ass on the line like that.

He was so engrossed in his vision that when she spoke, he thought the voice was in his own head. The voice said, "It's beautiful when it's this rough."

"You," he said gently as she settled into the deck chair next to his. He was pleased to see her, yet as always she threw him off-balance.

Julia Royal hugged her blue windbreaker around her. A sudden breeze fluttered the collar. "I love to watch the sea get its back up."

"Sure chases the tourists away."

"Yeah, but you're still here." They both smiled. "I still don't know who you are," she said abruptly, looking out to sea. "I thought I did, but now I'm not so sure."

Without realizing it, he was fingering chords on the guitar. "When you find out, let me know."

"You're so flip. It's what I said before."

He heard a plaintiveness in her voice that disarmed him. He let out a long breath. "You're right. I don't mean to be. But you've been so . . . you know."

"Yeah, I know," she said. "Maybe I don't know how else to be." She started to get out of her chair.

"Don't leave," he said, pressing a hand gently on her arm. "Please. Just sit with me awhile."

She hesitated a moment, then sat and leaned back. "You really wanted me to like you."

"You drive me crazy in about sixteen ways." He shook his head and laughed. "You're what my dad would have called 'a tough out.' "

She looked at him quizzically. "A tough out?"

"It's a baseball term, for a guy that can always get on base no matter what you throw at him or how the infield shifts." She still looked puzzled. "You know, a scrapper. Somebody who never gives up. It's a compliment, really."

"Okay, if that's what it is."

"Never mind. Anyhow, sure, I wanted you to like me. I mean, I still do."

"Well, shit. Know what? It worked." She smiled and indicated the guitar. He was still playing soft chords. "You going to sing me?"

"I'm not much of a singer."

"Yeah, and I'm not much of a listener. Except maybe tonight. And you're the only singer I've got."

"Like I said, a tough out." He felt for the chords and played in slow cadence. "The water is wide," he sang, his voice low and resonant, soft in the wind, "and I cannot cross o'er."

The sun was gone now, and there was just the ambient light from inside the inn. The gloom was at once melancholy and calming and carried his voice softly, clearly. "Nor have I wings to fly so high. Give me a boat that can carry two." The guitar was smooth and familiar under his hands, and he felt the music thrum against his body.

When he finished, she said, "That's pretty. 'And we shall row, my love and I.' "

He turned and watched the breeze riffle her short hair, her eyes squinting at him, as if she were sizing him up, making up her mind about something.

"That's a pretty beat-up little guitar," she said. She laid a hand on the scarred, pumpkin-colored spruce top.

"Like me," he said.

"You should take better care of it," she said, holding him with her eyes.

"Well, it's had some hard traveling."

"Yeah, I know all about that." She caressed the top of the old guitar, tracing each scratch with her finger, and through the wood he could feel her hand against his body, or imagined he could.

"It wasn't supposed to turn out this way," she said, still petting the guitar. "I wasn't supposed to like you. You're not supposed to be here. You're not even my type."

"I never thought of you as having a type," he said.

"Well, if I did, it wouldn't be you."

He laughed and shook his head. "Can't say I blame you. I'm kind of a bum. You know, a vagabond, always on the move."

"I'm really mad at you now."

"You've been mad at me for weeks. But you know what?"

"What?" She stopped touching the guitar and leaned back, still looking at him, unblinking.

"I don't think it's me you're mad at."

She leaned forward and kissed him on the mouth.

In a life full of unexpected turns, he had never been so taken by surprise. She clasped his hand firmly in the two of hers, lifted him out of the chair, and led him to his own room. He leaned the guitar against the wall, and she faced him in the dark and kissed him again.

She said, "I wondered what that would feel like."

He felt both thrilled and terrified. "You scare the hell out of me," he whispered. "I just don't know what to make of you."

"Then don't make anything. Just hold me."

"I can do that."

In the night, a fast storm broke over the island and took out the electricity. The rain swept over Lifeboat Station #17, and Nick and Julia lay awake side by side in his room and watched the lightning flash across the windows, heard the thunder roll up the coast and shake the house. He held her close as she wept without even knowing why, and he kissed her tears. Something had come loose inside, and he felt her shuddering sobs in his own chest.

For a long time, all they did was lie together, clinging tightly, each holding the other as closely as a secret. And then after a while, she was done crying and he was kissing not just her eyes and salty cheeks but her mouth.

They made love tentatively at first, as if they were both brittle, fragile, and might break. But then Nick enfolded her from behind and held her. His hand cupped one of her small breasts, and he could feel the throb of her heart. She whispered nonsense words, and he answered with nonsense of his own, but for once they understood each other perfectly.

He held her all through the night.

She lay awake long after midnight, thinking, *Forgive me, Paw Paw. I never meant to betray you.*

At first light, he awoke and felt the feathering of her hair on his chest, heard her low, soft breathing, and cherished her. He fell back asleep holding her tight, but when he woke again she was gone, and he wondered if she had ever been there with him at all.

And someone had slipped a note under his door. He unfolded it and read the name in block letters: *PATCHETT*.

Well, that was one he already knew.

CHAPTER NINE

HATTERAS ISLAND, MAY 1942

1

The onshore breeze carried a discordant note, a spike of sound. Different from the rant of gulls. Not random but full of purpose.

Human voices.

Liam Royal squinted in the direction of the sound and saw the ghost of movement—a dark shape drifting toward shore. He watched as the others drank, passing the jar among themselves. There was only a sliver of moon in the cloudy sky. He wouldn't speak until he was sure of what he was seeing. He had famous eyes.

At first, it was just a blot, heaving on the sea. Foam sparkled around it, luminous under the clouded moon. Then it came clear: a little, fat boat, tossing in the breakers. The inflatable kind, big rubber sausage tubes for a hull.

It lifted on the crest of a wave and slapped down into the shallows, and human figures tumbled out, splashing, and dragged the bloated thing toward the high-tide line. It was a labor, and Liam understood at once by their lack of coordination that the men were not sailors.

He held up a big, flat hand. "Quiet," he said, and the others immediately quit joshing and listened, staring in the direction Liam was staring, straining to make out the shape.

A rubber boat.

Four men standing over it, hands on knees, breathing hard.

All the boys were watching now, prone on the sand like a squad of infantry, guns leveled. The men were not more than twenty yards away, close enough to hurl a baseball at them. For a frozen moment, the boys waited.

Hauling on the rope handles along the tubular gunwales, the four men dragged the boat higher, staggering and grunting under the load. Liam watched them approach, growing larger and taller with each step, like a trick of the eye. *Survivors,* he thought, *floating in out of the sea.* Not bodies this time, but men alive and vigorous with effort. He could hardly believe what he was seeing. He had imagined such a scene for so long that now he wondered if he were hallucinating. He rubbed his eyes and shook his head to clear it from the whiskey.

But the others saw it, too.

The figures stood up tall and became men and stripped off black oilskins. They worked clumsily and took a long time. They flung the oilskins into the sea, where the jackets and bibbed trousers bobbed like shadows. They all stood a moment catching their breath, then gripped the boat again and began moving across the beach, away from the water.

Without a word, Liam gripped his shotgun and crawled among the hammocks on hands and knees, and the others followed. The wind was carrying toward them, so there was no worry about giving themselves away to the intruders. Meantime, the men's voices grew louder and more distinct. One rose above the rest, more strident, in charge.

The boys lay just in earshot, and Liam tried to make out the words in between the smacks of the surf. He could hear the voices clearly, yet they were speaking nonsense. Maybe the whiskey was fuddling him.

Then one of the men stumbled and recovered himself and said, "*Gott im Himmel!*" and it came across clear as a curse: They were speaking German.

Liam cocked his head and kept a leery eye on the men, as if by staring he could comprehend their speech, of which he understood not a word. He could sense his companions around him, motionless, their eyes and guns focused on the men hauling the rubber boat toward them, and he felt a quickening of all his senses, the way he did when hunting ducks on the sound—the thrum of pulse in his ears, the whine of nerves, then a great calming force spreading down his arms into his hands, steadying his legs, as his breathing slowed and the world shrank to the narrow alley of distance between him and his quarry.

He watched through a fluttering curtain of sea oats.

The men were almost on him now, but the sea oats screened him perfectly. In a few more steps, they would overrun him, still bearing the boat. Liam rose out of the dark so quietly that at first they didn't see him, so intent were they on their chore.

"Stand fast!" he ordered. The force of his own sudden voice startled even him.

There was confusion. One of the men stumbled backward and dropped his end of the boat. Another turned and made a step toward the surf line, but Chance was already there, shoving a gun barrel into his face, and the man raised his hands wordlessly in the universal gesture of surrender.

Littlejohn, Patchett, and Tim Dant now materialized with leveled weapons, and they all stood still for a long moment on both sides, as if nobody knew what to do next. The wind was kicking up, snapping Liam's collar and scouring sand into his eyes. By morning, it might come a true mullet blow, some real dirt. The world was changing fast. It was the sky always changed first. The wind blew the clouds clear of the moon, casting the scene in a sudden clarity of hazy light.

"Put down the boat," Liam said over the wind, without any expectation they would understand him. He was about to enforce the order with his fists when the men obediently lowered the raft to the sand and then stood as if at attention—*Maybe they* are *at attention,* Liam thought. *Maybe they're soldiers.*

The man closest to him, a square, muscular man with a blond, brushy mustache, said, "Please, lower your weapons. It's all right, son."

Chance said, "By God, they speak English."

The man with the mustache smiled. "Of course we speak English—

we are Americans." The words were English, but the accent carried a stiff German precision.

Liam wasn't buying it.

2

The man with the mustache grinned. The others shifted nervously, saying nothing, letting him talk for them.

"We are Americans," he said again. "This is the truth."

Liam held the shotgun loose in his big hands. Something was not quite right about the scene. The men were dressed in rough civilian clothes, dungarees and work shirts, like any merchant sailors. One wore steel-rimmed spectacles. Another wore a slouch hat. All except the one were clean-shaven.

The man wearing spectacles unhitched them from his ears and wiped spray off the lenses using a pocket handkerchief. The man in the slouch hat bent to tie his shoelace.

Liam looked at the man's black shoes, how they reflected the moonlight. He looked at the other men.

New shoes. All the men wore new shoes.

3

Liam leveled the shotgun and closed his left hand around the barrel to steady the weapon. The other island men picked up his cue and raised their rifles. Liam said again, with deliberate menace in his tone, "Stand fast!"

The four men beside the boat looked bewildered. The one dropped his glasses onto the sand and did not pick them up. Each in turn looked at the stocky blond man, as if for orders. That one took a confident step forward and held up his hands, palms out. "Please, don't shoot," he said quietly but with a firm authority in his voice, as if he were used to being obeyed by subordinates.

Chance said, "I guess we'll shoot whoever we want," and Patchett laughed nervously, his fingers opening and closing on his weapon.

Liam said, "Kneel down and put your hands behind your heads," and his friends fanned out around the four men. "Check them for weapons," he said to nobody in particular.

Dant and Littlejohn handed their rifles to Patchett and frisked the prisoners a little too roughly and came up with two pistols.

"Loaded for bear," Patchett said, and giggled nervously.

Tim Dant pulled a steel flashlight out of his jacket pocket and studied the contents of their pockets "Look at this," he said, and held up wallets with American driver's licenses, union cards, ration books, a few hundred dollars in small bills.

The boys began rummaging through the boat. Wrapped in oilskin were four leather portmanteaus full of clothes, shaving gear, and papers.

Dant held up one sheaf folded like an accordion and let it fall open. "Map," he pronounced. "Looks like Portsmouth and Newport News."

Littlejohn discovered a railroad timetable and more maps—Chicago, the upper Chesapeake Bay, the Mississippi River Valley. They studied them by flashlight, making out what they could. Some were large-scale local maps, full of detail: buildings, docks, and other structures; railroad tracks, airports, power lines, water mains. Penciled neatly onto the maps at strategic points were the names of factories, training camps, and shipyards, along with other notations—in English, the writing too small to read.

Dant hauled out a heavy suitcase and sprang the catches. "Radio set," he said. "Good old German engineering."

Liam watched the stocky leader. He was handsome—strong jaw, alert blue eyes, short-cropped hair. When the man spoke, Liam heard a haughtiness in his voice, as well as an anger just barely under control. From the man's muscled build, Liam guessed he was a mechanic of some kind, unlike the other three, who seemed softer, indoor men. "I guess they're not seamen."

Tim Dant found another satchel wrapped in oilskin and opened it. "Holy crapola!" he cried out, and suddenly everything got worse.

4

Liam stood before the men kneeling in the sand. The breeze was a wind now, stinging all their faces with sand. The men squinted against it. Liam said, "Just who the hell are you?"

The leader stood and dusted sand off the knees of his stiff dungarees. "This is nonsense," he declared, and the island boys took a step back. "I told you—we are Americans, like you."

"I doubt it," Chance said. "Maybe you're Americans, but you're nothing like us."

Next to him stood Tim Dant, holding the open satchel filled with rubber-banded stacks of hundred-dollar bills. He counted. Fifty stacks, one hundred bills to a stack. Five hundred thousand dollars. The bills flapped in the wind.

Liam said, "Counterfeiting is a crime, whoever you are."

The leader smiled. "I assure you, it is the real McCoy. You don't believe me? Take it." He shooed them with his hands. "Go on. Just take it. Don't ask questions. Just leave us alone."

"Get back on your knees," Liam said, and the man slowly dropped to the sand, glaring at him with unblinking eyes. The clouds had scraped the moon clean, and it shone a cat's-eye light, casting the men's faces in livid shadow.

5

"I'm seeing, but I ain't believing," Tim Dant said, looking back and forth at the men and the money. "Who the hell are they, bank robbers?" All of a sudden, he was shivering, his voice uncertain.

Patchett chimed in, "Saboteurs, by God."

"Saboteurs? Like spies?" Littlejohn said.

"Yeah," Chance said, "except they blow up stuff."

"He's right," Liam said. "The maps, the money, all of it." He glanced over at Chance, who had a tight grip on his .30-06. "Going for the shipyards, maybe, or a tank factory."

"You got their number, all right," Chance said. "Not just killers, but cowards."

Liam nodded. The whole plan unfolded clearly in his mind's eye: Two teams of saboteurs. Dressed in American clothes, with American driver's licenses. Carrying enough cash to buy anything—or anybody—they needed. The damage they could do, over and over again. They would be invisible. The boys had heard of such teams landing up north, in New England. Never here, on home ground.

Littlejohn said, "We ought to turn them in."

Liam nodded. He was feeling sober now, and his mouth was dry. The wind was in his ears.

Tim Dant said, "They've got American IDs."

Patchett said, " 'Course they do."

"You think they're really Americans?" Chance said. "Why should we believe anything these bastards tell us?"

Before Liam could answer, the leader said loudly, "Okay, so you caught us, Mister Big Shot. We have committed no crime. We have done nothing wrong—"

"Shut up!" Liam said. He needed quiet to think. Between the wind and the voices, his head was a boiling rush of sound.

"You won't get another chance like this," the blond man said. "Take it. Go on. You want to, don't you? Don't all of you?" He looked around, and the others stared back, then glanced at Liam. "Take the money, I tell you! Let us be on our way."

"The hell you say," Liam said. He stepped toward the leader, shotgun leveled, hand on the grip, finger where it could reach the twin triggers.

The leader stood up defiantly. "This is foolishness. You don't know who you are dealing with."

"I can sure guess." Liam kept advancing. He couldn't help it. He made no conscious decision to crowd the man, but somehow he could not abide the fact that the man was standing proud and defiant instead of kneeling in the sand like the others.

The leader put his hands out to fend off the gun barrel. He touched the muzzle with his palm, then grabbed it as if trying to push it away.

Liam braced to hang on to the gun. His hand didn't move, but when the man yanked the barrel, both triggers pressed against his finger, and the gun went off. The blast opened the man's chest, and he flew backward, the sudden explosion of light and noise overwhelming the night. Liam staggered a step from the recoil.

There was a long pause in which nobody did or said anything. The concussion and bloom of hot smoke were carried off on the wind. The dead man lay on his back with his arms flung over his head, as if he had been caught in exercise. The other men froze, mouths agape.

The boys stood staring. Liam had no breath. His ears rang from the double concussion, and the sound of breaking waves seemed faraway, muffled. The windy shore was a sudden vacuum, and then all at once his lungs filled again.

The night had been torn in two, *before* and *after*, but the parts had not yet fallen away. In that eternal moment, the world was making up its mind. Liam would recall later that even the wind seemed to still and the thrashing surf to go mute. He would never cease to marvel at that gap in his life, in all their lives, a void of breathless time in which he was no longer alive, and then, all in an instant, he was alive again.

A weird, otherworldly calm settled over him, over all the boys. Nobody shouted or cried out. They simply waited for what would come next. Liam understood he had fallen into the abyss between *then* and *now*. He should do something, say something, make a move, to bring this moment back under control.

But he could not. He had never before known a moment when he could not.

It was the most significant scene of his life, and he was a spectator.

6

The other captive men rose from their knees, broke for the open strand, running, and the island boys instinctively fired after them. Tim Dant shot the one wearing the hat, and the hat flew off his head.

Littlejohn and Patchett together killed the third man, who had gotten farthest away. The man without his spectacles staggered a dozen paces and, for reasons Liam would never understand, stopped and turned. He stared at Liam. He was not even a moving target. When Chance Royal fired, the man's head burst apart above the left ear.

7

Chance had a fierce, triumphant look in his eyes. Liam breathed deliberately, still marveling that he could. He felt a great weight bearing down on his chest, a concrete heaviness in his legs. He didn't say anything for a long moment, and the others stood beside him and waited to be told what to do.

Finally he crooked the shotgun over his shoulder and said hoarsely, "Well, boys, I guess we have a secret to keep."

They hardly had to discuss what to do next: Slash the boat and bury it, along with the four valises and the radio.

Drag the bodies, shoeless, to the water at the turn of the tide, before dawn.

Burn the maps but leave the ration books and IDs.

Let the men float among the crabs for a day or two before the tide fetched them back in and left them in the sun to be found. They would be just more unfortunates, casualties of the U-boat war. There would be no autopsies. They would be buried and forgotten, like so many others.

But the money, that was a different problem.

Brick Littlejohn said the obvious: "Well, we can't give 'er back." He meant, *Not now.*

The rest of them agreed that this was so. What was right or wrong, what was even possible, had changed in the course of a few seconds.

The money ruined the purity of the act. Nobody said so. It was a truth so apparent that it occurred to all of them at once, irrevocable and absolute.

If they kept the money, they could not pretend, even to themselves, that they had acted as patriots. Yet if they turned it in, there would surely be questions, an investigation, a judgment by off-islanders. The men they had killed weren't armed—not when they were shot. They might indeed have been what they claimed to be—loyal Americans on some strange mission for the government. Unlikely, improbable, but what if it were true? The boys had gunned them down in a sudden, unpremeditated, almost accidental frenzy.

Fueled by whiskey—that's what everyone would say, the last damning fact. The white lightning that was meant to celebrate their turning from boys into men.

But even in the moment, Liam understood the other truth of it: If the men had simply remained still, nobody would have fired on them. If they had simply knelt there. Not done anything at all. That would have saved their lives. Action had doomed them. Bursting into flight, they had excited the primal hunter's urge to kill the thing in motion. There had been no intent, no premeditation, just animal reflex.

Yet at the center of the frenzy had been a killing calm. They had all felt that, Liam most of all. He had looked down the barrel of his shotgun and watched the insolent man tug on it and known in the instant just before it happened exactly what was going to happen.

Then the gun fired itself.

That was an excuse, he knew, but it was also true. He had fired by accident, the only time in his life he had ever made such a mistake, yet he had seen it coming, had one fraction of a second when he could have changed the outcome.

But he had simply watched the moment happen. And in so doing, he had made the other killings somehow not just necessary but also inevitable.

And now they had a secret to keep.

They could not touch the money until after the war. None of this needed to be spoken either. The war would be their alibi, the best alibi in the world. By the time the bodies were discovered, they would be gone from the scene, doing their patriotic duty, unconnected from these men, this beach, this night. And in doing their duty, they might redeem themselves, redefine their lives beyond this one wild, unanticipated moment. They would bring back from the war the right to forget this night, these men, this killing. They would bring back the right to start over as honorable men.

No one must ever know where the money came from. It was an impossible windfall in a place like this, where most of their neighbors lived by barter and cash was rare. So they must be careful to hoard their treasure and spend it quietly, a little at a time, until no one remembered they had ever been poor.

This would require patience and loyalty and discipline—and luck.

Liam said, "If any of us doesn't make it back, his share goes to his family, right." It was not a question, and they all agreed solemnly. It would not have occurred to any of them to do otherwise—as it did not occur to them that they might not return.

Meantime, they must find someplace to stash the money. Parvis Patchett would stay behind—no point in pretending any longer—and he would have their trust, their fortune. For now, they loaded it into the trunk of Patchett's restored Packard Runabout.

Tomorrow he would drive them to the recruiting station. But that would be a formality, Liam now knew. They had been mistaken to think they were going off to war. They were already at war. The war had found them and taken them into itself, and they were already long gone from the island.

It was a trick of dark magic: Five boys had gone out into the dunes to get drunk together and simply disappeared.

Who came out of the dunes were killers, already grown old.

CHAPTER TEN

HATTERAS ISLAND, 1991

1

It could not have been the company, could not have been Fannon. He would not have risked being killed in that Land Rover careening down the bridge. And anyway he trusted Fannon.

And the boat, the inverted valve on the bilge pump? It was hard to imagine anybody staying aboard for a ride out into the ocean, knowing it was rigged.

A mechanic had come aboard the night before to work on the fuel filters. The regular mechanic was tied up on the *Lady NorthAm,* and fuel filters, those were basic stuff. So they hired a local man, a guy by the name of Chuck Gandil who came well-recommended, and he was down there twenty minutes or so until the engine was humming like it would run forever. He was an affable guy, a small-boned fellow with blond tousled hair, wearing a baseball cap and a blue jumpsuit.

But who hired him? And why? The name rang some kind of bell in the back of his mind, just out of reach.

And the dark blue pickup truck gunning its engine out by the cemetery, bearing down on Nick out of the rain and missing him only because he still had some of his old third baseman's reflexes? Surely that was meant for him—not Fannon, not anybody else. It was all meant for him. Maybe it had nothing to do with oil.

But why? That's what Nick wanted to know.

Diogenes had told him there were Patchett girls married off all over the island. On an instinct, he called Diogenes Lord and asked him a simple question: "Does the mayor have any grown daughters?"

2

Caroline Dant asked Nick an unsettling question: "Do you own any shares of NorthAm?"

He sat across her kitchen table from her, sipping strong, sweet coffee, just the way he liked it. It was worth the drive just to sit in her kitchen, and for a moment he could almost pretend he hadn't come on darker business. Let them share small talk for a few minutes. "Do I look like the kind of guy who plays the market?"

She shrugged. "I thought maybe, you know, profit sharing."

He sat up straight. "Forgot about that," he said. A few shares a month were added to his portfolio automatically, in lieu of a pension. Fannon always said stock was better than a pension. The world needed oil. The world would keep on needing oil as long as there were automobiles and airplanes and power plants. Yeah, but would it keep on needing NorthAm?

"It always goes up, doesn't it? The stock value."

He sipped and nodded. "So far. Just like beachfront property." And with the Cape Point Reserve, the stock would go through the roof. It occurred to him for the first time that he might get rich. What would that even mean? A life of leisure? Funderburke was rich enough to own an estate at Lake Forest, right on Lake Michigan, but he seemed happiest working twelve-hour days at the office, and Nick suspected he would be miserably bored in retirement.

Caroline Dant laughed. "Until a hurricane."

"Now you've got me worried." He smiled. She was talking figuratively, but he imagined a real hurricane, what would happen. He thought about the rig, so gargantuan and yet so fragile, perched on three spindly legs in that mass of seething water. There was unsettled weather all over the Atlantic, but no hurricanes yet—it was still early. Just small patches of low pressure, disorganized, whirling into compact microsystems, then breaking up over open water. But the fact that fierce weather could be so local gave him pause. An ocean storm could rise quickly, unforecast, out of a clear blue sky and never touch land, never make it onto the six o'clock news.

"Maybe you should be," she said. "There are some things I sure wish I had worried about."

"You don't seem the worrying type," he said.

"Yet I never married," she said wistfully, out of the blue.

He would never have raised the subject—it was far too private. But the line between private and public was getting blurrier all the time. "You don't have to . . ."

She smiled sadly. "It's all right. I had my chances. But I was always solitary, you know? Being alone was precious to me, and I was worried I would lose that, with a man. With someone who was always, you know, *there*."

He simply nodded.

"I was a great reader. I would read anything by anybody, any time of day or night. I carried books to church. Even in school, I was always reading something else besides what the class was supposed to be reading."

"Yeah," Nick said, "I was that way a little bit." But he didn't say the rest—how he knew it was partly a result of loss, of being in a big, empty space by himself and making the best of it, living with his crazy grandmother above a candy store, a world removed from his friends at school, because he'd been somewhere they were not prepared to follow. Where no sane person would follow, given any other choice.

"And I was a headstrong girl, you know? Every time I tried having a boyfriend, he wanted to tell me what to do. 'Go here, do this, wear that. Don't talk to that boy, or that boy. Why can't you wear a dress instead of those old dungarees? Don't you want to look pretty for me?' "

The way she mimicked the callow voices had Nick grinning in spite of himself.

"Oh, Lordy," she said, shaking her head. "I was sure full of vinegar. But them days are long gone."

Nick said, "Oh, don't be too sure."

"Well, it's what I worried about, being stifled. Being kept down by a man. Now, lo and behold, I think I worried about the wrong thing," she said. "A person can be alone too much, and then it stops being so precious." She fixed her eyes on him. "You're good to give me company."

He put down his mug and flattened his palms on the table. There was something fundamentally decent about this woman. She seemed without guile, and yet they were both talking around it. Though he couldn't wait to give her the letter, he sensed it would change everything, and the one thing he didn't want to change was her friendship. It was the last thing he had expected to happen when he rolled down that bridge and dumped the Land Rover in the sand.

He waited until silence settled over them. "I have something for you."

"I know. Diogenes called." She took a long breath and smoothed back her hair along both temples, and he noticed how gray it appeared in this light. She looked older, vulnerable, as if, with the wrong word, she might break. "How long have you known?"

"I don't know much of anything yet," he said softly. "That's why I'm here." He carefully pulled out the envelope from his portfolio and heard her sharp intake of breath.

Caroline Dant froze, her hand half-extended, as if she could not decide whether she wanted to take the letter or not.

"Your father wrote it," he said. He turned it so the addressee was visible in penciled block capitals: *PETER DANT*.

"Oh, my." She dabbed at her eye with a finger. "He mailed it? The stamp. It hasn't even been canceled."

"He gave it to Isaac Lord, the mailboat driver."

"Why would he do that?"

"Maybe . . . I don't know." His voice was uncertain, without good answers. "Maybe he couldn't bear to tell your mother."

"Tell her what?"

He shrugged. "I don't know, like I said. Whatever it was he wrote. To his unborn son. To you."

"And how is it that you came to have it?" It was a soft question, but under the words lay a hint of distrust, the first he had ever sensed from her.

He shook his head. "I'm not entirely sure." He worked to find the right words. "It's the strangest thing—they think I'm some kind of messenger. That's what they said—*messenger.* That I was somehow meant to come here. Old Isaac Abraham, it was his idea. His word. His prediction, I guess." Or maybe the old minister had truly been a prophet, had seen into the actual future that would bring Nick to this island for the reckoning his Oma had waited for all these decades. "There was a mention in the will. It was Rosa, his granddaughter, who found the letter." He paused. "Caroline, please. I don't mean any harm to you. Of all people."

"I know, hon." She turned her back and started straightening up the counter, though it was already neat. "I guess you've read it by now."

"No, no. Mister Lord, Diogenes, requested that I give it to you without reading it."

"He doesn't know I was supposed to be Peter. A boy."

Nick nodded stupidly, since she could not see him. "So maybe I'm the messenger after all." He waited a long moment, heard the evenness of her breath, how she was controlling it, how her back moved with each inhalation, her shoulders slackened with each exhalation.

Without turning, she said, "Would you do me a kindness?"

"Sure, you know I will. Anything you want."

"Read the letter to me."

He took a breath. "I can do that." But really, he wasn't sure. Still, he couldn't deny her. He carefully withdrew the letter and unfolded it. It took him a couple of seconds to steady his hands on the brittle sheets. "My dearest unborn son," he began, careful to keep his voice under control.

It was a long letter and told in detail of five young men on the beach, of drunken celebration and a pact of honor gone awry, of murder and shame and regret. Of an instant of lightning and death, of drunken bravado turned lethal in the worst moment of the worst night in their young lives. Of deception and loyalty to each other and to family. Of money. A lot of money. Money that made their fortunes. Untraceable, genuine United States currency, clean as Monday's shirts. That was Tim Dant's own phrase.

It finished, "The weight of what I done is more than I can bear. Today I am going to sea for the last time. I leave it to you, and all my love."

The weight of what I done. Not even blaming the others, the older boys who had led him out there. And did he mean just that night, that moment of pure murder? Or had the war also left its weight on his conscience, a secret burden he would never reveal?

"So it's true," Caroline Dant said almost too softly to hear. "What Mama always said. He did it a-purpose."

Nick studied her back, square and muscled from manual work. She had been alone for a long time, and her house, the house of her lifetime, was that of a person who put things in their places and knew no one would be coming behind to disarrange them. He himself lived that way. It created a reassuring, yet disappointing, neatness, lacking the telltale signs of any loved one's presence. In that moment, he saw her as the most tragically alone person he had ever known, an arm's length away from his touch but a lifetime distant.

It was a struggle to know what to say next. Anything he said would be both too much and not enough to make this moment bearable. He took a long moment to compose himself. "I don't know why old Isaac never passed it on to you when you were old enough to understand."

"He was a character, that one. He was likely taking his orders directly from the Lord." She chuckled without mirth at her pun. "The other Lord. Or maybe . . . maybe he just saw what happened to my mother," she said. She stilled and stared back at him in the glass face of the cupboard.

Nick said, "You didn't, did you? Spend the money. Any of it. You were the only one."

"No, I didn't," she said, and turned, her flushed cheeks tracked by tears. "I didn't care how untraceable it was. *Clean*, what a word. I always knew it was dirty money. *Blood money*, my mother called it. She would never tell me where it come from. I never knew the particulars, just that it was rotten somehow. All part of my father's . . . evil. The evil that got hold of him. But he was a good man, wasn't he? Tell me you believe he was a good man."

Nick thought for a moment. "I think maybe he was the best man," he said. "The best man of all of them."

She nodded and wiped her face with a tissue. "Thank you for that, even if you don't believe it. It's a kindness."

"I believe it," he said. "You know me well enough for that. And you believe it, too, or you would have spent the money." Her father was better than the money—that was the truth that had defined her actions. Though she knew him only as a photograph and a mother's story, had heard his voice only now in his last, agonized letter, she would keep the damning evidence forever separate from his memory. "Maybe it would have made it easier if you had."

"People always think money makes it easier. Lo and behold, it just gives you more chances to go wrong."

He smiled weakly. "That's a point," he said. It was hard to argue. Without the money, her father might have survived the killing—but really there was no telling. "Anyway, I admire that you didn't."

That was true, as far as it went. But he had done some checking, and she sure could have used the money. Money didn't change people unless they were going to change anyway. Even now, though her name was on the marina, she did not own it. The Founder owned it. He had given up trying to make her accept ownership. She was too stubborn even for him, working for a small salary. It occurred to Nick that, in a technical sense, Julia was her boss, or would be soon enough.

"My mother didn't want it, but she wouldn't get rid of it."

"Maybe she thought that should be up to you."

"Whatever her reasons, she never moved it from where he left it." She pulled down the corpsman's bag from the high cupboard and laid it on the table in front of Nick. "Go on," she said. "Put your eyes on it."

Carefully Nick unbuckled the stiff strap that held the flap, turned it back, and loosened the drawstring that cinched the top of the sack. He extracted ten neat bundles of hundred-dollar bills and stacked them in two rows on the tabletop. They were not crisp but soft with handling. *That would be right,* he thought. The men in charge would have sent the saboteurs ashore with old currency, real dollars that looked like they had gone hand to hand for years. And probably they had, patient Nazi operators collecting the stash one bill at a time over the course of years, none of the serial numbers sequential, none of the bills connected to any bank's list of stolen cash or even to each other. It was a brilliant plan, in its way. New bills would have attracted suspicion as soon as the men tried to spend them. Nick had no doubt that the money was utterly untraceable.

Clean as Monday's shirts.

She explained the truth to Nick now, carefully, as if she were briefing him on the terms of a warranty or a will. "It paid for everything, you see. With Chance Royal gone, Liam kept a double share. The family did. And lo and behold, it's the foundation of everything they have. Which at this juncture is millions. And maybe more millions. You wouldn't know it to look at Liam, that old beach rat in his stained pants and his raggedy shirts, but he's worth a fortune. You got to be awful rich to dress that badly and still get into the places he gets into. He's got real estate and businesses and investments, who knows what. All of it come from that one night, everything they have. Maybe everything we all have."

Nick thought, *Mooncussers and wreckers—the dark of the island.* He nodded toward the stacks of old bills, hefted one and then returned it. "Maybe not everything. Were you ever tempted, you know . . . ?"

"To cash in?" She pulled a dishtowel off the bar and rubbed her hands in it, then carefully laid it back across the bar in a trifold. "Wasn't any morality tale, hon," she said. "What I have is my own, and I left no hurt behind me. But I'm nothing better than them."

"Don't sell yourself short."

She said, "Bless your heart."

"I mean it."

"Me, too," she said, and he understood she had somehow changed the subject. "I've been waiting for you," she said. "I didn't even know it, but I was." She exhaled a long breath. "Old Isaac Abraham knew what he was talking about, I guess. How about that? A messenger, for blessed sake." She swept a hand across the top of the bag. "Go ahead and take it."

"What?"

"You heard me. That's why Isaac Abraham waited on the letter, so you could do this. Get it out of this house once and for all."

He couldn't believe what he was hearing. "What am I supposed to . . . ? What do you want me to do with it?"

"That's between you and your conscience, hon. But I guess it was stolen from your grandfather."

Nick shook his head. "It wasn't his."

"Well, he was the last one had it. It wasn't anybody else's. I'm done talking about this, hon. Go on. Take it. You'll be doing me a kindness."

Nick slipped the money back into the corpsman's pack and tucked it under his arm, feeling all one hundred thousand dollars of its weight.

"And hon? It was that Lord girl found the letter?"

"Rosa. Yes."

"Tell her for me that I'd love to see her. It was a hard gift, but it was still a gift."

Nick nodded, set down the letter on the side table.

3

Two hours later, Fannon stopped him as he came aboard the *Rascal,* straddled the gangplank with arms akimbo. "The fuck you think you're going, mate?"

"Out to the rig. With you."

Fannon shook his head and didn't budge from his stance. "Not a good idea. Not today."

Nick smiled tightly. "What do you care? Anyhow, I'm not asking. Corporate called and wants a site report."

"Bucky can do that. I can do that."

"Well, corporate wants me to do it. And they still sign my paycheck." Unlikely as it seemed even to Nick, it was true. The message had been waiting for him back at the inn. Usually all communication to him came through Fannon, his supervisor, so it could only mean there was divided counsel back in Chicago. Somebody didn't trust somebody. Maybe it was the core samples coming back so quickly—too quickly? Something about this project had seemed off since the beginning, and now Nick was square in the middle of the equation.

"It wasn't corporate. It was Funderburke. That nosy little fucker. That's who signed your message. Come on, tell the fucking truth."

Nick felt a sense of panic, of something slipping away. "What if he did?"

Fannon relented, and Nick pushed past him into the main cabin, catching a strong, sour breath of bourbon. Fannon never drank during working hours, not unless he was at a three-martini lunch with a cab waiting to ferry him home. Never in the field.

The engines were already fired up, and after a couple of engineers and a relief crew swung aboard, the captain pushed her out of the inlet toward the open water. At the bar, the seas turned to a heavy chop, and Nick held on to steady himself against the rough motion of the boat.

4

Fannon paced the confined cabin, stumbling a little with the roll of the boat. Something was wrong, his manner all agitation and hostility. Fannon stepped out onto the fantail, and Nick followed him.

"Pretty early for getting boiled," Nick said. "What the hell's up?"

Fannon held on to a pipe rail, gripping it hard and swaying, unsteady on his feet. The boat heaved through the building seas, and off the stern the wake frothed in an arrow-straight furrow, as if they were plowing the ocean. Fannon leaned across the rail and vomited over the side, wiped his mouth with a handkerchief, and took several deep breaths.

Fannon stood staring out at the eastern horizon, so Nick said, "Never been on a job before where so many things went wrong. So many dangerous things."

"Aw, shite, man." Fannon shook his head and laughed without mirth. "You really are clueless."

"Then clue me in. I've been all over the island. There is no local organization protesting the drilling. The signs all came from the same printer in Norfolk. Paid for with Royal money. Just showed up one day, and people put them up. But it's not an organization, just a few pissed-off people."

"Well, maybe a few pissed off people are enough."

Nick grabbed him on the shoulder so that Fannon turned around. "Seems like you're pissed at me. What the hell did I do to you?"

Fannon faced him square. "The Land Rover, the goddamn boat—they weren't anything to do with the rig, mate. That's what the hell you did. I don't know what they were, but I think you've got enemies. I think it's bloody personal." He stared at Nick with narrowed eyes, mouth twisted in a meanness Nick had never seen in him before. "I could have been killed, yeah?"

Nick held on to the rail against the movement of the boat. The farther out they went, the rougher the water got. Now the gray sea was flecked with whitecaps.

"There's more to it than that, isn't there?" If corporate wanted him to report directly to Chicago, then confidence was breaking down. Something was wrong, more than just somebody with a grudge against Nick.

"All those fucking shenanigans you inspired got Funderburke's attention, yeah? Set off warning lights and bells and called out the fucking fire brigade."

"Funderburke? He's retired, sitting on a beach—"

"Well, he's back in the game, sport. Seems he got bored and flew back to Chicago. Something started scratching at his brain. Started going over the project with a fine-tooth comb. Wasn't taking anybody's word for anything. I tell him the sun came up in the morning, he wants it confirmed. Meddling fucker."

Nick's stomach went queer. "How bad is it?" He had to restrain himself from grabbing Fannon by the collar. "Fannon? How fucking bad is it?"

Fannon said airily, "Oh, I dunno. The company's fucking broke, if that's what you mean. The cupboard is bare."

"Insolvent?"

"Circling the drain for months now."

Nick felt the air go out of him. "Even before we got here?"

Fannon laughed. "Jesus, you just don't listen. What the fuck you think we're doing here? It's the fucking reason we're here!"

"One last gusher? There's no time. It'll take months—"

"Nobody expects a gusher, mate," Fannon said, almost sober-sounding. "Nobody expects fuck-all. There isn't any buried treasure."

"Then what the hell?"

Fannon said, "Everything was going fine. Everything was bloody sailing along according to plan. But all it takes is one guy, one bloody spoiler, to open his mouth." He pounded the rail with a fist. "And he was supposed to be out of the picture, retired, off in Cabo drinking Mai Tais. For fuck's sake."

Funderburke. Who trusted only Nick on site. It was all starting to sink in.

Fannon glanced into the cabin, where the engineers and roughnecks were settled into the ride, paying no attention to them. "Just getting the exploratory well on line jumped our stock five points. The core samples? Now it's through the roof. You have any idea what a new strike would mean? And if it's right here, no shipping it halfway round the bloody world."

First, figure out what you already know. Second, use what you know to figure out what you don't know. "So you're just pumping up the stock. There's no oil out there."

"Sure, there is." Fannon laughed. "Just read the geologists' reports."

Nick shook his head. His ears were ringing. "I can't believe this. The whole thing is bogus? Jesus, how could you—?"

"We can't afford the fucking rig. We can't afford the fucking payroll. Insurance, helicopters, boats. Christ, the operational side alone costs eighty thousand a day."

Nick sagged against the rail and propped himself up with his arms. He had given the company his loyalty. He had given it the data, the words, to win the trust of other people. "So the whole thing's a fraud?"

Fannon said, "Don't look like such a wounded puppy. We're just staging the company for sale."

"Staging? That's what you call it?"

"Split any hairs you like. The company is a shell. Why do you think we leased that piece-of-shite drilling platform? The company's been selling off assets left and right. Your profit-sharing is just a big fat IOU now, mate—or was. Now it's riding the crest." He took a breath. "We take care of our own. You'll get yours on the back end."

"I don't want to get mine on the back end. Jesus!"

"Suit yourself."

"Is it the whole shooting match? Or just this one hole?"

Fannon let out a long, exasperated sigh. "Does it matter? Even on the holes that are producing, we're losing our shirt. The cash reserves are gone! After that spill in the Andaman Sea, the stock was going into free fall."

"No, that was cleaned up. I saw it for myself." He had written the press release himself—ditto the story for the annual report.

"Well, you saw wrong. The cap just cracked again, and it's leaking. Only a matter of time before it shows up on the evening news."

"Who's the buyer?"

Fannon shrugged. "Does it matter? One of the majors. I'm not at liberty to say."

"They'll perform due diligence."

"Yeah, well. That's been taken care of, hasn't it? I mean, they got the core samples, don't they? And you can believe they're the real thing." He smiled. "You should know, mate—you helped me carry 'em down here."

The metal case, the so-called calibration equipment. Core samples of good wells swapped out from La Grange. So the fix was in before the rig was even sited. "You son of a bitch—you got me to help you."

"Yeah, you're in the shite, along with the rest of us." Fannon looked suddenly tired and pale, all used up, like he had been holding everything together for too long and now it was unraveling. "Anyway, they'll recapitalize the company. It's the only thing that makes sense."

"You think you're going to get away with it?"

"Why not? All the people who know anything can't talk. And whoever buys it won't want to talk either, or they'll look like idiots. Their stock will tumble right along with ours. It's all about confidence, mate. They lose the confidence of their shareholders, they're bloody well fucked, too."

Nick cursed. "That's why you wanted me with you in the field. To put my name on your fraud."

"To protect you, more like."

"If you say so."

"What are you going to tell Funderburke? He'll believe whatever you tell him."

"Don't put that on me! Maybe I won't even write a damned report! You're not dragging me into this any deeper."

Fannon was suddenly right up close. "You're already in up to your neck. Don't forget your own shares. You'll be as broke as the rest of us."

Nick was so angry he could hardly speak. Tears backed up behind his eyes, and his throat felt hot and thick. "There never was any choice, was there? You knew I couldn't resist coming down here."

"Yeah, well, that's always the best way, ain't it? The mark has to want to be conned."

"You bastard. I trusted you."

"Yeah, and I took care of you, didn't I? Now fuck off."

Before Nick could say anything else, Fannon leaned over the rail again and heaved.

5

Julia took the call an hour after Nick left for the rig. She was making up beds on the top floor and had to race down the stairs to the kitchen. She listened, out of breath. Nick's grandmother was failing. She had suffered a heart attack in the night and was not expected to live out the day. Nick ought to fly back at once.

She called the Coast Guard and asked the young petty officer who answered the phone to radio the rig and pass on the message.

She wished she could be there and hold his hand, tell him gently, but she knew in her heart there was no gentle way to tell such heartbreaking news. There was the moment before knowing, and then there was the eternity afterward, living with what you knew.

6

It started as blots on the radar, scattered storm cells that showed up as bright green patches scudding toward them out of the northeast. Fast, violent, and local. Cal Root and Bucky Malagordo tracked them from the control room of the rig, and before long they didn't need a radar screen. The cells had come together in a purple wall, foaming white at its base, a silver sheen of rain breaking out all across the front like a solid sheet of aluminum. The purple mass was spider-webbed by lightning.

"Jesus Christ!" Bucky Malagordo said, staring transfixed.

Cal Root said, "Oh, he's coming, all right."

7

Fannon had gone inside to slump on the gang bench. Nick remained on the fantail, gripping the rail tight as the boat porpoised through the confused seas. Spindrift slapped him in the face and wet his collar, running down his yellow oilskin jacket in chill rivulets, but he couldn't bring himself to go inside and face Fannon again. For the first time in years, he felt nauseous on a boat. He choked down the bile seeping up the back of his throat.

Everything was falling apart.

A feeling of dread settled on him, like the world was suddenly tilting out of balance and all the things he had counted on were now in random motion, and when it was over the pieces would settle into some new equilibrium, a different world, a harder place for him to be.

The wind was in his face now, and the ocean and sky seemed to merge into one swirling, watery mass. Then he saw it, big and blurry, darker than the weather around it. He thought at first it was land, a mountain rising out of the sea, but that was impossible. No land was in that direction until Bermuda, six hundred miles away. And it was drawing closer. Now he saw the orange rig, a haze of flickering lights, the spindle-legged tower dwarfed by the purple-black storm looming behind it.

Inside the cabin, men were stirring, leaning at the ports, watching the thing. A nor'easter, but worse, a localized vortex of wind and waves plowing toward the rig. A microsystem fueled by heated water and low pressure, pinwheeling through the atmosphere, scouring the sea beneath it.

They watched it come from more than a mile away now, the purple-black wall rising higher, pushing a black wave of water before it, a solid sheet of rain and hail pulverizing the water into froth. Nick lurched inside and stood beside the captain and Fannon.

"Face her into it!" Fannon ordered, suddenly sober, but the captain knew his job and was already aiming the bow straight into the howling wind. The sound changed at once, the dull roar turning to a keening screech, the wind shuddering the hull of the boat as the air pressure suddenly dropped and the cabin bulkheads popped and cracked.

"Backing down the engines!" the captain warned, and eased the throttles back by half so the motion of the boat settled down. He shouted, "We can't approach the rig in this! We'll ride it out and then go in later." Then he said to his crew, "Button her up, boys, it's going to get rough."

Without a word, two deckhands made their way aft and dogged the main companionway to the fantail, dogged the overhead hatches, and checked all the ports in the cuddy cabin at the bow. They remained standing beside the helm station, crowded now, men hanging on to overhead rails and handholds built into the console.

The little wipers flicked back and forth, barely clearing the windshield before a fresh burst of salt water flung itself across the Plexiglas. Nick's view of the rig was strangely strobed—an image, a smear of water, a sharp image again, like a succession of motor-driven snapshots. The rig loomed larger and larger, upright orange legs vivid against the dark of the storm.

With all the violent motion of the boat, it was impossible to tell, but Nick swore the rig was swaying.

Fannon said, over the roar of the wind and the slamming rhythm of the waves, "She's going to take a hell of a hit."

The captain said, "What the hell do you think *we're* gonna get?"

Nick saw details of the rig in flashing frames. The tiny figures in yellow jumpsuits scrambling along the catwalks. The drill tower, massive up close but from this distance strangely delicate-looking. The two lifecars, orange lozenges clinging to the side of the rig.

"Jesus, look at that!" one of the young engineers said, voice high-pitched. He pointed, but Nick already saw it: The rig had indeed swayed. All those millions of pounds of seawater, all that heavy wind, slamming into it, the advancing wall of storm just beyond it now, coming on fast.

The rig leaned. Slowly, so slowly, the back leg was uprooted, as if some giant hand were reaching up from the sea and lifting it.

Two things happened next, in such quick succession that to Nick they seemed simultaneous. The sky lit up as from a single vast explosion, blue and orange pulses of lightning veining out from the center so that the heart of the storm glowed for a long second. Then a shock of electricity arced into the rig and something on deck went off like a bomb, shooting a fireball into the sky and dousing the upper decks in flame.

In the glow of the flames and the cascade of lightning, Nick saw men scrambling into the lifecars. First one, then the second lifecar rocketed down the rails and crashed into the waves and disappeared.

"D'you see them?" yelled the captain. "Did they come up?"

Fannon said, "Can't see shite. Goddamn fuel cells are supposed to be grounded."

"Fourth of fuckin' July," the captain agreed grimly, and held on to the wheel hard.

Fannon grabbed the VHF mic and keyed it. "Mayday, Mayday, Mayday," he said, suddenly sober, then repeated it, and in a strange monotone gave their position. But no one answered, and Nick had no idea if anyone had heard.

Nick stood silent, hands holding on so hard he could feel his fingers cramping, but he couldn't let go. The other men shut up and watched, too. It was not a thing they could turn away from—such awesome, magisterial catastrophe.

The purple-black wall reached the rig now, and it leaned harder, still burning even with water sluicing across the decks and streaking off in waves of spindrift. Then the sea reared up black behind the rig, higher than the main platform, held there for an infinite second, frothing lip curling, enveloping the orange rig in its black shadow.

Then, ever so slowly, the great wave broke.

It seemed to take a long time to happen. The near leg, already damaged, twisted and bent and finally buckled, and the whole rig leaned at a crazy angle, hung there burning, water bursting windows and toppling gear. Then, almost gracefully, the rig toppled in a long, graceful fall, fires hissing out to black smoke, two orange legs poking into the air.

Then it was gone, as if it had never been there.

There was no sign of the two orange lifecars, and no time to look for them. The storm broke over the *Rascal* now. Her bow rose and plunged, and the men hung on. Then the great wave loomed above them.

For a fleeting second, Nick thought the boat would rise again on the wave, bob to the top, and ride down its back. But the wave broke on the cabin roof and held the boat underwater like a great hand. The light at the ports went all watery and dim, and the men yelled and cursed, but the rushing of the water was the only sound Nick heard. He was aware of the boat rolling to his left, then of being upside down, then of being back on his feet. His arms hurt, and something banged against his head, but he held on.

He felt men push past him in the darkness, felt wetness on his face, all at once felt the weight of water around his legs, filling his boots. He shucked them off and held on as the world went on roaring, caught in the maelstrom. It was both completely unreal and the most vivid moment he had ever experienced. He could not imagine its ever coming to an end.

He held his breath as long as he could. Then, with his head going light, he gulped a breath. Strangely, he breathed in air, not water. The boat was upright, the cabin filled to his waist, water flooding in through broken ports and an overhead hatch that had been ripped clean off.

He steadied himself, still not daring to let go. He tasted salt from a bloody wound on his forehead. The cabin was lit by an eerie dim blue haze. The roar of the storm was now receding off the stern. He looked that way. The companionway door was gone, the metal railings of the fantail twisted and broken. Inside the cabin, the engineers and roughnecks were gone. The captain floated, bloodied, against the aft bulkhead.

As carefully as he could, Nick made his way back to him and laid two fingers against his neck to find a pulse. But there was none. The man's head was stove in, and he must have died instantly.

There was no sign of Fannon. As far as Nick could tell, he was alone.

CHAPTER ELEVEN

HATTERAS ISLAND, 1991

1

Liam knew he must go out.

It was almost a relief, such certainty. He had been listening to his VHF scanner. The Coast Guard had been on the air all morning, answering distress calls. All the rescue helicopters from Elizabeth City were committed up and down the coast, far from here. The Hatteras station boat had been struck by a fishing trawler and was itself in distress. And now there was a Mayday from that oil-company workboat.

He looked out toward the beach, where the combers were rolling in hard in big, fast sets. Every seventh or eighth wave in the train was a goddamn whale. *Niver mind.*

He shoved open the big double sea-facing doors, pushing hard against the wind, then strode to the other end of his boathouse and opened the land-facing doors. He pulled the Jeep in that way, hitched it to the trailer, and pushed the boat and trailer out onto the sand. The sky was brimming with dark clouds, and before long a patter of rain pocked the sand. He hurried back and closed all the doors, then moved in a stiff, fast walk toward the inn, calling her name.

But she was already coming toward him, dressed in yellow foul-weather gear.

"You can't go out alone, not in this!"

"Niver mind, girl. I got my boys."

Through the curtain of rain, she made out three figures marching up the beach in black oilskins. When they got closer, she recognized the faces under the identical sou'westers: Poe Patchett in the lead, followed by Hank Littlejohn. Little Jimmy Littlejohn, his black reefer puffed out tight by his enormous belly, trundled along in the rear.

Poe Patchett said, "You might want to think twice about this, Liam."

Liam glared at him. "And just what are you supposed to be, the soul of caution?"

Patchett flung his arms out like a marionette. "All I'm saying, this ain't the old days, and you ain't your old man."

"Now we got that settled," Liam said.

Little Jimmy slapped Patchett hard on the shoulder. "The sea's getting her back up, boys. Let's get her done."

Julia was already in the Jeep, and once the men were aboard she shoved the boat toward the breakers. She waited for the signal, and when Liam gave it she gunned the motor. The boat shot into the waves and kept going, clear of the trailer, cresting the train of combers, hanging on that last great wave in the train, then teetering across to the other side. The Founder held the wheel, the tails of his reefer flapping like black wings, the other men hunkered down and holding fast for life, the boat looking small now in the great sea, flying toward the heart of the storm.

2

The *Rascal* floated dead in the water, sinking.

The storm had blown past, leaving behind a weird jaundiced light and a restless sea. Compared to the roaring din of only an hour ago, the world was blessedly quiet. Water slapped the hull. Objects adrift inside it bumped against bulkheads. But there was no engine noise, no sound of pumps laboring to keep out the sea. Nick knew the boat had watertight bulkheads forward and aft, but how much air they had trapped in the roll-over and how long the vessel could float before the weight of water simply pushed her down into the sea, he had no idea.

He tried the radio, though he knew the batteries were probably underwater, shorted out. Had they been submerged when Fannon made the first call? He could swear he heard the ghost of a response to Fannon's Mayday, the crackle of an open mic, but he had heard no voice, and there was no reason to suppose anyone would come looking for him.

Somewhere out on the ocean were bodies, men he had worked with. He did not imagine any of them could have survived that thrashing monster of a wave. And what of the two lifecars and their seventy-odd men?

3

Of all the people I don't want to save, Liam told himself.

He fought the waves and the wind, stung by rain and feeling fatigue already, his age overtaking his will. He should be on site in half an hour, maybe a little longer. He was pushing the boat hard. That's what it was for. The NorthAm boat should be near the rig, and he had the Loran coordinates for that. Little Jimmy had been out there fishing for kings and noted the location on his chart.

Little Jimmy looked up from the Loran screen and pointed ahead. "You see that? Don't that make your asshole pucker?"

Ahead, the towering purple-black thunderhead floated toward them, laced with blue and orange lightning. Before it were intermittent sheets of rain, the edges of the front ragged, clouds beginning to fragment and trail off like smoke.

"Take a damned fool not to be afraid of that," Liam said.

Little Jimmy grinned. "Oh, you're a damned fool, all right."

Patchett said, "Remind me again what we're doing out here."

"Shut your pie hole, Poe. We're out here because we're out here."

Little Jimmy said, over the din of the motor, "She looks to be breaking up a bit."

"That's good," Liam said. "Better her than us."

4

Liam raced the boat toward the gathering black wave at an acute angle, and the bow rose while the engine labored. He shoved the throttle all out, staring at the looming wave. "Don't break, you bastard—don't break!" he said over and over out loud to himself.

The other men held on as the air was sucked out of the sky and a sudden chill wind slapped them hard. The atmosphere was suddenly full of water—spindrift pelting them in horizontal sheets mixed with rain and then hail that rattled the deck like pea stone. The windshield spider-webbed with cracks, and the men hunched against the onslaught like soldiers under fire, hiding their faces in the stiff black collars of their oilskins.

All but Liam. He held his head up to see, his vision a blear of gray. He swiped water out of his eyes and felt the boat under him working, climbing across the face of the wave. As long as the wave did not break, they had a chance. The motor had muscle, and the boat was built for this, for battering by a wild sea in pursuit of rescue.

The black wave did not break. It lifted them up and up until Liam felt like he was riding the sky, airborne—and then the boat slid down the back of the wave, slewing to starboard at the bottom of the trough. The wave train behind it was big and surging, but nothing compared to the one they had just crossed.

Liam laughed and howled into the wind. In a few minutes, the Loran told him they were on site. There should be a rig, orange lifecars, the *NorthAm Rascal.* He scanned the horizon, watched the turbulent, thrashing seas, all in wild motion.

He saw exactly nothing.

5

She waited on shore, as she supposed women had waited for centuries for their men to come back from the sea. As her great-grandmother had waited for Liam's father.

She put on a slicker and half-ran the steps down to the boathouse, now empty of the big craft that had taken up most of the space inside. She stopped next to the scanner and caught her breath, realized she was shaking. The boathouse seemed empty of purpose, like a firehouse after all the pumpers and ladder trucks have sped out toward the fire.

The Coast Guard was still trying to raise the *Rascal*, but there was no response. The operator sounded young, some twenty-year-old petty officer with a high voice that spoke in an off-island accent, the flat vowels of the Midwest in his voice. He tried to raise the rig. No response. There was radio traffic among other Coast Guard craft far out at sea—helicopters locating a turtled sailboat, a cutter picking up survivors from a foundering trawler.

She listened to the rain ticking on the roof. The worst of the storm had broken north, and the island was receiving only a kind of sideswipe. Out the ocean-facing window, she could see the waves lying down under the rain, the Jeep and trailer abandoned on the beach.

They had all gone off and left her, when she was the one who wanted to leave. *Don't cry*, she told herself. *Don't you dare cry*. And waited.

6

It was Poe Patchett who spied the *Rascal* lying low in the water, waves lapping across her aft rails. She had not long to live. The boat listed to port, settling by the stern, the heavy diesel engine now just a great anchor that would carry her to the bottom.

"Goddamn me, that's them," Poe Patchett said, sounding none too happy about it.

"Ready with boat hooks," Liam said, "starboard side," but he didn't need to say anything. The Littlejohn brothers, Hank and Little Jimmy, were already in motion, each wielding a boat hook, quietly making their way to the rail.

"Nobody aboard," Poe Patchett said, raising a hand in salute against the sudden glare of sunshine, a shaft of buttery light piercing the gloom.

Liam said, "Don't be too soon, Poe."

He eased the boat toward the *Rascal*, but all at once there came a sudden crack sharp as a gunshot, and a tearing sound. The *Rascal* tipped up and made a half-turn, then slid under the waves. A body floated free, and Liam ignored it, maneuvering his boat clear of the suction of the larger wreck. The boat slid toward the slick where the *Rascal* had been, pulled into the swirling water, and for a long moment Liam felt the boat stand on end, bow down, into the strange sink, and then just as suddenly she leaned back, fell hard on her keel, and the vortex was gone, the surface flat and oily.

Meanwhile the body popped to the surface, and Little Jimmy snagged it with the boat hook and hauled it toward them. He and his brother lifted it by main strength into the boat.

Poe Patchett regarded the man, the logo on his shirt, shook his head. "Company man," he pronounced. "Didn't do him no favors."

"That's all?" Hank Littlejohn said. "Just one? Where the hell is the rig?"

Little Jimmy grabbed his shoulder and pointed. "Over there! In the water!"

Just astern was a man struggling, afloat but just barely, head sticking up, arms thrashing. Before anybody could say more, Poe Patchett was over the rail and stroking to his side.

Little Jimmy turned to Liam. "Didn't even know he could swim."

Liam said, "He can't. Steady, now." He turned the boat and eased it toward the man in the water. Poe Patchett had the survivor under his arm and was holding his head out of the drink. The man looked unconscious or dead. The Littlejohns hauled him aboard and laid him out like a gaffed mackerel.

Poe Patchett crabbed over the gunwale and was back in the boat on his own steam. "Let me," he said, and began chest compressions.

He pushed hard on the man's sternum a dozen, fifteen times, and all at once a small geyser of water and bile erupted from the man's mouth. He coughed and convulsed, and they turned him on his side and held him till he quieted and opened his eyes.

Poe Patchett cursed. "Jesus Christ, ain't it always the way?"

Nick Wolf stared up at four shapeless figures in black coats and hats. The world under him heaved, and overhead banks of heavy, dark clouds scudded by.

Liam said, "What? You want to throw him back?"

The Littlejohns laughed.

Liam patted the steering console. "Goddamn good boat, I've always said so."

7

The Coast Guard located the two orange lifecars hours later, toward dusk. Seventy-three souls were accounted for—all the men on the roster when the storm hit. The other men from the *Rascal* were picked up—most of them injured but all of them alive—by Liam's boat and a Coast Guard boat that arrived on the scene not long after. Fannon's body was not found, and there was no confidence that it ever would be.

Nick drifted in and out of woozy consciousness and woke up finally under the glare of lights in the emergency room. He was wrapped tight in blankets, and a pair of gloved hands was sewing up the long gash in his forehead.

"That ought to keep your brains from leaking out," the doctor said, and Nick recognized the voice at once: Diogenes Lord. Dr. Lord said, "Relax, boy. This is my day job. The newspaper, that's just an investment."

Nick lay awake a long time, feeling weightless, wrestling with everything he knew and what to do about it, what he owed and to whom, and in his half-dream the world was full of gold flakes settling around him into stillness. Julia sat with him a long time. She told him the news about his Oma as gently as she could, but really there was no gentle way. The old woman had never recovered from her heart attack and passed quietly a few hours later.

He felt anger and embarrassment that he had let himself be played. Confusion about Julia, mingled with a fierce and surprising love. Hate and outrage and pain and a great weight of fatigue. And a crushing sense of loss and grief.

He watched the gold flakes swirl and settle, and as the hours passed in a gauzy reverie he struggled and dreamed and woke to more struggle, until after a long time exhaustion overcame him and he let it all go, felt light and whole and at peace.

And then he slept, through that night and the next.

8

Three days later, when he had recovered sufficiently to face him, Nick showed up at Poe Patchett's house. It was a grand gated villa, more than a house, with an interior courtyard, a pool, wraparound decks, and everywhere evidence of expensive bad taste. He mentally contrasted it with the boathouse where the Founder lived.

He recalled what Diogenes Lord had said: *It weren't natural, the way that man succeeded.*

"Wasn't expecting company," Poe Patchett called from a high deck. It was only ten in the morning, but he held a frosty cocktail in his good hand. "I know why you're here. You don't have to thank me."

The rescue, Nick thought. "That's not why I came. I came to ask you something. You coming down, or am I coming up?"

Poe Patchett waved broadly. "Come ahead, youngster."

Nick climbed two long sets of stone stairs and reached the third-floor balcony.

Poe Patchett, skinny and loose, tumbled into a wooden deck chair and slurped his drink. He wore a flowered orange shirt, open for three buttons, and sun-bleached khaki shorts stained with red and green paint. "That's quite a bandage on your head. Get you some refreshment?"

Nick stood facing him, felt the stiff breeze carrying ashore. "I want to know why."

"Why I saved you? Couldn't very well leave you out there."

Nick shook his head. "Why you tried three times to kill me."

Poe Patchett leaned back in his chair and took a long sip. "Three? I heard it was only twice. Mechanical failure both times. You got to know how to handle machines or they'll get away from you." He held up his mangled hand and waggled it.

"No, I'm pretty sure it was three."

"You've got a bad case of paranoia, my friend."

"And I'm pretty sure it was you."

A glint of something hard came into Patchett's eyes. "Pretty sure ain't proof. Pretty sure is bullshit."

"Pretty sure is enough to get a judge interested, and maybe he'll want somebody to look into it."

Patchett set his drink on the table a little too hard, and it sloshed onto his mangled hand. He licked the stubs of his fingers. "I already answered your question. I take care of my people. Just like my daddy before me." He glanced up at a bedroom window. Nick followed his glance and saw the curtains move slightly, as if someone were watching. "He always looked after those boys. Always did, always will."

Nick said, "I don't care about any of that. I came to ask a favor."

"Now you want a favor? From me? After you just threatened—"

"Nothing. I plan to do nothing." He opened his empty hands and dropped them to his sides. "But in return, I want a favor, Mister Mayor."

"If I'm not mistaken, I already done you a pretty big favor."

"Something else."

"Spell it out, son. I can't read your mind."

Nick did. Poe Patchett listened.

"That's all you want?"

They shook hands on it, and that was that.

As he started down the stairs, Nick heard Poe Patchett call after him, "How did you know?"

"Charles Gandil," Nick said. "I thought about that. Charles Gandil? Chuck Gandil? Then it came to me. You ever heard of Charles 'Chick' Gandil?"

“Can’t say I have.”

“Chick Gandil played first base for the 1919 Black Sox. Your grandson-in-law is an old neighborhood boy from the South Side of Chicago who used to have his own garage.”

“That’s a good one, boy.” Patchett laughed. “I’ll tell you another good one: It really was only two times.” He held up fingers. “Only *two*.”

CHAPTER TWELVE

HATTERAS ISLAND, 1991

1

Liam walked along the surf line, his legs heavy.

The sea was lying down again, and the air held the sense of something dying quietly. He was engulfed by an unutterable sadness as palpable as the pain in his back, a sadness that seemed to inhabit his bloodstream and be pooling behind his eyes. And he had no one to speak it to.

His whole life had been decided in one renegade moment all those years ago, before he even had a chance to be the man he would become. Or maybe it was exactly what had made him the man he was, and he never got to be that other man, the one he was meant to be, the son of a heroic father who had never wavered in his convictions or his actions. A father who would not understand a son who had been tested and failed in his secret character.

Instead Liam had become a kind of walking ghost, a man haunted and hiding, unable to inhabit his own life except in furtive moments alone in the deepest well of his heart. In those moments, he conjured himself as he believed himself to be, a good man capable of heroic action, a man bigger than his faults.

The rest of the time, he was merely impersonating himself, or an idea of himself that his family and friends could embrace. He was alone now, in truth had always been alone ever since that night. He had stepped through a doorway where no one could follow. He was rich now, a man who owned hundreds of acres of prime real estate and sold them at a high profit for vacation homes, places where people didn't actually live but pretended to live for a little while. He made more money contracting with Patchett to build the homes. Hundreds of men and women worked for him. His investments made money for him even when he wasn't paying attention, let alone working. But he had no use for the money anymore, if he ever had. Even the foundation couldn't give it away fast enough.

Out here on the beach, he was just a barefoot old man wearing rolled-up ragged trousers with empty pockets.

Chance had died in the war, just like Kevin before him. Probably, Liam understood, it was what Chance had wanted all along, the only way to quench his anger at Kevin's death. But it was a bitter pill nonetheless. While Liam was getting drunk at the Outrigger Canoe Club in Waikiki Beach, Chance was dying at another beach half a world away. He spoke the name out loud, softly: "*Chance*."

Tim Dant landed at Tarawa and fought through the end of the war at Okinawa, earned a Silver Star, and came home with shrapnel in his legs and darkness in his eyes. The careless kid who had gone off to war never came home. Before two years had passed, his fishing boat was found miles offshore on Pamlico Sound, bobbing on the swells, and Tim Dant was just gone, leaving behind a pregnant wife. Slipped over the side, or maybe it was an accident after all.

So many things turned out to be accidents.

Tim said he had written a letter, but it never turned up. Told Liam in an offhand way as he headed down to his boat that last time. But who could have known it was the last time? A letter to whom? What did it say? Liam had presumed it was just an ordinary letter about household things, until Tim didn't come back from the water.

"*Timmy*," Liam said out loud. "What did we do to you?" He remembered a storm-shattered morning, a carton of eggs, unbroken, after the typhoon. Unscathed, an unnatural thing.

Kevin and Chance and Tim Dant—none of them ever came home. Their graves were empty.

Brick Littlejohn went about the family business and never spoke of that night again. His first store, at Buxton, was a goddamn gossip factory, full of noisy prowsers passing the news, fishermen ringed around the old potbellied stove in winter. More windows than a goddamn greenhouse. Open to the air most days, a goddamn hurricane of a breeze washing all the voices out the windows to anybody passing by. You couldn't call Littlejohn a happy man, but he got rich and surrounded himself with friends and kept himself firmly planted on the island.

The business grew—two stores, then five, then a couple of restaurants—and his family prospered. People said he was a genius at the business: *Look how he built it up from almost nothing, a little general store into a whole franchise.* They elected him mayor, twice. If that night changed him, he never gave any outward sign. Liam thought, *All men carry things differently.*

Parvis Patchett turned out to be, of all things, a builder.

He spent the war roaming the beach and quietly building a new house for his family, already spending his share in dribs and drabs. But there was too much going on, and nobody paid any attention. He was lucky in that way. Nobody bothered to notice him, and nobody much cared what he thought or didn't think. He made no claim on truth or righteousness or even respectability, and the world left him alone.

When all the boys were home who were coming home, Patchett shared out the money. Liam collected Chance's share as well as his own.

When Tim Dant died, Liam kept waiting to hear that Tim's widow and parents had come into money, but the parents continued living in their two-bedroom cottage near the boat landing, and Tim's father, Ray, continued to work his crab pots and climb poles for the power company whenever he was needed. A couple of years went by, and one day he fell off a pole and broke his back. It took him many months to recover, and from then on he was a semi-invalid.

Tim's widow, Valerie, lived on in the shingled house on the hill that he had built for her, kept mostly to herself, raised her daughter quietly.

Liam invested in a small marina on the inlet and tried to give the title over to Ray and Susan Dant and their daughter-in-law, Tim's widow. He never said why, and they didn't ask. They just said no. He let them run it anyway. And now Tim and Valerie's daughter, Caroline, ran the marina and the garage Liam had added to take advantage of the postwar craze for automobiles. He had no idea what she did or didn't know. She hadn't spoken to him in years. The marina made him more money that he didn't need.

And he never learned what Tim Dant did with his share of the money. Maybe he took it overboard with him. Maybe it was the anchor that pulled him to the bottom.

2

Liam trudged up from the waterline feeling the absence of storm on his bare back and neck. The heaviness was gone from the air, and the light breeze soothed his sunburned skin. The sand felt cool between his toes, and the water hissed a dark stain onto the sand and then retreated. To him, the water was sadness itself leaking out of the world onto his beach.

The sound of the breakers receded as he made the dune line. He saw the figure of a man standing in the doorway to the boathouse. Nicholas Wolf. He had heard about Nick Wolf's visits to Caroline Dant.

Then, finally, he must know.

Liam's whole fortune had come ashore one dark night in the middle of a war, and he had taken it. That was all he was worth, the price of that taking.

He paused and sighed deep in his chest. *Just as well.* He felt the weight begin to lift off him, a sudden lightness come into his head. He almost felt dizzy. Not his heart—that would be a fist in the chest. Just the weight of knowledge lifting.

It was as if he had been holding his breath all these years and now at last could suck in a lungful of fresh air.

He stepped on the wooden landing onto which the great double doors opened and nodded at Nick Wolf. He plucked his old blue shirt off the railing and slipped his scarred arms through the sleeves and left the door open so Nick Wolf could follow him inside.

3

Liam filled the percolator with dark Colombian coffee and set it on the flame. He stood with his back to Nick and didn't speak while the water steamed and boiled and began to tick against the glass bubble of the pot. He waited until it was good and black and then poured two unsugared mugs and handed one across to Nick, who received it with both hands.

"Go on and say what you got to say."

His tone was flat, and Nick couldn't tell if he heard any malice under the words. "You think I've come to judge you?"

"Why else?" His name would be disgraced now—that would be Julia's legacy. That was the part he could not bear.

Nick shook his head, as if dealing with an imbecile. "My God, however can I do that?"

Liam just stared, perplexed.

"My grandfather was a goddamn Nazi."

"Well, there's a point." Liam sipped carefully and smacked his lips.

"And if he was doing what we all know he was doing on the beach that night, he was a traitor to his country. To your country. To my country."

"Still . . ." Liam couldn't bring himself to say it: *I shot him down. Turned a living man into an ugly mess on the beach, open to the wind and water.*

Liam walked to the bureau beside his bed, set his coffee down, and opened a box that had been there all these years. He had left it in plain sight, almost daring someone, anyone, to open it, but of course they hadn't. Not even Julia, his treasure. He lifted the lid on its hinges and pulled out a small bundle wrapped in a handkerchief. He held the pistol out for Nick to take.

"I promised myself, if anyone ever came for him," he said.

Nick slurped his coffee and set the mug on the counter. He walked over and held out his hand, and the old man laid the pistol in his open palm gently. It was surprisingly heavy for an object so small. Still loaded. It was a squarish black automatic, nothing special, compact enough to slip into a coat pocket. The kind of gun secret agents always pulled in the movies.

Nick said, "So he had a gun. Think about it."

"What do you mean?"

"Do you really believe he was going to walk away from it all? From his mission?"

In all these years, pondering every angle of his guilty conscience, Liam had never considered that he might not have controlled the situation, that any man could get the better of him. He saw the whole event as entirely within his power, until it wasn't.

What if the German saboteurs had turned the tables? Would they have let him go home? Let all of them simply go on about their lives?

No, he could see it vividly now, as if it were happening right in front of him. A gun pulled from a pocket, a starburst of flashes so quick he wouldn't even have time to hear them, all the island boys down on the sand, their lives disappearing before the sun came up.

In fact, they had missed the gun during the first search. It was only when they were moving the bodies that Liam had stepped on it in the sand.

"He was a fanatic," Nick said slowly. "A true believer. Have you ever met a true believer?"

For the first time, the Founder laughed. "Christ, I live on an island of true believers."

"What do they believe in?"

"Everything. Nothing. The sea." He let out a long breath. "The days of giants."

Nick waited for him to say more.

At long last, Liam said, "So now you know. I don't even care how you know. It's about time, that's all. About goddamn time. What are you going to do?"

"Do?"

"Knowledge carries a burden. After you have knowledge, you cannot pretend you don't have it. It doesn't work like that."

"You knew about the letter, didn't you?"

Liam nodded heavily. "Only that he had written it. Niver saw it. Don't know where he sent it. Niver turned up."

"But that's why you worked so hard to keep the Dants satisfied, isn't it? In case that letter turned up."

"I would have done that anyway, goddamn you."

"But that wasn't the case."

"You have it! What are you going to do?"

"What do you think?"

"You want to take it all down, don't you? Everything we've built." He closed his fists. "Ruin—just plain ruin." He could live with that, but he couldn't live with what it would do to Julia. Liam didn't know how much she knew. He knew only her blind, devoted love for him, how she had saved him after his wife died. He didn't want to leave her with shame.

"Yeah, well. Sometimes doing nothing at all is taking action."

"Goddamn you, boy."

"Look, whatever you think you owe me," Nick said as Liam Royal glared at him, "you settled up out there." He jerked his head toward the ocean.

Liam let out a deflating breath. "I really don't get you at all, boy." He resumed drinking his coffee as if it were a chore that must be completed. He felt a prickle of agitation. It must not be so easy. It was too important to be shrugged off. "Don't you think it was wrong?"

Nick still held the gun in his open palm, like something dirty he had picked up on the street and now had nowhere to discard. "I'm not the right one to ask."

Liam Royal pounded his coffee mug on the rough table, and drops splattered onto his shirt front. "Who the hell else, then? Tell me that! Who the hell else?" When Nick didn't reply, he stood, his face softening and some of the color draining out of his neck. "What are you doing here, then?"

"I came here on a job, that's all. Just a goddamn job. I didn't ask for this."

"Sure, you did. As if you had any choice."

Nick carefully wrapped the handkerchief around the gun and went to replace it in the open box. Three other items lay in the bottom. One was a card. He picked it up between his fingers. An Illinois driver's license in the name of Nicholas Walter Wolf.

"I left the seaman's card in his pocket. That's how they knew his name, to report it."

Nick nodded. He closed the lid over the gun and held onto the license. It had the soft, silky texture of having been handled often. A familiar feel, like the baseball cards he had carried in his wallet as a boy.

The second item was a harmonica, the shiny metal worn dull. Nick put it to his mouth and blew softly, but the reeds were dry, and the only sound he produced was a metallic *chuff*.

Liam glared at him across the short space of the room. "To remember," he said. "It was not a trophy."

Nick grabbed the third item in the box and held it up, opening its leather covers and flipping the pages. Five by eight inches, bound by a green rubber band. His project journal. He held it up.

Liam shrugged and cleared his throat. "Thought it was a diary. Wanted to know . . . wanted to know what you knew. Nothing to do with the damned oil."

Nick said, "You didn't take it."

"Naw," the Founder said, grinning sheepishly. "Had it took. I ain't a thief."

"Yeah, well." Nick held up the card. "You've spent your whole life wishing you had never met my grandfather."

Liam waved a hand toward the wall, toward nothing.

Nick said, "What do you want to do, give the money back? To whom? To buy what? Forgiveness?"

"I don't want your forgiveness!" Liam trembled with grief. "I did what I did! You should be angry with me."

"Maybe in time, I will be. Who knows? But not now." But Nick knew that was all gone. In the hospital, in two long nights of healing, he had felt it drift away like smoke. "I'm too damned tired for that now."

The Founder glared at him with such ferocity that Nick put up a hand to ward off the blow he believed was coming. The old man's face reddened, and his mouth quivered as if he were swallowing something bitter. But Liam Royal did not lift a hand to strike him. Instead he sighed deeply, all the force going out of him, and Nick could hear the wracking pain in his breath. "You have no idea," he said. "No idea at all."

But Nick did have an idea. He understood about moments that changed everything. He knew *before* and *after*.

Your life is going in one inexorable direction, and in your naïvete you think it will keep on moving in that clear, straight line toward some shining, ideal future. But you forget that things can deflect it.

They come out of the dark as suddenly as a car without headlights and slam into you. The angle of incidence equals the angle of deflection—the old physics postulate was true. Now your life is deflected at an acute or oblique angle in a direction for which you have no map.

Your parents are dead. You are adrift in the world, an orphan who will not have those loving eyes on you as you struggle up each rung toward adulthood, who will feel no guiding hands on your shoulders, hear no confidential consoling voice in hardship.

And what Liam knew: Your wife is dead and the bed is suddenly too big, and all those trivial, crucial things you had to say will go unsaid. You wake up and turn toward her to tell her of the strange and wonderful dreams you had, and she is just an empty space in the bed. And it is like being a child again, the awful terror of aloneness. Not like she has left the world, but like she and the whole world have left you behind and gone to a new place.

Or some stranger walks out of the sea onto a lonely, wind-scoured beach at midnight and ends up dead, and with him dies your own idea of who you are, of what you will finally do when it matters. You are not the person you were, not the person you were going to become, but some stranger now, an unrecognizable disappointment to yourself, a man defined by a momentary coward's choice.

"Tell me this," Liam said. "What the hell are you doing here?"

Nick said quietly, "I've come to ask you a favor."

4

Just beyond the open door, Julia stood and wept softly, as if her heart would break.

5

At Lord's Manor, Nick sat alone by the window, sipping an iced tea. The place was empty, the lunch crowd gone, too early for the dinner rush. He waited, knowing she would find him, and she did.

Rosa Lord slid into the booth across from him and quieted her hands on the tabletop. She stared at him frankly, her brown eyes clear and unblinking. She reached into her apron and pulled out a folded slip of paper, laid it on the table in front of him.

He unfolded it and read the single block-printed name in the familiar hand: *MACSWEEN.*

"He's the best," she said. "And believe it or not, he's German."

"German?"

"It's a long story from another war."

Nick nodded and folded the paper, tucked it into his shirt pocket. He sipped his tea, then said, "You've talked to Caroline Dant?"

Rosa nodded. "She even let me read the letter."

Nick was surprised by that—he had expected Caroline to guard her secret more closely. But maybe the time for that was past. It was nobody's secret anymore—and everybody's.

He thought about old Isaac Abraham hoarding that letter for all those years. Surely he had read it—otherwise, why not deliver it? Had he simply forgotten he had it? No, Nick couldn't believe any man would forget such a confidence. And in the end, Isaac had left definite instructions.

Maybe he had just kept waiting for the right moment, but the right moment never came. After the war, the Lords slid down the social scale as they lost property, while the other families suddenly made their fortunes. Even the Dants came into a marina—or everybody thought they had.

Or maybe Isaac had just watched the slow decline of Caroline's mother. Or maybe he was just being literal—there was no son Peter to give the letter to. Never would be. Who the hell could really say what went on in that old man's mind for all those years, when he was hearing the voice of God telling him personally what to do? Maybe he was just batty. Who could say for sure why anybody did anything?

"Why didn't you just come out and tell me what you knew?"

She shrugged. "That's not the way we do things here."

"You mean I don't understand because I'm from off."

"I'm saying I'm not sure I knew what I knew. Or what I was allowed to tell. Coming from a Lord, it would have seemed like digging up an old grudge. And I was . . . beholden."

"The fellowship."

"He's the Founder of my feast, too."

He drank his tea, tasted the tartness of the lemon wedge.

She went on. "And there was old Isaac's will."

"The messenger. You believe that? That he knew?"

"Yes. I think he had the gift." She paused and canted her head. "Don't look at me like that. Maybe to you it's all nonsense, just an old man's crazy superstition. But I happen to believe."

Nick nodded. "Okay, fair enough. But not just that. You think he knew about all of it?"

"I don't know—maybe. He was there when the bodies washed up."

"And you knew about me? My name?"

She shook her head vigorously. "No, no. Not for a long time. I had to find out if you were him."

"The messenger."

"If you responded to the clues. And then I followed you one day and you found the grave."

"In the rain?"

She nodded. "I thought that blue truck was going to run you down."

So he hadn't imagined it. Everything was turning out to be true.

She said, "At the grave, when you cried—you can't fake that. Then I was sure."

Nick was incredulous. He was sure he'd been alone in that hidden place. "Wait—you were there?"

"I stayed back in the bushes at the entrance. Didn't go all way in."

"You knew about that place."

"I told you, I study history."

"And how did my grandfather come to be buried as a crewman on the *Goliath*?"

"No big mystery there," she said. "I checked the roster of ships sunk during the war, and *Goliath* went down with all hands that same night. Probably sunk by the same U-boat that landed your grandfather."

"But the crew manifest . . . ?"

"The *Goliath* had just shipped from Galveston with a bunch of extra crew for the convoy at Halifax. They all hitched a ride at the last minute. Their names weren't on the manifest." She shrugged. "Everybody thinks there is some kind of absolute permanent record of everything, but lots of times there's not. It never gets written down at all."

Nick nodded, letting it all settle in. "You knew about the saboteurs."

She shook her head. "That was just a guess, an intuition. I found some old newspaper stories about landings up north, on Cape Cod. There was even a famous trial. I knew they always came ashore with money—real money, and lots of it."

"And you knew the names."

"The picture in Caroline's house is famous. It was printed in the newspaper back in the day and reprinted all over the place."

"So you really didn't know the rest of it?"

"I was just following the trail, connecting the dots. Seemed like a good way to spend the summer with my family and still make progress on my degree."

"And this will all be in your thesis?" *Just another kind of report,* he thought. He had finished his final report for Funderburke—what he knew and how, what happened that final day—and was done with reports, at least for a while.

"Not all history makes it into books." She smiled slyly. "You of all people should know that."

"I'm not sure what I know anymore. The rug has sort of been pulled out from under me."

She gazed out the window and said absently, "So I guess we're going to let them all get away with it."

Nick said, "I'm not sure anybody has gotten away with anything." He remembered Liam stricken, a man adrift, his life's work a single ongoing crime, his shame before Julia.

"I didn't know about your company, the rig and all. I'm so sorry."

"Don't be. Maybe it's for the best."

"Sometimes it seems like everybody's working an angle."

"Not me," he said. And that much was true. All the sharp angles had been filed off, rounded into a single, whole life. He felt empty and light, his insides exposed to the world. He didn't care anymore if people liked him, not in general. There were only particular people who mattered—their respect and trust and, yes, their affection.

"Well, anyway, I don't think you're from off. Not any more than me."

"How's that?"

She took his hand and smiled. "We both have somebody in the graveyard."

EPILOGUE

HATTERAS ISLAND, 1991

The service was simple—a few words from the local priest, MacSween, the short and fussy funeral director in his dark suit presiding over the practical details, the plain black-walnut coffin lowered into the sand beside the grave that had held Nicholas Wolf for all these decades. Nick played a verse of the coming-home song on his guitar, the song his Oma had always loved. He did not sing the words. At that moment, he had no voice.

Poe Patchett had arranged it all, just as he promised. They laid her to rest beside her errant husband. The pall bearers were Nick, Liam Royal, Poe Patchett, Caroline Dant, and the two Littlejohns. Nobody said much, and when it was over they all dispersed, the men already yanking the crooked knots out of their ties.

Nick and Julia walked back along the beach, barefoot, each holding their Sunday shoes in one hand.

Out on the beach, it was easier to talk somehow, the breeze carrying away their words, no one to listen and overhear. They walked side by side, not touching hands, bare feet quiet on the smooth, wet sand.

"What do you want?" he said without looking at her. He had already forgiven her small lie, the one in service of the greater lie.

"The same two things every woman wants," she said.

They walked a few more steps, and he waited. The sea was down, the breakers slapping onto the beach as if spent. The storm was all blown out.

"Two things impossible to have at once."

"Oh," he said. "Story of my life."

"To stay—"

"And to leave."

"It's not fair," she said.

The lighthouse rose far off above the dunes. They both stopped and looked as though it were a new thing, something that had sprouted overnight.

Nick said, "I don't know about fair. I haven't seen much that was fair."

"You don't think people get what they deserve?"

He thought about his grandfather, going away to find the war and then bringing it home with him, to this place. If what happened to him was fair, then how about what happened to Oma—all those years left waiting, a woman alone, dreaming of her lost man as if he were alive and coming back to her, never giving up hope, though he was dead all that time? He said, "I think people get what they get. Sometimes we're lucky."

"Yes," she said. "I don't know if I'm lucky."

He shrugged her off. "You're just tired of carrying around that heavy name." He thought of his own name, spelled out on his Opa's tombstone. His name had been part of the lore of the island for half a century, yet he had never known. Did that make him an islander at last? *You're an islander only if you have somebody buried in the graveyard,* she had said only weeks ago, but before. Before everything.

"You haven't even asked," she said quietly, not looking at him.

"I know," he said. "It doesn't matter."

"What I knew," she said. "How much I knew."

"It doesn't matter," he repeated. "Maybe it did before. But we're way past that now."

"All those years of knowing just enough," she said. "Waiting. Of course you would come."

Nick thought about that, and how everything would go on now just as it had before, yet it would all be different. Everything underneath the simplest transaction of everyday life would be charged with knowledge that no one would ever speak out loud. "Your parents?"

She nodded. "It's one of those things. You have to take sides. There's just no middle."

"No, I guess not."

"I guess we all knew you were coming someday."

"Maybe you were wrong to be so afraid of me."

She said, "He's a good man. He's not as strong as everybody thinks. I was afraid you would hurt him, really hurt him. Then what would he have?"

"I might have, once," Nick said. He had always thought home was a place, but now he thought of it as a person. "Then I met you. Maybe that was what all this was about—my coming, finding you. Maybe old Isaac Abraham was oblique in his prophecy."

She took his hand. "I'd love to believe that's true."

"You think he'll be all right? Your grandfather?"

"I don't know. It's an awful gift," she said absently.

"What?"

She stopped and held his face in her small hands. "Forgiveness."

He kissed her forehead.

"He wasn't a bad man, I bet. Your grandfather. Your grandmother loved him so much. You can't love a bad man that much."

"He tried to be a bad man, I guess." Nick shook his head, broke away gently, still not quite believing all the things he now knew for sure. "Tried his damnedest. Sure caused a lot of trouble in the end."

He had told her about his grandfather's plans to sabotage the railroad, the shipyard, the Pullman tank factory in Chicago. His Opa had changed overnight, gone from being a man who made things with his hands and his intelligence to being a man who was bent on destroying things. Nick still could not fathom that turn toward darkness, the ambition to create something traded for a dream of destruction. It was lucky his Oma had died without ever knowing.

She said, "Well, he didn't blow anything up after all, did he?"

"Sure he did." *Sabotaged this whole island,* Nick thought. *Blew a whole community into pieces.* Some of the pieces were gone now, and some were just scattered. But maybe there was a chance that the ones remaining could be joined again. Dants and Royals, Patchetts and Littlejohns, Lords and all the rest.

"I bet he was a lot like you," Julia said. "Stubborn. Sweet sometimes. Always looking for adventure someplace else."

He smiled. "*This* is someplace else."

For a moment, she didn't say anything. She started walking, and he kept pace. "You're going back." It wasn't a question.

He shook his head. "Back where? There is no back." His Oma was dead. The map of his previous life was now erased, all traces of it vanished into memory, an album of the dead. He could conjure them in any order, or no order, one at a time. Or in pairs. Mom and Dad. Oma and Opa. Even the *Rascal*'s captain, whose name he never learned, and Fannon, whom he had counted a friend.

Except for the pulse of memory, there was nothing to prove he had ever lived in Chicago. He had a couple of cartons of clothes and books, a photo album, and a ten-speed bicycle in a garage apartment. Nothing he couldn't live without, except the album. He had lived without all of it most of the time.

The rig was gone. Fannon had disappeared. A week after he went missing, a man had shown up on the island and said he was Fannon's brother.

Nick had no news for him. He said, "You've come all way from Australia for nothing."

The man looked puzzled. He said he came from a small town in Iowa, where Fannon was raised and his family still lived on a farm. *Iowa.* Nick couldn't even recall the name of the town. *Iowa.*

Who the hell was Fannon, talking about *salties* and *shite* and calling him *mate*? Who the hell was anybody?

NorthAm was bankrupt. He might get an offer from one of the majors, but he was tired of that life. He had a few dollars stashed away.

And he had Caroline Dant's unexpected gift. What to do with that? One way or another, that money was meant to stay on the island. Somehow, sometime, it could be put to good use. He could stay here and sort it out. Maybe, in time, the answer would come, when he understood what he really wanted.

At least his grandfather had known exactly what he wanted. And now both of them had ended up on this island. Nick didn't believe in fate, but he also didn't believe in coincidence. Like his Oma used to say, *There are no coincidences in life, Nicky. There are only patterns you don't recognize yet.*

Well, he would stay until he recognized the pattern.

Julia reached an arm around his waist, and he felt the gentle pressure of her hand on the small of his back. He said, "It's funny. All you want is to leave, and now all I know I want is to stay."

"Well, that's different."

He stopped and faced her. Her brown eyes were bright, all the sadness gone out of them. "You can go under a new name," he said, and kissed her long and slow, holding her tight against him, not giving her any chance to spin loose.

They left the beach at dusk, walking hand in hand among the camelbacks toward Lifeboat Station #17. The clouds were all gone from the sky when the sun disappeared west across the sound, leaving behind a star-dazzled night, the sea lustrous with remembered light.

ACKNOWLEDGMENTS

Thanks to my old friend Bob Reiss for his generous help in working out the story line. Thanks also to the fine crew at John F. Blair, especially Carolyn Sakowski, whose enlightened leadership has helped bring many wonderful books to readers; Anna Sutton and Debra Hampton, who worked tirelessly to help create this one; and Steve Kirk, the kind of sharp, smart editor any writer is lucky to have. Finally, thanks to my wife, Jill Gerard, my first reader, for encouraging me to write this novel in the first place.